I0778998

With thanks to Melanie Hoopes, who keeps all of William Kingsfield Publisher's chips neatly stacked, for joining me on my publishing voyage.

AUTHOR'S NOTE

When I began work on *Scare Card*, I had a dilemma; while Lizzy Ballard's story would pick up a month or more after her last scene in Book 3: *The Iron Ring*, whatever happened next to Lizzy's nemesis Louise Mortensen would happen seconds after we last see her in that book.

That meant that, if I were to present Lizzy and Louise's scenes in chronological order in *Scare Card*, the first several chapters would have to focus on Louise, and I didn't want Lizzy's fans to have to wait that long to re-engage with their protagonist.

My solution was to catch Louise's timeline up with Lizzy's in a novella: *Kill Box Checkmate (Book 3½)*

I had so much fun plumbing Louise's villainous depths in *Kill Box*, and setting the stage for her reappearance in *Scare Card*. If you love villains as much as I do—at least this particular villain—I hope you'll check it out *Kill Box Checkmate (Book 3½)*

In a twisty tale of betrayal and vengeance, a cunning scientist orchestrates her escape from the isolated estate of a sociopathic tycoon. When Louise Mortensen's kidnapper, Theo Viklund, drops dead, she glimpses her chance for freedom—by becoming him.

Joining forces with Viklund's sinister head of security and her hapless lab assistant, Louise makes a chilling pact to conceal her captor's death. Once Louise assumes Viklund's identity, her path to freedom will be ensured ... but first, she must access his biometrically-protected computer accounts.

The key seems out of reach ... until Theo's brother arrives, searching for the truth behind Theo's disappearance. Will he provide Louise the clue she needs to unlock Theo's riches and his secrets?

Louise finds herself navigating a high-stakes web of deception, treachery, and murder. And the closer she gets to claiming absolute power, the deadlier her web becomes.

In this exhilarating thrill ride, a devious antiheroine with a murderous past must unravel a conspiracy of lies to claim a prize worth killing for.

Scare card: A card that creates uncertainty and anxiety because of its potential to make strong hands weaker or turn weaker hands into stronger ones.

From Blinds to Bets: Poker Basics for Beginners by Thomas Koenigsfeld

1

———

As the young woman stepped through the sliding glass doors of the Mesa Blanca Resort, she sensed the man at her side scanning the space, although it was designed to look more welcoming than dangerous. The décor of the hotel-casino's lobby was reminiscent of the Phoenix landscape outside. The yellow-gray of its tiled floor mimicked the surrounding mountains' granite peaks. Stylized shapes suggesting saguaro cacti decorated the walls. The domed ceiling was the indigo of a sky just before true darkness fell, sprinkled with pinpoints of light arranged into easily identifiable constellations. It was always evening inside the casino. She guessed that a team of consultants had decided it was the best ambiance for keeping players at the tables.

She crossed to the hallway leading to the restrooms, while the man, as usual, waited for her in the lobby.

Even the women's room was opulently decorated, although the light was brighter, allowing visitors to fix makeup or adjust clothing as needed. She caught a glimpse of herself in a full-length mirror. Her short hair was a sun-bleached gold tipped with bright red, and although she liked the look, she knew she should change it—it was unusual enough to attract unwanted attention. Her dramatically applied makeup—eyes lined with black, lips stained a plum purple—was also attention-getting but not unusual among the casino crowd. She had picked her sapphire-blue dress because it was the classiest-looking offering at Target, but now she realized it hugged her slender frame a little more closely than she would have liked. The Zuni bear pendant at her throat was her only jewelry; once she saved some money, she supposed she should invest in some flashier accessories to finish off what she thought of as a costume. She was still not entirely comfortable in the high-heeled sandals she wore to exaggerate her height, and she tried to adjust her walk from her natural limber stride to a more mature saunter.

She entered one of the stalls and hung her wrap on the door's hook. Opening her beaded evening bag, she took out what looked like a pencil case and unzipped it to reveal a glass vial and a syringe. Drawing the prescribed amount of liquid into the syringe, she injected herself in the bicep, then repacked the vial and slipped the case into her bag. After blotting away a tiny drop of blood, she draped the wrap around her shoulders, dropped the syringe into a sharps container by the sinks, and washed her hands.

When she reached the lobby, the man fell into step beside her. He was in his early thirties, medium height and slender, with black hair combed back from a sun-weathered face and dark, watchful eyes. He wore a pressed shirt, neat jeans, and leather boots. The only noteworthy part of his outfit was his belt buckle: a ladder design in turquoise and silver, overlaid by an etched outline of the head of a snake, its eye a dot of red coral.

"All juiced up?" he asked with a smile.

She raised her closed hand for a fist bump. "Good to go."

They entered the casino and went to the board operator's station.

"Good evening, miss," said the attendant. "Good to see you again." He turned to the man. "And good to see you again, as well, Mr. ..." He raised his eyebrows expectantly.

"Riva."

"Mr. Riva." He turned back to the woman. "Texas hold 'em, five-ten table?"

"Yes, please," she said.

He scanned the room. "Table seven, seat three."

There were three other players at the table: a fiftyish man in a Los Angeles Lakers jersey, a gray-haired man holding an umbrella drink and wearing a Hello Kitty sweatshirt, and a fortyish man in a sport coat and open-necked Oxford shirt. She took her assigned seat, Riva standing behind her, and nodded greetings to her fellow players. She was used to the surprised looks her arrival usually caused—despite the dress and makeup, she knew she looked younger than the legal gambling age. But if anyone asked, she had an ID attesting that she was twenty-one.

She removed a roll of cash from her purse, counted out twelve hundred-dollar bills, and put them on the table.

The dealer, who was probably not much older than twenty-one himself, pushed the bills into the drop box with a paddle and slid her chips across the table, dealing her in on the next hand.

Each player received two cards, face-down. As she checked her cards and then scanned the faces of the other players as they checked their own, she could feel the effects of the injection start to kick in.

Lakers, Hello Kitty, and Sport Coat placed their bets.

She pushed her cards toward the dealer. "Fold."

She watched the remainder of the game with little interest. Lakers took the pot.

Hand followed hand, and she folded each time, losing only the fifteen dollars of her compulsory bets.

"You're going to have to stick it out at some point, sweetheart," said Lakers with a sneer.

She nodded without looking at him. "I will."

On the next deal, she called Sport Coat's ten-dollar bet, Lakers raised to twenty, and she and the other players matched his bet.

The dealer then dealt three cards face up: a four of hearts, a seven of clubs, and a king of diamonds. This was the "flop"—she loved the bizarre terminology of poker—which the players would combine with their own two face-down cards to make a hand.

Hello Kitty bet twenty and Sport Coat called. She herself raised to forty, and they all met Lakers' raise to eighty.

Next came the one-card "turn": an eight of diamonds.

She tried to suppress a smile. She glanced around the table to see if anyone had noticed her expression—no one would accuse her of having a poker face—but they all had their eyes on their own cards.

Hello Kitty tossed in his cards. "Fold."

Sport Coat bet fifty.

She pushed in chips. "Raise to one hundred."

Lakers didn't bother hiding his smirk. He obviously thought she was responding less to the cards and more to his taunt about her tentative play. He pushed in chips. "Call."

Sport Coat, evidently agreeing with Laker's assessment, also called her bet.

The dealer dealt the final card, the "river": a king of spades.

Sport Coat bet fifty.

She pushed in chips. "Raise to one hundred."

Lakers' smirk became a predatory smile. "See your hundred, raise to two hundred."

A few bystanders must have sensed a change in the energy at the table and stopped to watch. Riva positioned himself so that no one could step too close to her.

Sport Coat looked at his cards again. His hand drifted to the pile of chips, then returned to the tabletop, drifted to the chips again, and back to the table. After a few moments, he puffed out a breath and threw in his cards. "Too rich for my blood."

Lakers grinned. "I understand—you don't want to take candy from a baby. But I don't mind."

She pushed in more chips. "See your two hundred, raise to four hundred."

Lakers chuckled and shook his head. "Call your four hundred, raise to eight hundred."

Hello Kitty and Sport Coat stirred in their seats—one with concern, the other with excitement.

She would have raised again, but she only had a few chips left. A phrase she recalled her father saying years ago—*it takes money to make money*—drifted through her mind. If she *had* money, she wouldn't be doing this. She pushed in chips. "Call."

"Show your hands, please," said the dealer.

Lakers flipped his cards over. "Kings—three of a kind." He draped his arm over the back of his chair. "What've *you* got, baby?"

She turned over her cards. "Straight. Four through eight."

Lakers' smile froze.

Sport Coat barked out a laugh. "I'll be damned."

Hello Kitty smiled and raised his umbrellaed glass in a salute.

The dealer began moving the pile of chips toward her, but she raised a hand. "That's enough for me." She turned her gaze to Lakers. "I think I'll take my candy and go play somewhere else."

The dealer colored up her chips, consolidating her pile of

smaller-denomination chips into a few higher denominations. He passed them to her, and she handed one chip back to him. "Thank you."

He winked at her. "Thank *you*, miss."

She slid off her chair, and she and Riva headed for the cashier's booth.

"I have to say, that was fun to watch," he said with a grin.

She grinned back. "I have to say, that was fun to *do*."

"You didn't want to keep playing?"

"We were drawing a crowd. Plus, the juice was already fading. I don't think this latest batch is as strong as the last one." She rolled her eyes. "And I don't want to try to rely on my non-existent knowledge of poker strategy."

She cashed in her chips and put the money—about twenty-five hundred dollars—in her evening bag.

She and Riva were crossing the lobby toward the entrance when she heard a shout.

"Hey, Casal!"

She sensed Riva tense, and they turned to see a man approaching. Riva stepped forward.

"How the hell are you?" the man said as he reached them. "You remember me, right?" He held out his hand to Riva, but his eyes were on her. "It's your old buddy—Marcus."

Riva ignored the extended hand. "You've got the wrong guy. My name's Riva."

Marcus dropped his hand, returned his gaze to Riva, and knit his brow. "Riva?" His expression cleared, but only partially. "Like Oscar?" Then he grinned. "Or Olivia?"

"Not like anyone," said Riva, his voice tight.

Marcus shrugged. "Sure, whatever you say. Not like that." He turned back to the woman, his eyes scanning her like she was standing on a stage equipped with a pole. "Not like Olivia Riva."

Riva took a step toward Marcus. His voice was quiet when he

spoke. "You wouldn't want to end up in Williams for harassing a pair of people just looking for a relaxing evening at the casino, would you? Or should I say, you wouldn't want to end up *back* in Williams."

Marcus took a step back and raised his hands. "Sure. Whatever you say."

"Whatever I say ... what?"

After a moment, Marcus said, "Whatever you say, *Riva*."

Riva turned away from him and put a hand on the small of the woman's back.

"Casal," Marcus said under his breath.

Riva wheeled back toward Marcus, but the woman took his arm. "Leave it," she whispered.

He hesitated, then turned back to the door, and let her lead him outside.

The day had been a typical one for Phoenix—a scorcher, even in the spring—but the evening was cool. She pulled her wrap tighter around her shoulders.

As they crossed the parking lot, Riva asked, "Could you tell what Marcus was thinking?"

"He was wondering why you were with me instead of Olivia."

"Yeah, I gathered that," he said. His tone was joking, but she could tell he was irritated. "Anything else?"

She wrinkled her nose. "Nothing I want to describe."

When they reached a Dodge Grand Caravan marked by a long silver scrape down its side, he opened the passenger door for her, then climbed into the driver's seat and started up the van.

She slipped the strap of her crossbody bag over her head and pulled off her shoes with a grateful groan, then examined herself in the mirror on the back of the lowered sun visor. "Man, I barely recognize myself."

"If you barely recognize yourself, it's less likely anyone else will recognize you either."

She sighed. "Yeah. And I know I wouldn't look old enough without the makeup." She rubbed her foot. "But I am starting to have second thoughts about the heels. A couple of inches in height couldn't make that much difference in terms of someone recognizing me, right?"

"Probably not. Although it does make me a little uncomfortable that the attendant knows my name. And if fellow ex-cons are recognizing me, that's no good either. We might need to give this place a rest for a while."

"Yeah."

As he pulled out of the parking lot, she took her phone from her bag and hit one of the contacts in her favorites list.

"Hey, Pumpkin!" answered a man's voice, sounding breathless. "How are you doing?"

"I'm good. How are you?"

"Just getting in a little bit of exercise."

She knit her brow. "Don't overdo it."

She heard a wheezy laugh. "Don't worry about me—the Sergeant is making sure I don't overdo it."

"Or underdo it," came a woman's brisk voice in the background.

She laughed. "I'll bet." She glanced at the roll of cash in the bag. "I had a good evening at the casino." She continued, her tone embarrassed. "Although I suppose that shouldn't be a surprise—I do have an unfair advantage."

"I'm sure you don't put your advantage to use more than you need to," the man said soothingly. "Are you being careful?"

"Philip came with me."

"Say hello to him for me."

"I will. And I'll send a money order soon."

"Why don't you keep it, Pumpkin. I'm doing fine."

She knew he wasn't doing fine, but he would never admit it.

He continued with a laugh. "I can see your name in lights: Lizzy Ballard, Card Shark."

Her own laugh was a bit sheepish. "It helps to be a mind reader, Uncle Owen."

2

————

Louise Mortensen walked briskly down the central hallway of Theo Viklund's sprawling home-cum-head-quarters, the tread of her low-heeled Christian Louboutin pumps muffled on the thick carpet. As the corridor began a gradual downward slope, the décor became more utilitarian, with cork tiles replacing carpet and plain drywall replacing raw silk-papered walls.

She reached the door at the end of the hallway. There was no longer a guard stationed there, as there had been during her first visit to the suite two months earlier. Lucas, the head of security, and Maja, the head of housekeeping, had sent most of Theo's staff back to Sweden, planning to replace them gradually with a new contingent. Hopefully, the new employees, unfamiliar with the old normal under Theo, wouldn't notice the oddities of the new normal under Louise, Lucas, and Maja.

She opened the door and stepped into the suite.

The living area was a single large room. In the middle stood a Danish modern dining table and four chairs—three more than when Theo had been in residence. Beyond that was a sparely equipped galley kitchen. To the left was a well-appointed personal gym. To the right was an enormous desk, also Danish modern, and a conference table with a professional-grade video conferencing set-up. As beautifully appointed as the rest of the complex was, Theo's suite was devoid of color or decoration. This, in addition to the lack of windows, had no doubt inspired the name the staff had given the space: the bunker.

Louise thought longingly of her own comfortable suite, with its floor-to-ceiling windows looking out onto the woods surrounding the house. She had briefly considered moving Theo's desk from the bunker to her suite, but it wasn't worth the risk that such a move might disrupt the biometric sensor attached its top. And it would be hard to reconcile such a change with the story Louise, Lucas, and Maja were giving the staff: that Theo, grief-stricken at the death of his beloved niece, was sequestered in his quarters.

She sat down at the desk and tucked a strand of hair—auburn threaded with silver—behind her ear. From a small, lab-grade refrigeration unit next to the chair, she removed a glass container that might at one time have been used to bake meatloaf. From the container, she lifted a hand, severed a few inches above the wrist. She suppressed a shudder; even as a medical doctor, she found its rubbery texture disquieting.

The sensor that gave access to Theo's computer accounts performed three biometric checks, and they had to be performed periodically, even if the computer was in use.

One check was for temperature, and with some experimentation, Louise and her lab assistant, Edmund Rinnert, had determined the optimal temperature at which to keep the hand: high enough to satisfy the sensor but low enough to slow deterioration.

Another check was for a heartbeat, and for that Edmund had constructed a device that passed a tiny electrical impulse through the hand. Louise clipped the device's slender wires to the hand's rapidly fraying muscles and tendons, and flipped a switch on the device, which emitted a low hum. The fingers of the hand twitched.

Yet another check was of the palm print, and Louise pressed the palm onto a metal disk next to the computer keyboard with some trepidation.

Biometric signature - Print: Failed
Biometric signature - Temp: Passed
Biometric signature - Heart: Passed

"Damn." The hand's deterioration must be warping the print. Theo's hand was reaching the end of its useful life—if one could refer to a severed limb as having a "useful life"—and she would soon lose her opportunity to retrieve any more money from Theo's accounts. Then she could retire from her role as unofficial treasurer of a group of conspirators and return to her preferred role of scientist. The lab Theo had outfitted for her research never seemed as appealing as it did after a few hours in the bunker.

However, the lab she truly missed was the one she herself had outfitted at the Vivantem fertility clinic in Philadelphia, the lab where she had developed, administered, and monitored the official procedures performed on the clinic's patients, and the unofficial ones, as well. She had suspected her days at the lab were numbered when authorities began to probe her involvement in the death of the Pennsylvania Attorney General, whose office was investigating the clinic. She knew those days were gone forever when she put a flame to the drapes of her Pocopson home, burning it to the ground, along with the incriminating evidence it contained.

Louise supposed it was poetic justice that her difficulties had begun when her husband, Gerard Bonnay, had died at the hands of Elizabeth Ballard, a product of the Vivantem experiments. Or, Louise thought, with a twist of sorrow in her gut, not so much at the *hands* of that young woman. It was Ballard's *brain* that had dealt the fatal blow.

She repositioned the severed hand on the sensor and succeeded in passing the check on the third try. She returned the hand to the refrigeration unit, then tapped in the text passcode: *Järnring*, Swedish for iron ring.

The resulting screen displayed none of the elements one might find on a standard computer. In fact, there were only three icons: stylized renditions of a globe, a bank vault door, and a mailbox.

The globe provided access to an incognito browser, and since she had gotten access to the computer, Louise had brought herself up to date with news from outside the compound. She had arrived at the compound thinking her long-time colleague Theo Viklund was offering her sanctuary, only to learn that he was actually expecting servitude. But once she gained access to news sources, she reluctantly admitted she had been wise to accept his invitation to take refuge in his elegant compound in western Maryland. It had proven to be a prison, but Louise had found a way to eliminate her warder—an option she doubted she would have had at the type of prison that awaited her outside the compound.

The bank vault icon provided a list of links, some to banks or investment firms whose names Louise recognized. On her first foray into Theo's accounts, she was relieved to find that clicking on these links opened the accounts with no further sign-in needed. She had transferred money from those into five separate accounts. One of these was to cover maintenance of the compound, and even in the couple of months since Theo's handless body had been relegated to a freezer in the lab, and despite the dramatic reduction in staff, the household account was depleting with alarming speed.

Louise had divided the rest of the money across four other

accounts: one-third each to her and Lucas, the remaining one-third split between Maja and Edmund. Maja had seemed willing to take the lower amount on the basis that Louise and Lucas were shouldering most of the risk of their plan. Edmund wasn't aware that his portion was lower than Louise and Lucas's and the same as the housekeeper's. In fact, he had argued to Louise privately that Maja shouldn't get *any* money. Louise reminded him that if Maja hadn't agreed to help cover up their murder of Theo, Louise and Edmund might be the ones in the lab freezer.

In addition to the familiar names on the list of financial institutions behind the bank vault icon, there were ones neither Louise nor Lucas recognized, and these required a second level of sign-in. Access to several had been permanently revoked when Louise used up the allotted password attempts. A few reset after twenty-four hours, and on these she continued to experiment. Occasionally, she stumbled onto a correct password and transferred the money from those accounts, but she had not gained access to a new account in over a week. Today's attempts were no more successful.

It wouldn't be long before the expense of maintaining the compound and the futility of remaining there would make venturing beyond its guarded boundaries worth the risk.

Taking a deep breath, she clicked on the email icon.

3

———

Lizzy swiped the cotton ball across her eyes, then rinsed her face and patted it dry with a hand towel. She'd be relieved when she was old enough to pass as legal to gamble without the makeup. The fake ID Philip had gotten for her from a former prison colleague showed her age as twenty-one, but she suspected some of the casino staff, not to mention her fellow poker players, assumed she was closer to her actual age of seventeen.

So far, the ID had passed muster at the casinos, but with no paper trail behind it—no social security number, no birth certificate—Lizzy wasn't confident using it to apply for a more traditional teenager job, like working at a fast-food place or helping out at a kids' camp. Distasteful as it was, cheating at poker was the best option she had for paying back her godfather, whom she called Uncle Owen, for all the money had spent over the years to keep her fed, clothed, and safe. She knew she could never repay him for all the hardship and heartbreak he had endured because of her.

Now her reliance, and her indebtedness, had expanded to include Philip. Lizzy had met Philip—he was then going by

Castillo, having changed his name from Casal after his release from the Williams Correctional Facility—when she had fled to Sedona to elude Louise Mortensen. When events came to a head back in Philadelphia, Philip had heeded Owen's plea for help and come east. That visit had culminated with Louise's mansion in flames, her henchman dead in its basement, and Philip with a bullet in the shoulder. It has resulted in Lizzy heading back to Arizona to wreak vengeance on Tobe Hanrick, the man responsible for killing Philip's prison mentor, Oscar Riva.

She could hear two voices from the living room: Olivia Riva, Oscar's daughter, and Philip. Philip had adopted Oscar's last name when he and Lizzy had gone into hiding after Philip killed Hanrick. Lizzy suspected Philip regretted the choice since strangers assumed he and Olivia were married. Lizzy didn't doubt they loved each other, but neither of them seemed interested in marriage. That assessment was based on normal observation, since even when Lizzy was under the influence of the steroid drug—which she jokingly referred to as "the juice"— that enabled her mind-reading ability, Philip's thoughts were never accessible to her, and Olivia almost always had her mental defenses up around Lizzy.

As Lizzy wiped moisturizer over her face, she could hear that her unusual ability was the topic of their conversation. Philip and Olivia's voices were lowered but still audible through the apartment's paper-thin walls.

"You didn't object when she put it to work to help *you*," said Philip.

Lizzy winced. While she and Philip had hidden out in Arizona, they had accompanied Olivia on a few meetings related to her pro bono legal services. More than once, Lizzy's ability to read minds had averted what might otherwise have been disastrous situations for Olivia's clients.

"I wasn't entirely comfortable with that, either," said Olivia. "But in those cases, she was using her ability to prevent someone from cheating. In this case, she's the one doing the cheating."

Lizzy draped the hand towel over the shower curtain bar. Based on the ragged holes in the drywall, the bathroom had had a towel bar at one time but replacing it hadn't reached the top of Lizzy and Philip's fix-it list yet. She wiped a last smudge of mascara from under her eye, then stepped out of the bathroom.

Philip sat on the couch, one arm stretched across the back cushions, the other holding a bottle of Corona, his expression carefully neutral.

Olivia stood next to the sliding doors to the rickety second-floor balcony. Her arms were crossed, but when she saw Lizzy, she dropped them to a less combative posture. "Hello, Lizzy."

"Hey, Olivia." Lizzy headed into the galley kitchen. "Can I get you anything to drink? Or eat?"

"No, thanks."

"Philip?"

"I'm good."

Lizzy got a large bottle of seltzer from the refrigerator, twisted the cap off, and drank. She wondered if she should find an excuse to leave the apartment, or if that would be rude.

When she emerged from the kitchen, Olivia said, "I hear you had a successful evening."

"Yeah, it was good."

"You know she's sending most of the money to Owen, right?" Philip said to Olivia. He gestured to take in the apartment. "It's not like we're living high on the hog from her winnings."

Lizzy and Philip were borrowing the apartment from a prison acquaintance of Philip, but the acquaintance was due to be released soon, and they'd need to find new, and equally cheap, quarters.

Olivia re-crossed her arms. "You know you'd be welcome to stay with me."

Philip sighed. "I know. And I appreciate it. But it seems risky. Who knows who Mortensen might have out there looking for me and Lizzy."

"Not just Louise," said Lizzy. "Theo Viklund might be looking for you, Philip."

After the gun battle at Louise's Pocopson home, Viklund had spirited Philip out of the hospital and tried to recruit him as an ally. Guessing correctly that Philip regretted having asked Lizzy to kill Hanrick, Viklund had sent Philip back to Arizona, accompanied by his niece Rey, with a promise to help Philip kill Hanrick himself. Philip had escaped from Rey's supervision and, assisted by Lizzy's mind-reading ability, had slit Hanrick's throat in the abandoned Sedona trailer park where Hanrick was holding her hostage.

"And if Viklund and Mortensen have joined forces," said Olivia, "he might be looking for you as well, Lizzy."

"Seems like it might be time to relocate again," said Philip to Olivia, "and not just because of Viklund and Mortensen. We ran into Marcus at the casino."

Her eyebrows rose. "Marcus? From Williams?"

"Yeah. I told him my name was Riva, so he knows I'm trying to lie low, but not before he yelled 'Casal' across the lobby."

"Idiot," Olivia muttered.

"And the casino attendant remembered me," said Lizzy.

Olivia knit her brow. "If you're getting known around here," she said to Lizzy, "maybe you *would* be better off somewhere else."

"Maybe going back east wouldn't be any worse than staying here," Lizzy ventured.

Philip nodded reluctantly. "True. And I know you're ready to go home."

Lizzy's throat tightened, and she took another drink of seltzer. It wasn't so much getting back to Pennsylvania as returning to the small circle of friends who had become her defenders. That included not only Uncle Owen but his brother Andy and Owen's majordomo, Ruby DiMano. If Lizzy left Arizona, she would miss Philip—he was her best friend—but Owen, Andy, and Ruby, even though unrelated to her by blood, were the closest she had to family.

Olivia glanced at her watch. "Speaking of home, I have to get home to do some research."

Philip stood. "Still working? It's ten o'clock."

"My boss has some big project going on in D.C., and he needs me to do some research for it." She picked up a leather briefcase from a tattered easy chair. "Are we still on for dinner out tomorrow, or is it a better idea to hole up here with takeout?"

Philip shook his head. "I am *not* spending the rest of my life eating takeout. Let's just go somewhere new, where no one's likely to recognize us."

"Sounds good." Olivia slung the strap of the bag over her shoulder. "How about you, Lizzy? Want to join us?"

"No, thanks. Andy's coming for a visit tomorrow. You guys have fun."

Lizzy headed for her bedroom—at least she could give them a few moments of privacy. She closed the bedroom door, but she could still hear murmured conversation through the flimsy walls. She was grateful that when Philip and Olivia spent the night together, they did it somewhere other than Philip's bedroom, right next to Lizzy's.

She was lying on her bed, watching a YouTube video about how to hang a towel bar, when there was a knock on the bedroom door.

"Come in."

Philip opened the door. "I know it's late, but I'm hungry. I'm going to defrost some chili and make cornbread. Interested?"

She slipped her phone into her pocket and jumped up from the bed. "Sure. Want any help?"

"The cornbread's just from a box—I can handle that—but if you want to make a salad, that would be good."

She followed him to the galley kitchen and began assembling a salad as he stirred the bread mix.

"Since I'm getting recognized in Phoenix," he said, "maybe Andy can take you to the casino while he's here."

"Two trips in two days—I really am turning into a high roller." She raised an eyebrow. "But after Andy goes back to Philly, who's left to take on the job of being my minder?"

He sighed. "Olivia."

"Philip, I really don't need an escort. I can go by myself."

"I feel better having someone there with you."

Lizzy began to marshal her arguments: what could possibly happen in a crowded casino that would put her in danger? Just as important, how could she put anyone else in danger? For most of the time she was at a casino, she was "juiced" on the mind-reading drug, which inactivated the power she otherwise had: to cause another person's brain to bleed using the power of her mind. She had named this "the squeeze."

But she saw Philip's point. Although the casino crowds provided some protection for her, they also provided plenty of opportunities for more mundane but still upsetting interactions. She normally didn't take the juice until she was ready to join a game, and until then, those around her were in danger from the squeeze. Lizzy had learned the hard way that she couldn't always control herself in such situations, and it was others who paid the price.

"I suppose it's better to have someone with me," she

conceded, "but I don't think Olivia would be excited about being the person to help me cheat at poker."

"Lizzy, you're not …" He jabbed the buttons on the microwave. "Okay, you *are* cheating, but it's for a good cause. And it's not like Olivia and her clients haven't benefited from your ability."

"I'm sorry everything's so unsettled for the two of you," she blurted out. "You and Olivia could actually live together—and eat out wherever you wanted to—if you hadn't helped me out—"

He turned to face her. "Lizzy, nothing that happened is your fault. It's Louise Mortensen's fault. If she hadn't manipulated your mother's fertility treatment, you wouldn't have the abilities you do, and you wouldn't be in the situation you're in. You don't need to shoulder the blame for what she's done. She's the one who should pay the price for the pain she's caused."

They worked in silence for a few minutes, sliding past each other in the tiny kitchen, then Lizzy said, "I guess Olivia would feel better about things if we weren't sharing an apartment."

"Maybe," he said. "But that's her issue, and mine—not yours."

4

———————

The next day, Lizzy was standing on the balcony overlooking the apartment's parking lot when a silver Mustang pulled in.

"I think he's here!" she called back into the apartment.

Philip grunted an acknowledgement.

Lizzy's guess was proven correct when Andy McNally climbed out of the Mustang.

Like his older brother, Owen, Andy was six-four. Unlike Owen, he didn't carry any excess weight. And although he also shared Owen's reddish-blond hair, Andy's was thicker, and his mustache was a more luxuriant version of Owen's patchier one.

He spotted Lizzy on the balcony and waved.

She waved back but, conditioned by a lifetime of trying not to attract attention, restrained herself from calling out to him.

She stepped back into the apartment and hurried to the door. "He's here!"

Philip set aside the book he was reading—something by Carl Hiaasen—and rose from the couch.

Not waiting for Andy to reach the apartment, Lizzy met him on the stairway and threw her arms around him. The fact that she was standing two stairs above him helped make up for the height difference. "I'm so glad to see you!"

He tightened his arms around her. "Me too, kiddo."

He followed her up the stairs and to the apartment, where Philip was waiting for them at the door.

"Andy," Philip said, extending his hand. "Good to see you."

Andy grasped Philip's hand and gave it a quick pump. "Good to see you, too."

The three stepped inside, and Lizzy couldn't help noticing Andy sizing up the apartment ... and probably feeling some relief that he had booked a hotel room.

"We're borrowing this place from a friend of Philip's," she said.

"We figured it was better not to have our names on a lease," said Philip. "Never know what systems Mortensen and Viklund might be able to tap into."

Lizzy waved toward the couch. "Want to sit down?" she asked Andy. "Something to drink? Or eat? We have ..." Her voice drifted off as she realized that she didn't have much to offer Andy.

"Actually, I wouldn't mind going out to grab a bite," said Andy. "The food on the flight was mediocre at best, even in business class."

"Why don't you guys go," said Philip. "I'm going to be meeting up with Olivia in a little bit."

Lizzy suspected that Philip had two reasons for this excuse. First, he wasn't in a position to argue with Andy over who would pick up the check. Second, he no doubt knew that Andy and Owen weren't thrilled by the fact that Lizzy was sharing an apartment with a thirty-year-old man and was using the opportunity to remind Andy he had a girlfriend.

"That sounds good," said Lizzy. "Maybe we can get together for dinner. Maybe pizza," she added hastily, to assuage any concerns Philip might have about the expense of the meal.

Philip followed Lizzy and Andy to the door, where he raised his hand for her usual fist bump.

When Lizzy and Andy reached the Mustang, he opened the door for her, then got in the driver's seat.

"Nice ride," she said.

"I just can't stomach leaving a rental car lot in a Hyundai Accent. Any recommendations for lunch?"

She got out her phone and tapped, then turned it so he could see the screen. "Is this okay?" She gestured to her shorts, T-shirt, and flip flops. "I'm not dressed for anything too fancy."

"Looks good." He plugged the address into the car's GPS.

As they drove, she noticed Andy periodically deviating from the route and keeping an eye on his rearview mirror. She was glad he was being cautious but felt a twinge of guilt that she was the reason for the caution.

When they were settled in a booth and the server had delivered an iced tea for her and a gin and tonic for Andy, Lizzy said, "Tell me everything that's happening at home."

He smiled. "Ruby is keeping Owen in line."

She laughed. "I can imagine." Her smile faded. "How is he doing? Really."

"He's doing okay. It's going to take him a while to recover completely"—Owen had suffered a Louise Mortensen-induced heart attack and a Tobe Hanrick-inflicted stab wound to the leg —"but on the bright side, he *has* lost a lot of weight."

"And you're living in a new place."

"Yeah, an apartment in Center City."

She leaned forward and lowered her voice. "Are you guys safe?"

"We're being careful. My new place bills itself as high security, and Owen got a better burglar alarm in the Lansdowne house."

"You could get bodyguards."

He laughed shortly. "That would be pretty—" He took a sip of his drink. "—extreme."

Lizzy suspected he had been about to say *expensive*.

He continued. "I don't really see that we have much to worry about from Mortensen. What would she get out of coming after us now? Especially because we've demonstrated that we're not interested in running to the authorities."

"What about Theo Viklund?"

He shrugged. "I don't know what problem Theo Viklund would have with me or Owen or Ruby. It's you and Philip who need to be watching out for him."

They spent some time speculating about the possible relationship between Louise and Theo—had she been his guest at the compound, or a captive, as Philip had been?

They suspended the conversation when the server delivered their meals: a tofu poke bowl for Lizzy and ahi tuna for Andy. The server, whom Lizzy guessed to be in her late twenties, seemed to be sizing up her two customers and trying to decide what the relationship was. Lizzy knew that Andy was about ten years younger than Owen, who had been her father's college roommate. She supposed the age difference between Andy and herself wouldn't have been so noticeable if she had been dressed for the casino, but in her casual clothes and without makeup, she knew she looked no older than her seventeen years.

After the server left—with an extra-friendly *hope you enjoy your meal* for Andy—Lizzy asked, "You brought more of the juice?"

"Yup."

"You can take it on the plane?"

"Owen packaged it up to look like insulin."

"Too bad someone can't deliver it in person every time I need a new batch."

Owen had tapped into his expertise as a neurobiologist and his access to the facilities at William Penn University, where he taught, to analyze and replicate the drug Lizzy had taken from Louise Mortensen's protégé, Mitchell Pieda. He had lessened its concentration, which not only lessened its unpleasant side-effects but also shortened its shelf life. Owen usually mailed small batches to a Phoenix P.O. box rented in Olivia's name.

Andy smiled. "I don't mind having an excuse to see you in person, and a trip to Arizona is a nice break."

They chatted about news from Philly while they finished their meals.

After the server had taken Andy's credit card, Lizzy said, "Pretty soon, I'm going to be able to treat *you* to lunch."

He laughed. "A gentleman never lets a lady pick up the tab."

She swatted him on the arm. "That's so old-fashioned. You just watch. When I get back to Pennsylvania, I'm going to take you and Uncle Owen and Ruby out to dinner at Morimoto."

"So, you're cleaning up at the casinos?"

"I'm doing okay. It's sort of slow going because I'm trying not to attract attention by winning too much at once. Speaking of which, would you come with me tonight? Someone recognized Philip, and he wants to lay low for a little while."

Andy frowned. "Who recognized him?"

"Someone from Williams."

His frown turned into a scowl. "The prison?"

"Andy ..." she said, her tone cautionary. She dropped her voice to a whisper. "You know why Philip was at Williams."

Lizzy thought back to what she knew about what had sent then nineteen-year-old Philip Casal to prison: finding the son of a local rancher doing something "not very nice" to an animal, drawing a knife with the intention of scaring him off, and discovering that the other teen had a knife as well. It turned out that Philip was better with a knife than his opponent was.

"If the guy's father hadn't had connections," she continued, "I doubt Philip would have gotten in as much trouble as he did."

Andy sighed—he knew the story as well. "I agree it did seem like Philip got shafted on that one. I'll lay off."

They fell silent again until the server returned with Andy's credit card and receipt.

It looked to Lizzy like she had written her phone number on the customer copy.

5

———

Afdter spending the morning in the lab and lunching in her suite, Louise made her daily visit to the bunker. She applied the hand to the sensor and was relieved when it unlocked the computer on the second try. She made her usual foray into the financial accounts, trying unsuccessfully to access the links that had resisted her earlier attempts. Then, locked out of Theo's untapped accounts for the next twenty-four hours, she turned her attention to his email.

As with everything else on Theo Viklund's computer, the email interface was unlike any Louise had ever used, not only in design but in content. There were no folders other than the inbox, and although some of the emails were years old, there were only a few dozen threads, one for each of Theo's contacts. The messages were brief, and only hinted at what Theo's business with each contact was. He must have been communicating with them in other ways as well.

She scanned the messages and scowled. She pulled her phone from the pocket of her tailored dress and tapped a number. "Can you come by the bunker? I have a question about one of Theo's business associates."

A few minutes later, the door opened, and Lucas stepped in. He was a muscular man with the fair complexion of all of Theo's Swedish staff and a military-style crewcut, dressed as usual in khaki pants, a button-down shirt, and a sport coat that hid the gun in his shoulder holster.

"Do you know who *Billy* is?" Louise asked without preamble.

He frowned. "Probably Billy Chapel. Why?"

She gestured to the monitor. "I've been trying to close out the email threads that were active when Theo died. In most cases, it was easy. I replied as Theo and just told them I was no longer interested. One of the correspondents pressed a bit, but when I didn't respond, his emails stopped coming. The exception is this person who's signing his emails as Billy. Who is Billy Chapel?"

"He controls the drug trade and prostitution in Baltimore."

"Why would Theo be interested in some hoodlum?"

"He's not a hoodlum," said Lucas, surprising Louise with the sharpness of his response. "Don't make the mistake of underestimating him. He took over Baltimore before he was thirty, and now he's looking to expand—way beyond the East Coast."

She waited to see if he would say more, but he was silent. "The emails are so vague." She noticed she was twisting her wedding ring on her finger and forced her hands to be still. "Did they communicate via phone?"

"I imagine so."

"Do you know what they talked about?"

"I never overheard their conversations."

She scanned the email open on the monitor. "Chapel is talking about Theo's niece like he knew her. *Sorry to hear about Rey. She was a sweet girl.*"

"Viklund would sometimes send Rey to meet with colleagues after he stopped leaving the compound. Maybe she paid a visit to Chapel."

Louise tapped her fingers on the desk. "If Chapel knows Rey Viklund, maybe I can use the same story on him that we used on the staff: that Theo's so distraught by Rey's death that he's gone into seclusion."

"Maybe."

She leaned forward and read from the monitor again. "Another email from Chapel says, *Thanks for taking care of Phoenix for us.* What does that mean?"

"I know Viklund had some business interests in the southwest. Maybe he was working on those with Chapel."

Louise realized that *business interests in the southwest* might refer to the Arizona congressman Theo had sent Mitchell Pieda to kill, although she didn't feel compelled to share that suspicion with Lucas.

And Lucas's suggestion gave her an idea about another of the emails: *That clusterfuck in AZ didn't help our cause.* With a jolt, she realized Billy Chapel might have owned the mine to which Theo had sent Mitchell to disperse a group of protesters—and where Mitchell had chosen to kill himself instead. She kept that suspicion to herself as well.

"And how about this one?" she asked Lucas. "*Glad to hear you found an operative that wasn't as lily-white as the rest of them.*"

"Viklund sent someone to Arizona on an assignment—maybe the assignment was for Chapel."

"And who did he send?" asked Louise, although she had an idea who it was.

"Guy named Philip Castillo," Lucas said, confirming her suspicion.

Castillo had been a fellow guest of Theo's at the compound and had subsequently disappeared. "So Castillo was working for Theo ..."

"*Working for* might not be quite right. Viklund sent Rey to

Arizona to keep an eye on him—not something you do if you're certain of the person's loyalty."

"True." She sighed. "Originally, I tried to put Chapel off with the *no longer interested* message, but he's not giving up. Then I decided to just stop responding—"

Lucas shifted uneasily. "Maybe not the best idea."

She shot him a look. "Good to know ... although it would have been better to know earlier."

He crossed his arms. "I would have let you know earlier if I had known you were fielding emails from Billy Chapel. How did he respond?"

Louise gestured Lucas over to the monitor and pointed to the last two emails from Chapel.

The first read: *Ball's in your court, Viklund.*

The last read: *Cat got your tongue?*

"It seems clear I need to respond," she said, "and the least complicated approach would be for me to give him the story of Theo going into seclusion."

"Claiming that Viklund is hiding from the staff was enough of a stretch. Do you think Chapel is going to believe he's too upset even to reply to emails?"

"If you have a better idea," she said tartly, "I'm happy to hear it."

Lucas ran his hand across his close-cropped hair. After a few moments, he said, "No, that seems like the best thing to do. Not much Chapel can do to argue against that, and the less we have to do with him, the better."

"I'd be happy to avoid any interactions with *any* of Theo's former colleagues, but would Chapel be especially problematic?"

"I think so."

"Why?"

"He has no ..." Lucas knit his brow.

After a moment, Louise took a guess. "Scruples?"

"That's right. I've spoken to some of the men who have worked for him and heard rumors about those who no longer do ... including what he's done to those he suspects of being anything less than completely loyal."

To Louise's shock, Lucas had gone pale. This was a disconcerting reaction from the man who had captured Louise during her escape attempt and returned her to the compound and to the threat of having her thumb amputated as punishment.

She nodded. "I'll be as diplomatic with him as possible."

After Lucas left, Louise opened the browser and typed in *Billy Chapel.*

As Lucas had reported, Chapel was suspected by the Baltimore authorities of controlling the city's drug trade and prostitution. He was also suspected of extorting money from various small businesses—mainly bars and bodegas—and of money laundering and bribing city officials. All attempts at prosecution had failed, mainly because key witnesses changed their stories, disappeared, or, in one case, ended up floating in the James River.

Definitely a man with whom she was anxious to terminate communications.

Louise clicked back to the email program and spent some time crafting her response.

Mr. Chapel, I am a long-time friend of Theo's. As you know, Theo's beloved niece, Rey, was murdered, and the news plunged Theo into depression. He has gone into seclusion and, with Rey no longer available to serve as his second-in-command, he has asked me to fill that role.

I regret that any plans you had in process with Theo must be cancelled.

Sincerely,
Louise Vivant

She didn't want to give Chapel her actual last name, with all the problematic information an online search of it would reveal, and the use of a variation of *Vivantem* amused her. She read the email once more and hit send.

She clicked back to the browser and searched for a story she had been monitoring—one whose gory sensationalism had dominated public attention a couple of months previously when a hiker discovered three bodies in an abandoned trailer park in Sedona. Two of the victims were escapees from the Williams Correctional Facility. One was an ex-con who had done time there. The police had found a connection to another former inmate at Williams: Sedona psychic counselor Philip Castillo, who disappeared around the same time.

What the authorities didn't know was that Rey Viklund had also been killed around that time.

Louise couldn't imagine Theo had sent Philip to Arizona with Rey for the purpose of killing Rey—Theo had seemed genuinely fond of his niece. But had Philip and Rey fallen in with the Williams group, and perhaps walked into—or instigated—the murders in Oak Creek? Or had Castillo killed Rey in order to get away from Theo? That was a motive she could understand, if not condone. After all, she had killed Theo to get away from him.

In any case, there had been no recent news reports about Philip Castillo's disappearance. Considering his connection to the murder victims, it seemed likely he was dead as well.

6

———

Lizzy leaned toward the bathroom mirror as she applied eye liner, eye shadow, mascara, and lipstick. She thought ruefully that most teenage girls probably learned how to put on makeup from their friends. She dropped her gaze as her vision blurred with unshed tears. Or from their mothers. After a moment, she drew a long, ragged breath, and raised her eyes. Maybe it was just as well that, as with so many other things, Lizzy had to rely on the internet for her information. She forced a smile: her mother might have disapproved of the amount of makeup her daughter wore, even if—or maybe especially because—it was a necessity for her visits to the casino.

Makeup done, she went to her bedroom. The sliding door of the closet wobbled on its track as Lizzy forced it open. Lizzy had made room among the clothes of the official tenant—currently in prison—for her own: her two casino dresses and her wrap hung on the rod, and a small pile of jeans, T-shirts, shorts, and underclothes lay neatly folded on the floor, since the room's dresser drawers were full. Her few shoes were set in a row next to the closet.

She slipped on her red dress and fastened her Zuni bear necklace around her throat. Then, with a grimace, she retrieved her sandals from the closet and strapped them on. She looked forward to stopping at the discount shoe store and picking up a pair of flats.

From the stacked milk crates that served as a bedside table, she retrieved her cross-body bag—its pretty beading had caught her eye at Target—and checked its contents: phone, fake ID, the key to the Caravan, a lipstick, and the case she had taken from Mitchell Pieda, which contained convenient slots for syringes and the vial containing the steroid drug.

She grabbed her wrap from the closet. As she maneuvered the closet door shut, she heard a knock on the front door of the apartment, then Philip and Andy's voices coming from the living room. After a last check of her appearance in the closet's mirrored doors, she stepped into the living room.

The two men stood near the front door. Philip's hands were tucked into his back pockets, Andy was flipping the rental car key back and forth on its fob. Lizzy knew they would never be buddies, although each would have readily acknowledged the debt he owed the other.

She knew Andy was grateful to Philip for rushing to the abandoned Sedona trailer park to rescue Lizzy from Tobe Hanrick, and for providing sanctuary to Lizzy and Owen while they recovered from that encounter. She was sure Andy would also acknowledge the value to Lizzy of Philip's mentorship. But she also suspected that Andy harbored some resentment that Philip's guidance had proven more useful to Lizzy than what he and Owen had been able to offer, and it was Philip's connection to Lizzy that had put her on Hanrick's radar.

She knew Philip was grateful to Andy for providing him an alibi in the police's investigation of the arson and murder at Louise Mortensen's Pocopson home, and for acting as Philip's liaison to Lizzy while Philip was in the hospital. In Sedona, Andy had participated in the rescue of Philip and Lizzy from Hanrick. But Philip must have been aware of, and resented, Andy's disapproval of his and Lizzy's living arrangements, and the lack of trust in Philip it reflected.

And, she thought with some amusement, Andy's reaction when he saw her probably gave Philip another cause for annoyance. Andy's eyes widened almost comically. "Holy cow, I didn't expect you to look so ..."

Philip rolled his eyes. "... adult?"

"Yeah," Andy replied, flustered. "Adult."

Somewhat relieved that she hadn't yet taken the juice and therefore couldn't read Andy's thoughts, she said, "I have to look twenty-one to gamble."

"Don't they ask for an ID?" Andy asked, apparently grateful for an excuse to move the conversation off Lizzy's appearance.

"Yup. Philip got me one. Uncle Owen sent me the money for it." She sighed. "Yet another thing he had to pay for."

"Liz, you know Owen doesn't expect you to pay him back—" began Andy.

"I know he doesn't," she interrupted. "And I know you don't either. I know you've been helping cover my expenses. But I want to." She draped the shawl around her shoulders. "Ready?"

"You bet." He opened the door for her.

"Don't stay out too late, kids," Philip said, his tone sardonic.

"We could get take-out Thai for a late dinner back here," she said.

"I'm having dinner with Olivia tonight. Why don't you let Andy treat you to a nice dinner out?"

"Sounds good to me," said Andy. "Although it would be great to see Olivia."

"We could ..." Lizzy began. She was going to say, *go on a*

double date, but that comment, even as a joke, wouldn't improve the tension between the two men. "... have dinner together tomorrow."

The three agreed to the plan, she fist-bumped Philip, then she and Andy went downstairs and out to the Mustang.

"Where to?" Andy asked.

"Philip and I had been going to Mesa Blanca, but let's try Cactus Flower."

Andy tapped the destination into his phone. As they pulled away, he asked, "So, what's the plan? What am I supposed to do?"

"I'm going to be playing Texas hold 'em. You can gamble if you want ... although maybe at a different table. I don't want to try to keep from knowing what cards you have."

"Can you tell what cards everyone has?"

"Not everyone, but most. And the fact that the other players don't know about me being able to read their minds helps because they don't have any reason to put up mental barriers."

"And if people *do* know you can read minds?"

"It depends on whether they care. Uncle Owen knows, but he doesn't really care if I know what he's thinking, so he's easy to read. Olivia knows I can do it, but she doesn't want me to read her mind, so she puts up mental barriers, which makes it harder."

"But not impossible?"

"No. Sometimes things slip through."

Andy arched an eyebrow. "That must be interesting." After a moment, he said, "So those are the two determinants? Do they know and do they care?"

She shrugged. "I think some people are just unreadable, even if they aren't actively putting up barriers. Philip is like that. Sometimes there are people at the poker tables who are like that, too. I don't have any special advantage over them, and I'm just not that good at poker without being able to read people's minds, so I usually lose to them. That's okay, because if I won all the time, it would look suspicious."

They drove in silence for half a minute, then Lizzy said, "You know, I say *mind reading* but it's really more like *thought hearing*. It's not like I'm seeing into people's deepest, darkest secrets. It's more like I'm eavesdropping on the things they might say out loud if they thought they were alone. Like *Man, this hand sucks* or *I can't believe I got a full house*." She smiled. "Which is why it would be better for you to gamble at another table."

"I'd be so easy to read, eh?" His tone was joking, but she could detect a hint of nervousness. "I think I'll pass on the gambling and consider the Mustang my splurge for this trip. Plus, I gathered from Philip that I was supposed to stick with you."

Lizzy grimaced. "Philip's always worried that someone's going to bother me and ..." Her voice trailed off. "... pay the price," she concluded, trying to keep her voice steady.

When Lizzy's mother, Charlotte, had begun suffering small strokes, no one—least of all little Lizzy herself—recognized that she was responsible. The experiment that Louise Mortensen had performed during Charlotte's Vivantem fertility treatments had resulted in Lizzy's brain-squeezing ability. Whenever Lizzy experienced the inevitable upsets of childhood and got mad at her mother, Charlotte's condition worsened. When Lizzy's parents finally realized what was happening, they appealed for help to Owen McNally, who was not only her father's former college roommate but also a faculty member of William Penn University's Department of Neurobiology.

But even Owen hadn't been able to avert the inevitable tragedy, when seven-year-old Lizzy, feverish and fretful with a cold and angry at Charlotte for denying her the beagle puppy she wanted so desperately, had unintentionally inflicted the stroke that ended Charlotte's life.

And Lizzy could trace a direct route from her mother's death to her father's—Louise had had him killed to remove him as an impediment to her goal of taking advantage of Lizzy's ability to pursue her own ends.

Charlotte and Patrick Ballard's weren't the only deaths for which Lizzy felt responsible.

There was celebrity lawyer Lucia Hazlitt, whose only crime was pathological self-absorption and the inability to resist insulting Lizzy's father in front of sixteen-year-old Lizzy. Anton Rossi, the test subject Louise and her husband, Gerard Bonney, had locked in a room with Lizzy, having told him that she was a prostitute instructed to feign reluctance at his advances. Gerard himself, who had tried to defend himself from Lizzy's mental attack while Louise watched in horror via a video monitor. Louise's enforcer, George Millard, whose death had ended the gun battle between Millard and Philip, but not before Philip had taken a bullet in the shoulder.

There were others whose encounters with Lizzy had not proven fatal, as far as she knew. The biker on the Sedona trail, who had almost run Lizzy down and then blamed her for the accident. Wilson, the Walmart security guard, who had accused Lizzy of shoplifting and then followed her to her van and accosted her.

And against all these, the one man whose death she might have forgiven herself for: psychopath Tobe Hanrick. She had driven cross-country to Arizona's Williams Correctional Facility, where Hanrick was being held for the torture killing of a young woman. She intended to kill Hanrick to avenge Oscar Riva's death and had injected herself with the steroid drug she had taken from Louise's protégé Mitchell Pieda, thinking it would boost her squeeze ability. Instead, as she sat across from Hanrick in the prison's visiting room, she discovered that the drug rendered the squeeze ineffective. In its place, it bestowed on her the ability to eavesdrop on others' thoughts.

If it wasn't for the fact that the squeeze had saved lives—her own and Philip's—as well as taken them, she might have been tempted to stay on the drug all the time to keep those around her safe. But even she wasn't enthusiastic about risking whatever the long-term effects of the steroid-based drug might be.

Andy, unaware of the turn her thoughts had taken, said, "So what's the etiquette of being an observer at a poker table?"

"No talking, no coaching, no moving around too much. No pictures or videos. Don't touch the table or the chips—or me, I suppose, because people might think you're sending me signals." She considered. "That's about it."

"When do you inject yourself?"

"Right before I start playing."

"Do you need help with that? I've given a lot of shots in my day."

"No, thanks. I've gotten pretty good at it—plus you'd have to come into the restroom with me. I used to inject myself in the van, but one time someone saw me doing it and must have thought I was shooting up. I saw them talking to the security guy at the door and we had to leave."

They completed the drive in companionable silence. When they arrived at the casino, the parking lot was packed.

Lizzy started unbuckling her sandals.

"You're taking your shoes off?" asked Andy.

"If we have to park far away, I don't want to have to walk all the way to the casino in these heels."

"You don't have to do that. I'll drop you off."

"Hey, that would be great—thanks."

She rebuckled the sandals as Andy pulled the Mustang up to the entrance. He hopped out to open Lizzy's door.

She laughed as she climbed out. "You don't have to be so formal about it."

"I take my escort job very seriously."

She looped the strap of her evening bag over her shoulder. "I'll go to the restroom and give myself the shot, and I'll meet up with you in the lobby."

7

———

As Andy drove away, Lizzy stepped into the lobby of the Cactus Flower resort and headed for where she guessed the restrooms would be.

It quickly became apparent that she had guessed wrong and had ventured into a service corridor. She turned around to retrace her steps—and almost walked into Marcus. She let out a startled squawk and sidestepped to avoid him but stumbled on her heels.

He grabbed her arm. "Hey, if it isn't Philip Casal's—sorry, Mr. Riva's—young lady friend. Had a drink or two? Wouldn't want you to fall down."

She looked pointedly at his hand. "Thanks, but I haven't had anything to drink, and you can let go now."

Marcus's grip tightened. "Did Phil leave you all by your lonesome?"

"Mr. Riva isn't with me tonight," she said, entertaining a vague hope that Marcus was looking for Philip and not for her.

"Well, that's a crying shame," said Marcus with a leering grin.

"But I'm here with someone else."

"New night, new date, eh?"

Lizzy glared at him.

"I'm surprised Phil is willing to share you with someone else."

"He's not *sharing* me."

"Oh, yeah? Does he know about your new beau? If not, this new guy better watch out. I hear Phil is pretty slick with a knife when he's not happy with the situation."

She tried to twist her arm out of Marcus's grip.

He grasped her other bicep. "And where is this date of yours?"

"He's parking the car."

"Really? I'm surprised he left you to wander around back here with the other workers—and by that, I mean the *official* ones. I understand from some of my lady friends that you can get to the rooms from the service elevator. More discreet than taking the guest elevator up. Fewer prying eyes."

She looked up and down the corridor, hoping that one of those lady friends, or just an official casino employee, would walk by, but the corridor was empty. "I'm not going up to a room. I was on my way to the casino."

"Good hunting in the casino? Do you look for the high rollers?"

Lizzy tried again, unsuccessfully, to pull her arms loose from Marcus's grip. "Listen, I don't know what you're implying—actually, cancel that, I know *exactly* what you're implying—but I'm not a prostitute. I came here to gamble, and my date is going to show up any minute."

"Funny, I don't see him. Maybe he changed his mind. Maybe he found a 'date' he liked better." His eyes ran down her body. "Although that's hard for me to imagine."

Lizzy opened her mouth to object, then clamped it shut. She

forced her features into what she hoped looked like an expression of tired resignation.

She sighed. "Okay, you're right. I guess the guy I was supposed to meet stood me up. I'm really just looking for a good time." She looked at him slyly. "Maybe with you?"

He grinned. "Now you're talkin'."

He started to pull her into an alcove housing a housekeeping cart and a bag of dirty linens.

"Not here," she said quickly. "Come on, I have some standards."

He frowned. "I don't have enough money to pay for a room at this place."

"I have somewhere better: a van, all tricked out in back like an RV. It has a bed and everything. It's in the parking lot."

He scanned her again from head to toe and back. "Sounds okay to me. How much?"

"A hundred."

"Oh come on, girl, what do I look like? One of your high rollers?"

"Okay. For you ..." She mimicked his assessing head-to-toe scan. "... fifty."

He nodded. "That's more like it."

He let go of one of her arms and turned her toward the back of the hotel and began hustling her down the corridor.

"Not this way," she said. "Out the front doors."

"Why?"

"Look at these shoes! I'm not going out the back and then have to walk around the whole building to get to the van." She simpered at him. "Have a heart."

He sighed. "Fine, out the front." His hand tightened on her arm. "But I don't want you having second thoughts about my discount or trying to alert the guard."

"Are you kidding?" she laughed. "I have just as much reason to keep from attracting attention as you do. Probably more."

Lizzy was completely unprepared when he punched her. Her breath whooshed out of her lungs, and she doubled over, barely keeping her balance on the high heels.

"What the hell was that for?" she gasped.

"Just a little extra insurance against you having second thoughts." He jerked her upright and spun her toward the front of the building. "Let's go."

When they emerged into the lobby, Lizzy expected to see Andy waiting for her, but he wasn't there. What would happen if she and Marcus got outside, and he found out there was no bed-equipped RV waiting in the parking lot? What if he dragged her between two parked cars or behind a dumpster? Lizzy was pretty sure what would happen—and it wouldn't be what Marcus expected.

Lizzy realized that their path to the front entrance would intersect with that of a security guard who was strolling across the lobby. She had no intention of getting anyone else involved in this debacle, but Marcus obviously believed otherwise.

He jerked her to one side, behind a tree in an oversize planter, and turned his back to the guard and the lobby. "Don't get any ideas. We'll wait here until he's out of the way."

At that moment, the front doors whooshed open, and Andy McNally entered. He scanned the lobby and spotted Lizzy and Marcus. His expression darkening, he strode across the lobby toward them.

"You should go," she said to Marcus, her tone urgent.

"Now you're in a hurry, too?" he asked with a grin, reaching out his other arm to envelope her.

His grin disappeared when Andy reached them, grabbed Marcus's arm, and twisted it back and up, almost to his shoulder blades.

Marcus's shout was a mixture of surprise and pain. "What the hell?"

Still holding Marcus's arm behind his back, Andy spun him away from Lizzy. Marcus struggled briefly, but yelped again as Andy levered his arm higher.

The security guard hurried across the lobby toward them. "Sir," he said to Andy when he reached them, "please let go of that gentleman's arm."

"I wouldn't call him a gentleman," growled Andy, not shifting his grip on Marcus's arm.

The guard, whose name badge read *Reggie*, sighed. "That may be true, but you still need to let go of his arm."

After a moment, Andy let go, giving Marcus a little shove that sent him staggering toward Reggie.

The guard steadied Marcus with a hand on his bicep but didn't let go even when Marcus had regained his balance. "What seems to be the problem?"

"This man was harassing my ..." Andy glanced toward Lizzy and then back at the guard. "... daughter."

Lizzy raised her eyebrows in surprise.

"Your daughter, eh?" said Reggie. He turned to Lizzy. "You all right, miss?"

"Yes, I'm fine."

He turned to Marcus. "Were you bothering this young lady, Marcus?"

"She came on to me—I swear to God!"

Andy's hands tightened into fists.

Reggie said hastily, "Marcus, why don't you explain that to me somewhere else. I'll meet up with you right outside the doors in a minute." He pointed Marcus toward the casino entrance and, like Andy, gave him a little shove to speed him on his way.

Marcus scurried across the lobby, rubbing his shoulder and

casting baleful glances back toward Reggie, Andy, and Lizzy. When he got outside, he kept going. Evidently, he had no intention of waiting around to present his case to Reggie.

The guard shook his head. "Sorry about that. We do our best to chase him away when we see him, but he just makes the rounds of the other casinos and shows up back here eventually. It's hard to keep an eye on everyone who comes in." He cast his gaze speculatively between Andy and Lizzy, and Lizzy realized that Andy's description of her as his daughter might have raised another set of alarm bells with Reggie.

She hooked her hand under Andy's arm. "Thanks, Dad."

Andy patted her hand. "No problem, sweetheart."

Reggie sighed. "Well, I sure hope Marcus didn't ruin your visit to Cactus Flower, and I hope you folks enjoy your evening." He touched his brow in a mini salute, and ambled toward the doors, no doubt to confirm that Marcus had left the property.

Lizzy unhooked her hand from Andy's arm. "I could have taken care of that myself," she said with a frown.

Andy raised his eyebrows. "I thought the whole point of having someone with you was so you *didn't* have to take care of that kind of thing yourself."

"You might have hurt his arm."

"You'd really be sorry if I hurt that asshole's arm?"

"It's not just hurting his arm. You'd attract attention. It's never a good idea to attract attention." She noticed that Reggie had turned from the front door and was watching them. She tried to smooth the anger out of her features. "And now Reggie thinks we're arguing."

Andy also tried to relax his scowl. "We *are* arguing."

Part of her wanted to call it a night—not only didn't she want to spend it arguing with Andy, but her knees felt weak as the adrenaline left her system, and her stomach hurt where Marcus had punched her. If she asked Andy to take her home now, he might believe that she was rattled by what had looked like an upsetting but certainly not violent encounter. She doubted that Philip would—his ability to ferret out the truth was one of the traits that had enabled him to bill himself as a "psychic counselor" in his Sedona business.

She slipped her hand back under Andy's arm and turned him away from Reggie. "We might as well go ahead with the plan for the evening, especially since Reggie will be on the lookout for Marcus." She looked around the lobby. "I just have to find the restrooms."

"You didn't stop in the restrooms yet? How long was that guy bothering you?"

She squeezed his arm. "Not long."

Lizzy located the restroom, went into one of the stalls, and gave herself the injection. As she packaged up the vial and disposed of the used syringe, she noticed that her arm was showing the marks of Marcus's fingers. She was glad she had the wrap to cover them with.

She rejoined Andy and hooked her hand under his elbow. "I can't believe you told the guard you're my dad," hoping to lighten the mood. "That's a bit of a stretch, isn't it?"

"Unfortunately," he said ruefully, "not much of a stretch, since I'm two decades older than you are. After all, my brother was your dad's college roommate."

"But you're—what—ten years younger than Uncle Owen?"

"And sometimes act younger—am I right?" he said with a grin.

She laughed. "Sometimes."

8

The morning after her visit to the Cactus Flower casino —which was not as satisfying, either financially or psychologically, as her win over Lakers at Mesa Blanca —Lizzy was eating breakfast in the apartment, Andy having scheduled a brunch meeting with a University of Arizona medical colleague. She heard a key turn in the lock, and Philip stepped into the apartment. He was wearing the same clothes he had had on when she and Andy left for the casino, and he looked more cheerful than he had in days.

"Hey," she said through a mouthful of cereal.

"Hey to you," he said, tossing his jacket over the back of the other chair at the table.

"Did you and Olivia have a nice dinner?"

"Yeah. We ended up cooking in."

He didn't elaborate, and Lizzy hid her smile behind another mouthful of cereal.

"I'm going to make coffee," he said, going into the galley kitchen. "Want some?"

"No, thanks. I have tea."

She heard cupboard doors open and close and the sound of running water. "How did *your* evening go?" he asked.

"Marcus was there," she said.

The water shut off and he appeared at the kitchen doorway, half-filled carafe in hand. "I thought you were going to Cactus Flower."

"We did."

"And Marcus was there?"

She nodded.

He scowled. "What the hell?"

"The security guard said Marcus makes the rounds of all the casinos."

Philip's expression darkened further. "What security guard? What happened?"

Lizzy hadn't intended to tell Philip about the incident right away—these kinds of things always sounded less ominous a day or two later—but it had just slipped out. "Marcus was ... bothering me."

Philip set the carafe on the kitchen counter and sat down at the table. "Bothering you how?"

"You know," she said, not meeting his eyes, "just bothering me." The last thing she needed was for Philip to go after a fellow ex-con for punching her.

"Where was Andy?"

"He was parking the car."

"He was supposed to stay with you."

"The parking lot was really full, and we would have had to park far away, and I didn't want to deal with it in my high heels, so he offered to drop me off."

"Lizzy," he said, exasperated, "it doesn't do any good for someone to go to the casino with you if they don't stay with you."

"I had to go to the restroom to give myself the injection. I figured I could do that while he was parking the car, but I ran into Marcus. Should Andy have come into the restroom with me?" She had tried to make it sound like a joke, but her irritation was showing.

"Come on, Lizzy—"

"Anyhow," she interrupted him, "when Andy got to the casino, he took care of Marcus."

"'Took care of' how?"

"Jeez, Philip," she burst out, "what do you care? I'm fine. Andy's fine. We took care of it. It doesn't matter how."

He sat back and crossed his arms. "It does if a security guard got involved."

They glared at each other for a few moments, then Lizzy sighed.

"Andy twisted Marcus's arm up behind his back, and the security guard, Reggie, came over to see what was going on. It was pretty clear Reggie believed that Marcus was the one at fault —it sounds like Marcus has a reputation—and Reggie made him leave the casino."

"It would be better if Andy wasn't manhandling people in public," said Philip angrily.

"Reggie didn't even ask us for our names. He just thinks that Andy was some guy defending his daughter."

"His daughter?"

"Andy told the guard he was my dad."

Philip let out a snort of disbelief, which morphed into a chuckle, then a more expansive laugh.

Lizzy couldn't help smiling. Philip wasn't a frequent laugher, and it made her happy to see it, even if it was at Andy's expense.

When his laughter died away, Philip shook his head, still grinning. "Well, Andy gets credit for taking a blow to the ego for the good of the team." He stood. "Maybe some coffee will make me less testy."

He disappeared back into the kitchen and a minute later Lizzy heard the burble of the coffeemaker.

Philip emerged from the kitchen. "Okay if I hop in the shower?"

"Yup."

He was back, hair wet and in different clothes, almost before the coffee had finished brewing. He filled a mug and rejoined Lizzy at the table.

"Had you injected yourself before Marcus bothered you?" he asked.

Lizzy flopped back in her chair. "Not this again."

He waved a hand. "I'm not going to give you grief about whatever happened. I'm just curious."

She rolled her eyes. "No, I hadn't injected myself yet."

He took a sip of coffee. "So you could have squeezed him."

"I could have. But I didn't."

"Any sign that Marcus was suffering any aftereffects from your encounter?"

"Not that I noticed."

"You could have squeezed him, but you didn't."

"That's true. But it wasn't that serious a situation. I mean, it wasn't life and death."

"But that hasn't always made a difference in the past," he said gently.

Lizzy thought back to the people who had suffered in circumstances that couldn't possibly be considered life and death. Of the encounters in which Lizzy had injured or killed someone with "the squeeze," less than half might have qualified.

Philip laced his fingers together on the tabletop. "Did you think about using your power on Marcus and stopped yourself?"

She considered, then shook her head. "It wasn't so much a matter of stopping myself—it just didn't seem like it was necessary when we were in the casino, and I knew if he got me outside and I was in real danger, I could squeeze him."

"And it didn't happen spontaneously."

She shook her head again.

He leaned forward. "Lizzy, you and I have spent a lot of time trying to figure out ways for you to control your power—"

"And see—it's working!"

He shrugged. "I'm sure our conversations didn't hurt. But I think that you getting older, getting more confident, getting more comfortable in the world is going to be a huge help—has already been a huge help. I think the fact that you didn't squeeze Marcus is more to your credit than to mine."

She dropped her eyes to her hands, clasped around her mug of tea. "That's nice of you to say, but ..."

After a moment, he prompted, "But what?"

"I may be getting better at controlling it in most situations, but it's not going to protect people completely—especially if it really *is* a matter of life and death."

"Yes, I agree. It's not a solution. But it's a promising development."

He rose from the table and went to the kitchen to refill his mug—and, she suspected, to give her a few minutes with her thoughts.

When he rejoined her, he asked, "How did things go at the poker table?"

"Not as good as I hoped. The other players' thoughts were a little jumbled to me."

"You think that was because you were rattled from the encounter with Marcus?"

"That's what I figured." She frowned. "Plus, I think Uncle Owen might have lowered the concentration of the juice ... *again*." She sighed. "But I shouldn't win all the time anyway, so no harm done. I didn't actually lose money, just didn't leave with as much as I had hoped." She took a sip of tea. "Who *is* Marcus, Philip? Was he part of Tobe Hanrick's gang?"

"No, he was just some guy at Williams. He definitely wasn't in the gang that killed Oscar. The only thing dangerous about Marcus is that he knows me as Philip Casal—and knows I'm not going by that name anymore." After a moment, he added, "But just to play it safe, if the Phoenix casinos are Marcus's stomping ground, we should probably think about moving on to other pastures."

"How about Atlantic City?" asked Lizzy, only half joking. Atlantic City was only an hour-and-a-half from Owen's Lansdowne home.

Philip leaned back in his chair. "I'd feel better steering clear of the East Coast for a little while longer—or at least until we can figure out what Theo Viklund and Louise Mortensen are up to."

Philip's phone buzzed, and he pulled it from his pocket. He read, then asked, "We don't have any plans for today, right?"

"Right ... unless you want to come with me and Andy. We're going to the Desert Botanical Garden."

"That's okay—Olivia wants to meet me for coffee."

Lizzy laughed. "She can't get enough of you."

Philip raised an eyebrow, but it was accompanied by a smile. He tapped out a response to the text, drained the last of his coffee, and stood. "I'm going to meet her down the street—it'll give me a chance to get some exercise. Have fun with Andy."

She extended her fist, and he bumped it with his.

9

———

After Philip left to meet Olivia, Lizzy washed her breakfast dishes and showered. She had just gotten a text from Andy letting her know that he was on his way, when the front door opened, and Philip entered the apartment, his expression less cheerful than when he had left.

"I didn't expect you back so soon," she said.

"I already talked with Olivia. She wanted to tell me that she's going to D.C."

"For vacation?"

"No, for work."

She raised her eyebrows. "Permanently?"

"Not officially, although it might become permanent, depending on how things go there."

"Are you going with her?"

He stuffed his hands in his pockets. "I don't know. Although I'm happier having a continent between us and Mortensen and Viklund, as Olivia pointed out, a continent isn't a big deterrent to a guy who owns a jet. And we can't hide out here forever."

"You said Theo's plane took off from Hagerstown, Maryland. Since his compound must be near the airport, Philadelphia would be further away from it than D.C. would be, and if we were in Philly, you could take the train to D.C. to visit Olivia."

He smiled at her wryly. "You really want to get back there, don't you?"

She dropped onto her usual place at one and of the couch and heaved a sigh. "I'm so grateful for everything you and Olivia have done for me, but I do really miss Uncle Owen and Ruby and Andy. Other than you, they're as close as I've got to family." She didn't mention Olivia, not because she didn't feel grateful to her for everything she had done to help both Philip and Lizzy, but because she felt Olivia might not be entirely comfortable being categorized as "family" to Lizzy.

Philip sighed and sat down on the other end of the couch. "I'm probably being overcautious. The East Coast *is* a big place."

She sat up. "Does that mean we can go?" she said, trying to keep the excitement out of her voice.

This time, his smile was more relaxed. "Yes. Let's give it a try."

She broke into a grin. "When can we leave?"

"Well, Olivia's leaving pretty much right away, so we might as well do that, too."

She jumped up from the couch. "Are you guys flying?" She continued without waiting for an answer. "Even with the new ID, I don't want to try to use it to get past TSA, plus I need to get Ruby's van back to her, so I could drive back and meet up with you there."

"I'm pretty sure your godfather would have something to say about you driving across the country alone again. Plus, I don't have the documents I'd need to fly either—so I might join you on your road trip, if you don't mind."

"No, of course not—that will make it more fun." She started for her bedroom. "I'm going to pack."

He laughed. "When I said 'right away,' I didn't actually mean right this minute."

She laughed as well. "Okay, I'll try to cool it. Andy will be here pretty soon—we can let him know. And then we can call Uncle Owen and Ruby." She bounced on her toes. "And we need to plan the route—maybe we can do some sightseeing on the way!"

Andy arrived a few minutes later. Perhaps not surprisingly, he was not as excited about the idea of Lizzy driving cross-country with Philip as Lizzy was.

"How about the train?" he asked when the three were seated at the kitchen table. "They usually don't ask for an ID."

"But what will we do about Ruby's van?"

"Maybe Philip can drive it back."

Lizzy rolled her eyes. "Andy, Ruby gave the van to *me*, it's *my* responsibility to get it back to her."

"If both of us are driving," said Philip, "we can make quick work of it. Lizzy might get home faster than if she took the train."

"If we drove right through," said Lizzy, "it could take us less than two days. One of us could drive while the other one slept in the back of the van."

Based on Andy's scowl, she realized that introducing the idea of sleeping in the back of the van probably wasn't helping her case.

Philip must have realized it as well. He stood. "I'm going to let you guys discuss logistics. Lizzy, if you don't mind me borrowing the van, I'm going over to Olivia's place and give her a hand with getting things settled for her move."

"Sure," she said, fishing the key out of her pocket.

When Philip had left, Andy said, "Lizzy, I know you trust Philip, but ..."

She crossed her arms. "But what?"

"It's just a little weird for a teenager to go on a cross-country trip with a thirty-year-old guy."

She withheld the thought that floated through her mind: *No weirder than for a teenager to go to a casino with a forty-year-old guy.* "Andy, I know what you're thinking, but you really don't have to worry. Philip's in love with Olivia. He wouldn't do anything that would jeopardize that. Plus, he thinks of me as a kid, not as a potential girlfriend."

"That's what you assume, but how could you know? You said you couldn't read his mind—or listen in on his thoughts."

"I just know, okay? It's not that hard to tell how a person feels about you."

He dropped back in his chair. "Well, we do need to get Ruby's van back to her, and I know I'd feel better if you had some company on the road. Maybe *I* could drive back with you."

"You have a return plane ticket. Plus, Philip would still need to get to D.C. Maybe we could all drive back together ..."

Andy arched an eyebrow. "Maybe not." He sighed. "It's nice of Philip to offer to go with you. As long as you're sure about him and Olivia ... and him and you."

"I'm sure."

"Okay."

She got out her phone. "Let's call Uncle Owen and Ruby!"

Owen put his phone on speaker, and even before they had exchanged greetings, she blurted out, "I'm coming home!"

"Good heavens, Pumpkin, that's wonderful news!" Owen exclaimed.

"Yes, that *is* wonderful news," Ruby said less emphatically but no less sincerely.

Lizzy filled them in on the trigger for the decision—Olivia's at least temporary move to D.C.—and the plan for Lizzy and Philip to drive Ruby's van back to Philadelphia.

Accompanied by some hemming and hawing, Owen

expressed similar concerns as Andy, and Lizzy countered them with the same arguments.

Owen sighed. "I trust your judgment, Pumpkin—you do what works best for you." After a pause, he continued. "I agree that the East Coast is probably no more dangerous than Arizona for you and Philip, but Louise Mortensen might be keeping an eye on me and Ruby. I don't know that it would be safe for you to come to the Lansdowne house. Andy has a new place in Center City. It's supposed to be high security, with a doorman and people monitoring the CCTV ..."

"Bro," said Andy, "if Mortensen is keeping an eye on the Lansdowne house, she's probably keeping an eye on my apartment as well."

Lizzy was relieved that Andy himself had provided the excuse for rejecting Owen's suggestion. She couldn't imagine Andy's bachelor lifestyle would be enhanced by having a teenage roommate.

"We have some time to figure it all out," said Owen. They were all silent for several beats, then Owen said, with a hitch in his voice, "It will be wonderful to be able to see you in person, Pumpkin."

Lizzy felt her throat tighten. "It *will* be wonderful. I can't wait."

10

———

Once Lizzy and Philip had made the decision to relocate to the East Coast, Lizzy was so anxious to leave that Philip and Andy eventually agreed that there was no need to delay their departure. Andy rescheduled his flight to one leaving that afternoon, and after he left for the airport, Lizzy and Philip packed their things. It took barely half an hour.

They left Phoenix and headed north on Interstate 17, since Philip wanted to stop in Sedona before heading east.

"So what are we going to do when we get there?" she asked.

"I'm going to set things right with Eddie. Reimburse him for the couple months' back rent I owe him for the casita."

"You can't talk with Eddie. He'd either have to let the Sedona police know he'd seen you, or he'd have to keep the fact that he'd seen you a secret, and that's probably a crime, right? You are a 'person of interest.'"

Philip snorted. "That's the cops' polite way of saying they think I killed Hanrick."

Lizzy resisted pointing out that the cops' suspicions were correct.

"But you're right," he continued. "I shouldn't let Eddie know I'm in town."

"I can talk to him for you. No one has mentioned me in relation to what happened in the trailer park, so he wouldn't be breaking any laws by not reporting that he'd seen me."

"True." A minute ticked by, then Philip said, "I shouldn't have run. We were pretty careful not to leave any evidence behind in the trailer park. I should have gone back to work the next day and ridden it out."

"You couldn't have stayed in Sedona. Eventually the police would have realized you had a history with Hanrick, and that couldn't have ended well. Plus, where would Uncle Owen and Andy and I have gone if you hadn't been there to take us to where we could hide out and vouch for us with your friends?"

He sighed. "Yeah." After a few moments, he added, "But I still don't like having you take care of my unfinished business in Sedona."

"I don't mind. I'll enjoy seeing Eddie again," said Lizzy. "He's a nice guy."

"Yeah, he is. Too bad he used to be a cop."

"So what do you want me to tell him?"

"Tell him he can sell the contents of the casita, keep half the proceeds for the back rent—and for his trouble—and send the rest to you. Did Ruby get the P.O. box set up yet?"

"Yeah, she sent me a text a little while ago. It's near Uncle Owen's house in Lansdowne, but not too near. What about the stuff in your office—what do you want Eddie to do with that?"

"I'm assuming that when I dropped off the map, the landlord cleared the place out—probably sold what was in it."

Lizzy thought back to her visits to the office of *Philip Castillo, Psychic Counselor*. "That's too bad," she said. "You had some nice things there."

Philip shrugged. "The nice stuff is at the casita. Eddie should be able to get some good money for that."

A little over an hour later, they turned off the interstate and onto 179, scrub and grassland stretching out around them, mountains and mesas serrating the horizon. Soon they were passing through residential areas, negotiating a series of traffic circles, then following 89A toward Uptown Sedona.

As they neared the main tourist drag, Philip passed the turn that would take them to Eddie's house and Philip's casita. "I just want to check out the office first."

Philip's office was one of the last buildings before 89A began wending its way up Oak Creek Canyon toward Flagstaff. He slowed as they passed.

"It looks normal," said Lizzy, peering out the passenger window. "There are even brochures still in the holder by the door."

Philip pulled over a few dozen yards past the building and, leaving the engine running, opened the door. "I'm just going to give it a quick look."

"No, Philip—someone might see you." She opened her door. "I'll check it out."

"No, you stay—" he began, but she was already out of the car and jogging toward the office.

When she reached it, she looked through the glass-paned window. Everything in the waiting room was just as she remembered it: the rustic bench, the Equipale chairs, the woven rugs hanging on the walls, a kachina doll displayed on a shelf in each corner. The striped curtain that separated the waiting area from the room where Philip saw clients was closed.

Lizzy got out her cell phone and pointed it through the pane to take a photo, then jumped at the sound of a voice at her shoulder.

"You looking for Philip?"

The speaker was a tall woman with faded blond hair and bedecked in chunky turquoise jewelry. She was probably around forty, although her sun-weathered skin made her look older. A cigarette dangled from between two fingers.

"Is that his name?" Lizzy asked, flustered. "I just saw the sign for *psychic counseling* and thought that sounded cool."

"He's not here anymore. He disappeared. I should know—the jewelry store is mine," she said, jerking her head toward the adjacent store. She took a draw on the cigarette. "The police are looking for him," she said raising her eyebrows, inviting questions whose answers would demonstrate her insider status.

"Oh, yeah?" Lizzy was torn between the desire to avoid hearing whatever gossip about Philip this woman wanted to share and the knowledge that it might be useful information to bring back to him.

"Cops want to talk with him about a triple murder that happened in Oak Creek. So maybe not the kind of guy you would want to get any kind of counseling from, even if he was around."

"Well, if the police haven't had a chance to talk with him, they can't have the whole story—"

"I doubt he's going to be back," the woman continued, as if Lizzy hadn't spoken. "I'm surprised the landlord hasn't cleared his things out."

"Yeah, that is surprising. Well, thanks for the information."

Lizzy trotted back toward the Caravan, relieved to see that with the sunlight glinting off the windows, it would be impossible for the woman to recognize Philip as the man in the driver's seat. Before Lizzy reached the vehicle, she stopped to gaze out across the red rock vista, using it as an excuse to sneak a look back toward Philip's office. The woman was stubbing out her cigarette, which she dropped into a planter before disappearing into the store.

Lizzy hurried to the van and climbed into the passenger seat.

"Shit," said Philip. "It figures Mimi would pick that moment to come out for a smoke break. What did she say?"

"Just that the police want to talk with you." Lizzy scowled. "She doesn't seem very neighborly."

"Yeah, well ... she wanted to be more than neighbors, and I wasn't interested."

She laughed. "Everything in the office looks just the way you left it."

He raised his eyebrows. "Really? The landlord didn't strike me as the type who would let a moment go by before cleaning it out for the next tenant." He put the Caravan in gear. "Let's stop by Eddie's and then get out of here."

Philip turned the van around and drove a few blocks south. They passed the Cowboy Club, then made two rights, bringing them to a quiet residential street. They coasted past Eddie's house, behind which stood the casita where Philip had lived. Eddie's pickup was parked in the driveway.

"I'll let you off down the street," said Philip, "and wait a block or two away." He pulled over. "Text me when you're leaving his house and I'll pick you up here." He grimaced. "I really hate making you do this."

"It's no problem. And I'd like to have a chance to say goodbye to Eddie. He kept an eye out for me."

Philip raised an eyebrow. "Not as good an eye as I would have liked."

"It was my own fault that I left the casita. If I had stayed there like you and Eddie told me, none of this ..." Her voice trailed off.

"No second-guessing. What happened, happened. We make choices and we live with the consequences."

Lizzy nodded, then hopped out of the Caravan and walked back down the street. She turned into Eddie's driveway and knocked on the door of the rancher. A moment later, it opened to reveal a large, bald Black man.

"Well, if it isn't Philip's friend Lizzy," he said, his volume a few notches below his normal boom.

She smiled. "Hi, Eddie."

He stepped outside and scanned the area. "I was wondering if I was going to see Philip or one of his friends again. What can I do for you?"

"Philip isn't going to be coming back to Sedona."

Eddie frowned and stuffed his hands in his pockets. "I sort of figured."

"Can you sell what's in his casita and keep half of what you get for it and send half of it to me?" After a pause, she added. "And I guess the stuff that's in his office, too. It looks like it's just the way he left it."

"Yeah. I paid the rent."

Lizzy raised her eyebrows. "Really? That was nice of you."

He shrugged. "Philip was a good tenant, and an upstanding guy. If he came back, I wanted everything like he left it." He paused, then said, "The police searched it, you know. After they found Hanrick and those other guys from Williams in the canyon."

"Did they find anything? Anything they thought was interesting?"

"Not that I know of, but they wouldn't tell me now that I'm retired." He glanced around again, then lowered his voice. "Before they came, I packed up some things I thought he—or his friends—might want to keep. Hold on." He disappeared back into the rancher and returned a minute later carrying a copier paper box. "A man shouldn't have to leave his whole life behind just because he gets himself in a bit of trouble." He smiled and raised an eyebrow. "Or, should I say, the representatives of that man should have some mementos from his past."

She smiled. "Thanks, Eddie. I know he'd appreciate it."

"How about some of the bigger stuff? Like the rugs? Or the pottery? Do you want any of that?"

Lizzy thought for a moment about making an excuse to step away to text Philip, then remembered what Eddie had said about having paid the rent on the office. She felt pretty sure what Philip's answer would be. "No. You can sell everything. Will you be able to get the stuff out of the office?"

"That shouldn't be a problem. I know the owner, and he's the type who will be glad to have the place cleared out and not ask too many questions." He put the box on the step and pulled his wallet out of his pocket. "I can use some of the furniture and knickknacks in the houses I flip—nice décor to appeal to buyers. I can give you an advance on that." He counted some bills and frowned. "Although not much of an advance." He handed her some twenties. "How should I get you the rest of the money once the stuff is sold?"

Lizzy pulled a piece of paper from her pocket and handed it to him. "You can send it to that P.O. box."

"Will do." He tucked the paper in his wallet, then looked up and down the street. "You parked nearby? I can carry the box to your car for you."

"Thanks, but I can get it. I ... got a ride from a friend."

"Gotcha." He glanced at his watch. "Well, I'd love to stay here and keep you company until your ride shows up, but I'm doing some electrical work in the back bedroom. Which doesn't have any windows looking out on the street. Or the driveway."

She smiled at him gratefully. "Thanks, Eddie."

He raised two fingers to his brow in a salute. "Best of luck to you, Lizzy, friend of Philip." He disappeared into the rancher, and in a moment, Lizzy heard a radio or TV from inside, turned up loud.

She got out her phone and sent a text to Philip.

Leaving casita now. Eddie inside, away from windows.

She hefted the box and walked down the driveway.

Before she even had a chance to turn onto the street, the Caravan pulled up in front of the driveway.

She opened the back door, put the box in, then hurried to the passenger door and climbed in.

She didn't miss the longing look Philip cast back at the casita as they pulled away.

11

———————

The day after Louise sent the email to Billy Chapel, Theo's severed hand failed to unlock Theo's computer. Despite any efforts Louise made—varying the placement of the hand on the sensor or the position of the clips on the muscles and tendons, raising its temperature—the computer remained stubbornly locked. She thought back to Chapel's last message—*Cat got your tongue?*—and wondered what losing visibility to his emails at this moment would mean.

She called Lucas. "We need to see if Edmund can help. Can you bring him to the bunker?"

Lucas arrived a short time later, Louise's lab assistant in tow.

Edmund Rinnert's gray hair had almost grown out from the crew cut that had helped him impersonate Theo on a walk from the lab to the bunker. Fortunately, Edmund's nondescript appearance—medium height, medium weight, unremarkable features—and the fact that Lucas and Maja had cleared the route of household staff had enabled them to pull off the ruse.

"Good thing you have me here as your maintenance man," he muttered.

Louise understood that Edmund didn't have much reason to be cheery; after all, by helping her kill Theo, he had just traded one warder for another. Edmund spent his days in the lab and retired in the evenings to the apartment adjoining the lab. His moods shifted between sullen silence and angry demands that he be allowed to leave the compound. She never refused this request outright, but instead hammered home the point that they had to pick their timing carefully.

She never voiced her underlying reason for her noncommittal response: although Edmund had promised that he would not tell anyone about the compound and what had happened there, his reappearance after three years could hardly pass unquestioned, especially since he would reappear missing his left thumb. Louise also suspected Edmund would succumb all too readily to the temptation to tell his story, not only to the authorities but also to reporters or on some tawdry gossip show. No—she, Lucas, Maja, and Edmund would all need to leave the compound at the same time and then disappear in separate directions with their respective shares of Theo Viklund's money.

She cast a glance at Lucas. Based on his annoyed expression, she suspected Edmund had started complaining even before the pair reached the bunker. She was never sure what steps Lucas took to ensure Edmund stayed at the compound—she hoped it wasn't the threat of the amputation of his other thumb. She liked to think that she and Lucas didn't need to stoop to such crude methods in pursuit of their goals.

Edmund fiddled with the electrical mechanism for a few minutes. When he placed the hand on the sensor, the monitor displayed the confirmation message.

Biometric signature - Print: Passed
Biometric signature - Temp: Passed
Biometric signature - Heart: Passed

"Excellent work, Edmund. Thank you."

"I doubt I can keep it working for too much longer," he said, wiping his fingers on his handkerchief. "We better have a plan for what happens when we're not tied to this place by a piece of furniture."

"Yes, Lucas and I are working on that."

He jammed the handkerchief into his pocket. "Yeah," he said, glaring at her, "I'm sure you and Lucas will let me know what you decide."

Finding it preferable to respond to his words rather than his tone, she answered, "Yes, of course we will. Thank you, Edmund."

While Lucas escorted Edmund back to the lab, Louise returned the hand to the refrigeration unit, then settled down at the desk and opened Theo's email.

Her stomach flipped when she saw the sender of the one unread item: Billy Chapel.

I'm coming to the compound, and I expect to see Castillo when I get there.

She suppressed a shiver. She had hoped to put Chapel off, at least until she and Lucas—and of course Edmund and Maja— were out of the compound. At least the email confirmed her suspicions about the identity of Theo's non-Swedish operative.

Louise waited a few minutes, giving Lucas enough time to have escorted Edmund back to the lab, then called him and relayed the content of Chapel's email. "Since you obviously know him better than I do, we need to discuss how I should respond."

"I'll bring Maja as well. She had more direct interaction with him than I did."

Lucas and Maja arrived a few minutes later.

When Louise had first met Maja, she had been surprised that Theo's home, otherwise so elegant, was managed by a woman as inelegant as Maja. As with all of Theo's staff, Maja was Swedish, and Louise found it easier to imagine her sorting through produce at a farmer's market outside Stockholm, a basket hooked over her arm, than presiding over a complex as expansive as Theo's.

But the observation was far from a criticism. Maja had also defied Louise's expectations in the kindness she had shown Louise. When Lucas had taken Louise to the dispensary to await Theo's punishment for trying to escape from the compound, Maja had draped her baggy, hand-knit cardigan over Louise's shaking shoulders. More importantly, she had agreed to hide Theo's death from the rest of the staff and had even helped get her late employer's body into the lab freezer where it still lay.

Louise stood, and Lucas and Maja joined her at the desk.

"I filled Maja in on the situation with Chapel," Lucas said.

"Very good," said Louise. "I think the first question is whether Billy Chapel knows how to get to the compound. I was here many times in the past, and *I* wouldn't know how to get here."

"As far as I know," said Maja, "Herr Viklund managed Herr Chapel's visits as he did all his guests'—had his own driver bring him to the compound using an indirect route."

"But it's hardly foolproof," said Lucas. "Chapel could have had one of his men follow the car."

"Can we take care of him before he gets here?" asked Louise.

"If by 'can we take care of him' you mean, can I kill him," Lucas said testily, "then I'd say no. Killing him would be hard enough—his security is very good—but surviving afterwards would be just as hard. His men wouldn't let his killing go unpunished."

Louise turned to Maja. "I understand you're the most familiar with Chapel. Is there anything you can tell us that might help us prepare for his possible arrival?"

Maja pulled her cardigan more closely around her. "Not really. When he visited, he would sometimes ask for me if he needed something—a certain kind of food in the kitchenette in his suite or a certain kind of wine brought up from the cellar. I helped serve at dinner a few times when he was here."

"Did you hear anything during those dinners that might be useful?"

"No, not that I remember. They didn't talk about business when I was there—or if they did, it was in a way that someone who didn't know their business wouldn't understand."

"One of his emails made a reference to Rey. How well did he know her?"

Maja began to look flustered. "Not well, I don't think. I can't even think of a time he would have met her in person—at least here at the compound. Maybe Herr Viklund sent Rey to meet Herr Chapel outside the compound ..." She glanced at Lucas then back to Louise. "... but I don't think so. I think Herr Viklund would not have wanted Rey to spend time with Herr Chapel unsupervised."

"Why is that?"

"He is ..." She looked to Lucas "... *skrämmande*."

"Frightening," said Lucas.

Maja turned back to Louise. "He is frightening."

Louise twisted her wedding ring. "That is certainly good to know." She forced herself to drop her hands to her sides. "He wants to see Philip Castillo when he gets here. Is there some way we can track down Castillo? Just in case Chapel does show up?"

Lucas thought for a moment, then said, "A while ago, when Viklund was trying to locate someone, he hired a man to build a system that taps into the data feeds of a few big East Coast-based security companies and then apply facial recognition to scan for particular people."

Louise glanced toward Theo's computer. "From here? I don't recall seeing an icon—"

"No—Viklund left that kind of thing to the security team. I can run the scan. If we have a photo of Castillo, we can feed it into the system and see if he shows up."

Louise got out her phone, tapped for a few moments, then turned the phone toward Lucas, open to the About page on the *Philip Castillo, Psychic Counselor* website. "Here's his headshot. Will that do?"

"Yes, that's fine."

She sent Lucas a link. "I'd like to add another person to the scan. Elizabeth Ballard."

"We'd need a photo."

"I have one in my records." She drew a deep breath. "As long as the three of us are here, I'd also like to discuss possible courses of action. We've been tied to the compound for two reasons. First, it has proven to be an effective location to stay off the authorities' radar, at least so far. And second, we have no way of knowing what effect moving the desk would have on the sensor and our ability to unlock Theo's computer. But once the hand stops working, the second reason will be moot, and although we may be safe from the authorities here, I no longer want to rely on it as a refuge from Theo's business partners. I imagine none of us are enthusiastic about continuing to funnel money into the upkeep of the house and salaries for the staff. We need to start planning for our eventual departure. And to do that, I believe we need to understand what each of us wants in the long term."

Lucas and Maja exchanged looks.

"I'll go first, shall I?" Louise said. "My goal would be to replicate as much as possible the parts of my life at the compound that I appreciate. For example, the ability to do my research in a well-equipped lab—although admittedly that would be difficult to reproduce, since my needs are somewhat specialized. I'd also like to do my research in comfortable surroundings."

Lucas raised an eyebrow. "And you'd like to stay out of the hands of the authorities."

"Yes, of course. That as well."

"I would like not to have to deal with men like Herr Chapel," said Maja.

"And I," said Lucas, "want to stay out of the crosshairs of people who might resent things I've done for Viklund. Some of them have no doubt avoided taking action against me because they think I'm still under his protection. When we leave the compound, I'll need to disappear."

"To Sweden?" asked Louise.

He shrugged. "Wherever."

"What about you, Maja? I imagine you'd like to return to Sweden."

"Yes."

"Do you have any concerns about your safety in view of your association with Theo?"

"I could avoid anyone who might be interested in me."

"How about Rinnert?" Lucas asked Louise.

"Ah, yes—Edmund," she said with a scowl. "For a time, I thought that as long as he didn't know where the three of us went on leaving the compound, we could let him do whatever he wanted. But he does have his uses—if it weren't for him, we wouldn't have been able to use the hand to get into Theo's computer." She sighed. "Let's give that some more thought."

"And how about the rest of the staff?" asked Maja.

"Most of them haven't been around long enough to know anything that would be useful to Viklund's colleagues," said Lucas, "or to have done anything that would justify anyone taking revenge on them."

"That's not true of all of them," said Maja. "Elsa is one of the few remaining members of the staff who was here when Herr Viklund was alive, and she sometimes helped serve at dinners when Herr Viklund entertained guests."

Lucas frowned. "We can't start telling staff what we're planning. Elsa's a good girl, but I don't trust her to keep that kind of secret."

"We don't have to take her with us," countered Maja, "but we can't just leave her behind."

"We'll do what we can for her when the time comes," said Lucas, "but we can't give her advance warning."

"Lucas is right," said Louise. "Discussing this with anyone else—even, I'm sorry to say, with Edmund—will jeopardize all of us."

After a moment, Maja gave a single, curt nod. "If there's nothing further?"

"No," said Louise. "Thank you, Maja."

Maja left the bunker, easing the door shut with what seemed to Louise to be excessive care.

Louise sighed. "She's unhappy."

"She doesn't like to see people get hurt," said Lucas.

Louise arched an eyebrow. "Then she worked for the wrong man. I was always a bit surprised that Maja seemed as loyal to Theo as she did."

Lucas's expression darkened. "It wasn't loyalty that kept her here."

"What do you mean?"

Lucas was silent for a moment, and when he spoke, it seemed he had chosen to ignore Louise's question. "I had worked for Viklund for a few months—I was a junior member of the security staff, mainly patrolling the grounds—when my supervisor told us that Viklund was looking for a new head of the household staff. I thought of Maja. She was working at a hotel in Stockholm, but I knew she wanted to make more money, so I recommended her." He shifted his gaze to the computer. "I didn't really know what Viklund's business was. I guess I should have known that anyone whose name never showed up in the papers but needed a staff to protect him maybe wasn't completely ..." He waved his hand. "... up and up. But a good job is a good job. When they hired Maja, I was glad for her."

"Did she find the job to her liking as well?"

"At first. But working in the house, helping to serve at meals, she saw more than I did. Heard more. Not all of Viklund's guests were as careful about their dinner conversation as Chapel was. And once Maja had seen and heard those things, Viklund wasn't about to let her go." He paused, and his eyes shifted from Louise again. "I didn't know what she knew, and when there was an opening on the security staff, I recommended Maja's brother, Nils."

"Maja didn't object?"

He shrugged. "I didn't ask her." He was silent for a moment, then met Louise's eyes again. "Maja was angry when she found out I was responsible for Nils coming to work here. But he was smart and good at the job. He wanted to make his mark. After he had been here a few months, Viklund gave him a special assignment. Nils was supposed to befriend a journalist who was investigating a company Viklund had invested in. He was supposed to find out what she knew. He became ..." He cleared his throat.

"Attached to her?"

"Yes—attached." He drew a deep breath. "Viklund told him to kill her. When he refused, the young daughter of Nils' best friend in Gothenburg was ..." He glanced at Louise, clearly uncomfortable.

After a moment, Louise said, her voice stony, "Interfered with?"

He nodded. "Then strangled."

Louise suppressed a shudder. "What did Nils do?"

"He killed himself."

Louise realized she was twisting her wedding ring again, this time with enough force to raise an angry welt on her finger. She interlaced her fingers at her waist, forcing them to be still. "And Maja continued to work for Theo?"

Lucas's eyebrows lowered, and Louise thought he was angry at her for questioning Maja's decision, but then she realized his emotion wasn't anger but something she had never seen in his expression before: guilt. "What else could she do? She has family in Sweden, and any one of them—or their friends—provided leverage to keep her here and to keep her quiet. I think Viklund enjoyed the fact that he could command her complete loyalty—or at least a false version of it." He drew a deep breath. "Her service to Viklund puts her in danger from Viklund's colleagues as well. She thinks Elsa could be in danger because of what she might have overheard in the dining room, but Maja had much more interaction with visitors to the compound than Elsa did. His enemies, and even some of his friends, would want to know what she had learned about him and his businesses during that time. They wouldn't stop at much to find out that information."

Louise nodded. "We'll do all we can to keep Maja safe. To keep all four of us safe." She sat down at the desk. "You said you knew Maja was looking for a better-paying job. How did you know her?"

"She's my godmother."

Louise raised her eyebrows. "Really? I didn't know that."

"Not many do." He folded his arms. "I tell you that because you should understand that what happens to her is important to me. Family is important in Sweden. Not like here."

Louise wondered vaguely if Lucas intended that as a personal dig. "As I said, we'll do all we can to keep all of us safe."

He gave a single, curt nod, then headed for the door, but turned back at Louise's voice.

"You say Maja doesn't like to see people get hurt," Louise said, "but I can see how she might not have been too upset to find Theo dead in the lab."

Lucas's smile was grim. "Exactly."

12

The trip from Sedona to the East Coast was uneventful. Philip did almost all of the driving, while Lizzy watched the scenery or, if she got tired, slept on the little foldout couch in the back. When Philip needed a rest, they would stop, and he would sleep while Lizzy stretched her legs or went shopping for supplies. She suspected that Philip didn't trust her driving quite enough to feel comfortable being unrestrained in the back of the Caravan.

They reached Bethesda, Maryland in the mid-afternoon. The roadsides were dotted with flowering cherry trees, redbuds, and dogwoods, and Lizzy briefly considered but discarded the idea of proposing a quick side-trip into nearby D.C. to see the cherry blossoms there. Philip called Olivia, and they agreed to meet up for a late lunch at a sandwich shop near the office building where she was working.

Philip and Lizzy ordered for three, then took the food to one of the Formica-topped tables. Lizzy had almost abandoned her intention of waiting until they were all there before starting to eat when Olivia hurried in, her long black hair twisted into a bun at the nape of her neck, the bright spot of color of her red coral necklace a contrast to her dark gray suit.

Olivia gave Philip a sandwich-shop-appropriate hug and kiss, greeted Lizzy, and sat. "I'm so sorry I'm late, you guys. I was having some trouble extricating myself from a conversation." She gestured to her sandwich. "And thanks for ordering for me." She popped a potato chip in her mouth. "Tell me about the trip."

"Not much to tell," said Philip, "except that I've seen enough corn fields for a lifetime."

Lizzy started in on her chips. "I think I slept through most of the corn fields."

Philip described a thunderstorm they had driven through in Oklahoma and a deer they had narrowly avoided hitting in western Pennsylvania, but he, like Lizzy, must have noticed Olivia's distracted expression.

"Then there was the armadillo outside Pittsburgh," he said.

"Really? That's weird," said Olivia absently.

He rolled his eyes. "Liv ..."

She blushed. "Got it. No armadillo in Pittsburgh." She sighed. "I really am sorry, you guys. I know I'm not very good company right now."

"Work stuff?" asked Philip.

"Yeah. No." She wrinkled her nose. "Actually, I'm not sure. This guy who's supposed to be showing me the ropes wants me to take the lead in a meeting with someone who's much higher up the food chain, and who has a reputation for being hard to wrangle."

"That's good, right?" asked Philip. "It means he thinks you're up for the job."

"Maybe. I mean, on the one hand, it could be flattering that he thinks I'm qualified to handle it. On the other hand, maybe he's setting me up for a job he knows I'm going to screw up. I think he kind of resents me being here."

"If you could get me into a room with him, I could find out what he's thinking," said Lizzy.

Olivia waved a hand, "Oh, no, I didn't mean to be fishing for an offer of help."

"I'm sure you weren't," said Philip, "but she *could* help you out. She helped out with those two bastards in Phoenix."

"That was for a client."

"This guy might be trying to take advantage of you in some way," said Lizzy.

"It's hardly the same thing—this is just office politics," said Olivia. "I appreciate the offer, Lizzy, but it's certainly not worth having you take a dose of steroids just to save me a little awkwardness."

Philip's expression darkened. Lizzy guessed he didn't appreciate Olivia's implication that he had less concern for Lizzy's well-being that she did.

"Uncle Owen has really dialed down the concentration," Lizzy said. "I've never had any problems with it."

"Yes, of course," said Olivia. "I'm sure he made sure it's safe for you." She glanced quickly at Philip, who was still frowning, then returned her attention to Lizzy. "So, are you headed for Philadelphia after this?"

"No. It didn't seem smart for me to go to Uncle Owen's house or Andy's apartment, at least right away."

"If you need to stay here for a little bit ..."

"No, thanks for the offer, but I'm going to meet up with them in Atlantic City."

"Ah," said Olivia, her tone almost but not quite neutral.

"She has to earn money somehow, Liv," said Philip, exasperated, "and it's not like she has the paperwork she'd need to get a normal job."

Olivia picked up her sandwich. "I know, I know." She chewed

thoughtfully. "I wonder if there's a legitimate way to get the documents you'd need."

Philip picked up his own sandwich. "If you can think of a way, that would be great." He didn't do much to hide his skepticism.

"Thanks, Olivia," said Lizzy. "Let me know if you think of any alternatives. I sure wouldn't mind staying out of casinos for the foreseeable future."

Olivia asked for more details of the trip, and Philip largely let Lizzy provide the answers.

Eventually Olivia pulled out her phone and checked the time. "Philip, if we can head out now, I can drop you off at my apartment before I have to be back at work."

Philip gathered up their paper plates and deposited them in the trash, then the three went out to the Caravan. Philip retrieved his duffel bag and the box Eddie had given Lizzy and transferred them to Olivia's car.

"Thanks for the ride, Lizzy," he said.

She laughed. "You did most of the driving."

He smiled. "Then thanks for the company."

She was debating the best way to wish Philip goodbye, especially with Olivia there, when he resolved the issue by pulling her into a hug. "You take care of yourself."

She felt tears prick her eyes. "I will. You too." She stepped back and raised her hand, and they exchanged a fist bump.

Olivia didn't seem discomfited by the hug but appeared to be debating between a hug and a handshake for herself. She decided on a hug. "Yes, take care of yourself. And be careful."

13

———

Lizzy arrived at the Fortuna Hotel and Casino, a mile or so from the Atlantic City boardwalk, just before dark. She parked the Caravan in the parking garage, made her way through the hotel's opulent lobby, and took the elevator to one of the guest floors. She found the room number Owen had texted her and gave three light, quick knocks.

The door opened almost immediately to reveal Ruby DiMano.

Lizzy had been video calling with Ruby and Owen, but she hadn't seen Ruby in person since they had parted ways before Lizzy headed to Arizona, and the video hadn't captured the subtle change in Ruby. Although no one would ever call her curvy, a few extra pounds had softened the hard angles, and her mouth, which Lizzy was used to seeing pressed in a straight line, was more relaxed than Lizzy remembered seeing it. It looked like Ruby's life as Owen's majordomo agreed with her.

Ruby drew Lizzy into the room, closed and locked the door behind her, then gave Lizzy a quick, although heartfelt, hug. "It's so good to see you," she said, her voice raspier than usual with emotion.

"It's good to see you, too, Ruby," Lizzy said. She stepped back from Ruby, dropped her duffel bag on the floor, and swiped at her eyes. Then she turned to the room's two other occupants, who were sitting at a table near the window.

Andy grinned as he rose from his chair. "Hey, kiddo."

"Hey, Andy," she replied, but her eyes were on the other person at the table.

Just as video calls had not revealed the subtle changes for the better in Ruby, they had similarly disguised the changes for the worse in Owen. Owen had suffered a heart attack, courtesy of Louise Mortensen and an injection of potassium chloride, and a knife wound to the thigh, courtesy of Tobe Hanrick—it was clear he was still suffering the aftereffects of both. Although still a very large man, some of his fat had melted away. However, rather than making him look healthier, the slack folds around his face and neck made him look frail. His skin, beneath a patchy beard and mustache, was even paler than usual.

But his blue eyes sparkled as he heaved himself to his feet with the help of a cane. "Pumpkin."

She rushed across the room to him, but checked her momentum when she reached him to avoid knocking him back into his chair.

He folded her in his arms. "It is so, so good to see you."

When Owen released her, Andy gestured her into the chair he had been sitting in.

She dragged it closer to Owen's chair as he lowered himself carefully back down.

"How are you doing?" she asked him.

"Much better now."

She squeezed his hand. "Really ... how are you doing?"

He shrugged. "It's taking me a little longer to bounce back than I had hoped, but I'm feeling better every day. Ruby has been a tremendous help."

"You're the one doing the work, Doctor McNally," said Ruby.

"It's not much work—I mainly lie around."

"That's not true," Ruby said briskly. "You're doing physical therapy ... and resting up is part of the recovery."

He rolled his eyes. "So everyone keeps telling me." He turned back to Lizzy. "But I want to know how *you're* doing."

Lizzy recapped the drive from Arizona, emphasizing the parts she thought they'd enjoy most—mainly the scenery—and deemphasizing the parts she thought they'd enjoy less— anything reminding them that she had spent days on the road with Philip.

When she was done, she asked, "Are you all staying at the hotel?"

"Yup," said Andy. "Boys in this room, girls in the adjoining room. I feel like I'm at camp."

"I'll put your bag in our room, Lizzy," said Ruby.

Lizzy jumped up. "I can get it."

"You stay here and chat with the McNallys. I'm going to call room service and tell them to send dinner up." She picked up Lizzy's bag and passed through the adjoining room's connecting door.

"We're having dinner delivered to the room?" asked Lizzy, resuming her seat. "Fancy."

"I thought it would be more relaxing to eat in private," said Owen.

And probably safer, Lizzy thought. Not knowing what was going on with Louise Mortensen and Theo Viklund, they couldn't afford to let their guard down.

The conversation continued, now focused on what Owen, Andy, and Ruby had been up to. Lizzy couldn't shake the feeling that they were using the same approach she had: emphasizing the parts she'd enjoy more—mainly how normal and unstressful their lives were—and deemphasizing the parts she'd enjoy less—the danger and expense any involvement with Lizzy seemed to entail.

When Ruby returned, she was no longer wearing the beige shirtwaist dress she had had on when she answered the door to Lizzy's knock, but a light blue twinset, pearl necklace, and black skirt.

"Wow, Ruby, you look great!" said Lizzy.

Ruby blushed. "Since the younger Doctor McNally has other plans for the evening, I'm going to accompany you to the casino, and I thought I should dress up for the event."

"You don't need to do that. Of course," she added hastily, "you're welcome to come along, but it's not necessary."

"I'm curious about it," Ruby said, taking a seat on the bed.

They continued chatting, and a few minutes later there was a knock at the door. "Room service!"

Ruby went to the door and peered through the peephole, then unlocked the door and opened it. A staffer in a white jacket and black pants stood in the hallway next to a serving cart.

"Thank you," Ruby said, pulling a twenty from her pocket and handing it to him. "I'll take care of it from here."

"Are you sure?" asked the staffer. "It's no problem."

"Quite sure, thank you," said Ruby, already maneuvering the cart into the room.

Ruby closed and relocked the door, then Owen helped Ruby and Lizzy transfer the plates and silverware to the table while Andy fetched extra chairs from the other room.

The lowest shelf of the cart held a small white cardboard box. When Lizzy reached for it, Ruby shooed her away. "That's for later."

Dinner was lobster tails—Owen insisted on dipping his in butter, despite Ruby's disapproving looks—with baked potatoes and salads. Andy had brought along a six-pack of Victory

Hopdevil, and he and Owen each had two, Ruby had one, and Lizzy tried one and switched to a Coke from the mini bar. Owen finished her beer.

"Did you make more of the juice?" Lizzy asked Owen. "I think the batch Andy brought to Arizona must be almost expired."

Owen looked unhappy. "I did." He removed a small glass vial from his shirt pocket and handed it to her.

"Did you keep the concentration the same?"

He occupied himself scraping the inside of his potato skin with his spoon. "Pretty much the same."

"Pretty much? Uncle Owen!" she exclaimed, exasperated.

He set the spoon aside. "What's the worst that could happen? You can't read the other players' minds and so you can't win as much. You said yourself you can't win all the time, or it looks suspicious."

She rolled her eyes. "Yeah, but I can't lose all the time, either. It's not like I actually have any idea about poker strategy."

When they had finished dinner, Owen and Andy moved the dirty plates onto the cart, which Ruby pushed into the hallway. Then she opened the white cardboard box to reveal a small cake with *Welcome Home Lizzy* written in frosting.

"You guys, this is too much," Lizzy said, grinning.

"You coming home—or at least joining us on the East Coast —deserves a celebration," said Owen.

When Lizzy had finished her piece of cake, she fell back in her chair with a groan, then glanced at her phone. "I should get changed and go down to the casino."

Andy stood. "I'm going to head out. Meeting a local colleague for drinks."

"Okay," said Lizzy. "Have fun."

In the adjoining room's bathroom, she put on her blue dress, the Zuni bear necklace, and the high-heeled sandals—she still hadn't had a chance to buy low-heeled replacements—and applied her makeup.

When she emerged, Ruby was in the bedroom, brushing at a bit of cake icing on her sweater. She cocked an eyebrow at Lizzy. "You certainly look very grown-up."

"That's the hope."

"I miss the crazy color combinations you used to come up with," said Ruby, in an uncharacteristic display of nostalgia.

Lizzy smiled. "If I win enough tonight, let's go out and buy some fun clothes."

The corners of Ruby's mouth quirked up. "Yes. Let's."

Lizzy put the case containing the vial and a syringe into her cross-body bag and grabbed her wrap from the bed, then knocked on the connecting door.

"Come in!" Owen called.

He was working on his laptop. When he saw her, his eyes widened. "Good heavens—you look so grown-up."

Lizzy smiled wryly at him. "That's what I hear."

He hoisted himself to his feet. "Do you—" He cleared his throat. "Do you want me to give you the injection?"

"I can do it," said Ruby. "I gave my brother-in-law injections when he was sick."

"Ruby, I don't mean for you to—" he said, embarrassed.

"It's no problem, *Doctor* McNally."

Lizzy wondered if it was her imagination that Ruby seemed to put a little ironic emphasis on *Doctor*. Lizzy sometimes wondered how Owen had made it through medical school in view of his general squeamishness. She supposed it was the reason he had gone into teaching and research rather than medical practice.

"Actually," Lizzy said, "I want to wait until I've checked out the casino so I'm ready to go when the juice kicks in. I'll give myself the shot once I've done that. What are you going to do while we're all gone?" she asked Owen.

"They have a classic movie channel."

She raised herself onto her toes and kissed his cheek. "Have fun. We'll be back in a couple of hours."

14

Louise was enjoying a respite in the lab, entertaining herself with a perusal of files on the supposedly secure servers of the CDC. Access to such information had been one of the perks of her association with Theo.

She was also cheered by the anticipation of a perk of her association with Lucas: documentation to back up a false identity for when they left the compound. He had described two options. One was to purchase a stolen driver's license whose previous owner bore some resemblance to Louise. This could be done quickly and cheaply, but the license would have limited utility. The second was to commission a full set of documents that reflected information of her choosing. This would be expensive and take time to create, but the results would stand up to almost any official scrutiny.

She chose the second option and gave Lucas the information she wanted the documents to reflect. They couldn't have the forger bring the documents to the compound, and Lucas advised against sending a member of the already limited staff to pick them up, saying there was too great a risk that it might telegraph their escape plan. Louise herself didn't trust some of the newer security staff not to take a peek at what they were delivering. She asked that the documents be delivered to Philadelphia, where she would pick them up. She knew that going to the location where authorities were still on the lookout for her was risky, but she felt that the benefit of familiarity with the area outweighed the risks.

Her mood had been further improved when, earlier that day, she had been able to access Theo's computer and had not seen any new emails from Billy Chapel.

She looked up from the monitor when Lucas entered, carrying an iPad.

"Where's Rinnert?" he asked, glancing around the lab.

Louise gestured toward the door that led to two spartan apartments. "He turned in for the night. Why? Do you need him?"

"No," said Lucas, lowering his voice, "but I don't need him interrupting."

"Once he retires for the evening, he rarely comes out."

Lucas nodded. "Maja says he uses so much NyQuil, she's tempted to get it by the case."

Louise sighed. "I suppose there's not much for him to do in the evenings."

Lucas glanced toward the door, then lowered his voice further. "I believe we've located Ballard on the security video scan."

Louise raised her eyebrows. "Excellent. Where is she?"

"Atlantic City. At a casino."

"A casino? It doesn't really seem like her thing. Was she with Castillo?"

"No."

Lucas handed Louise the iPad. It displayed the grainy image of a paused video showing two women. The younger one sat at a poker table. The older one stood behind her, head turned as if to scan the area for threats—a hundred-pound bodyguard. "Yes, that's Elizabeth Ballard. And Ruby DiMano. But what's Ballard doing?"

"Playing Texas hold 'em."

Lucas reached over her shoulder to tap the screen, and the video played.

Louise watched, silent, through several hands, the pile of chips in front of Ballard growing larger, the expressions of the other players—all men—growing more morose.

"She's winning," Lucas said.

"Yes."

"A lot."

"Yes. Is there other video of her?" Louise asked.

Lucas swiped through various views: Ballard and DiMano stepping out of an elevator. Ballard and DiMano crossing the lobby. One showed Ballard alone, coming out of the ladies' room.

Louise stopped the video and zoomed in on an object Ballard was slipping into a beaded cross-body bag.

Lucas leaned toward the screen. "What is that?"

Louise's first impulse was to deny that she recognized it—the low resolution of the video would make that explanation all too believable—but she knew she needed Lucas's help to deal with the situation at the compound, not to mention the situation with Billy Chapel. Trusting him with this information was a lesser evil than trying to deal with those situations on her own.

"It's something I gave to Mitchell Pieda." She turned her chair so that she was facing Lucas. "What do you know about Mitchell?"

"I know Viklund sent him to Arizona to take care of a bunch of protesters at a mine. You know about that—you watched the drone footage."

Louise tamped down a twinge of guilt. "And do you know *how* Mitchell was intended to take care of the protesters?"

"I know that whatever he planned to do, it didn't require him to be armed."

Handing the iPad back to Lucas, she cast another glance toward the door to the apartments. "Let's go back to the house."

She closed down the computer, slipped on her coat against the chill of the spring night, then preceded Lucas out the door and down the path to the house. She caught a glimpse of a man standing in the shadows next to the path. Evidently Lucas wasn't relying on NyQuil-assisted slumbers or the threat of another amputation to ensure Edmund stayed at the compound.

As they walked, Louise thought back to the story she and Edmund had told Theo when they had lured him to the lab to lace his tea with poison: that they were investigating the possibilities of cloning non-human primates, dangling the hint that they might venture into human cloning as well. In reality, Louise had no interest in cloning, except as an interesting thought exercise. In her current circumstances, she was less interested in results that would benefit science generally and more interested in results that would benefit her personally—and quickly.

She had often thought how useful it would be to have Mitchell Pieda's clairvoyance and stroke-causing abilities at her disposal. With Mitchell dead, Elizabeth Ballard was the only surviving subject of the Vivantem experiments, and Ballard would hardly be willing to apply her abilities in support of Louise.

Louise would never regain access to her Vivantem lab or have the opportunity to experiment on women seeking fertility treatments. And even if she did, she couldn't afford to wait the years it would take the babies born of such experiments to reach an age where they would be of use to her.

What she needed was a way to create Mitchell's and Ballard's abilities in otherwise normal adults.

When she and Lucas reached the house, she led the way to the conservatory and closed the door behind them.

During the daytime, the transition from the conservatory to the woods beyond the glass walls was difficult to distinguish. At night, however, the darkness outside created an eerie mirrored backdrop to the bushes arranged along the walls and the tree branches arching overhead. The impact of the reduced staff was evident here, as in every other part of the house. The plantings, which had been carefully tended when Theo was alive, were straggly. Leaves littered the central brick patio area, as well as the cafe table and two chairs that stood there.

Louise turned to Lucas. "Mitchell Pieda and Elizabeth Ballard were both products of my work at the Vivantem fertility clinic. My goal was to produce babies who demonstrated clairvoyance, and Mitchell had that ability. He also had another ability—the ability to create strokes in others."

Lucas raised his eyebrows. "How?"

"Through the power of his mind. He called it 'the crush.' I developed a drug that increased this ability. Vivantem gammadexasone."

"Vivantem gamma ..." Lucas's voice trailed off.

"V-sone for short."

Lucas nodded slowly. "That's how Pieda killed the congressman who was interfering with the mining operation."

"Yes."

After a moment, Lucas added, "And how he killed the Attorney General—the one who was investigating you and the clinic."

"Yes."

Lucas considered, and Louise thought she could detect the slightest hint of a smile. "Handy resources."

"An untraceable weapon."

"And Ballard?"

"That thing she was putting in her bag on the video—I believe it's the case I gave Mitchell to store the V-sone and a syringe. When my Pocopson house burned, I saw Pieda near the house with Ballard—she must have gotten it from him then. But any V-sone I gave Mitchell would have lost its potency by now. Ballard's godfather and his brother are both doctors—I suspect they found a way to formulate more of the drug."

"And now she can ... crush people's brains?"

Louise smiled tightly. "Oh, Ballard doesn't need drugs to increase her ability. She just needs the right circumstances. Fear. Anger."

"So why is she taking the drug?"

"Mitchell was born a clairvoyant and only gradually developed the ability to cause strokes. Ballard was born with the ability to cause strokes and, as far as I knew before tonight, never displayed any clairvoyance. But if she took the V-sone, it might have triggered a previously dormant ability. I think that's how she's winning at poker."

"Killing people in a way that's untraceable *and* reading minds? That's quite a combination."

"Indeed. And if Billy Chapel shows up at the compound and just happens to suffer a stroke, his people could hardly blame us for that, could they."

Lucas laughed mirthlessly. "Well, they shouldn't—can't say they wouldn't." He shrugged. "But still a better option than putting a bullet in the back of his head."

"Is Ballard still at the casino?"

"Not in the casino, but she and the old lady are staying at the hotel." After a pause, he asked, "Who *is* Ruby DiMano?"

"Gerard arranged for the Ballards to hire her as a housekeeper when the strokes that Elizabeth was giving her mother caused Mrs. Ballard to be sufficiently impaired to need assistance."

"DiMano worked for your husband?"

"For many years." Louise arched an eyebrow. "Before she turned."

Lucas nodded. "DiMano isn't the only one at the hotel with Ballard. We also found video from earlier in the evening of Andrew McNally leaving the room."

Louise didn't bother hiding her surprise. "Ballard's room?"

"The room next door. It looks like Ballard and DiMano are in one room and McNally is in the other."

Louise scowled. "Is Owen McNally there?"

"Could be. I'll check to see if he shows up on the videos from earlier in the day."

"If Ballard's staying in Atlantic City overnight, maybe she's planning to gamble some more. It must be how she's earning a living. She can't rely on her godfather funding her forever." She twisted her ring. "Can you send someone to Atlantic City? If she leaves before we have someone there, we might not be able to pick her up again, correct?"

"We might catch her on another video feed, but it's not a sure thing. If I sent a man now, he'd be there within four hours, but we're already operating with a skeleton security staff ... and what happens if Chapel isn't bluffing and shows up at the compound? We'll want as many men here as possible."

"I know." She sighed. "But it's worth the risk. Ballard might be the best weapon we have against Chapel."

She described her plan to Lucas.

He nodded, considering. "We could make it look like a mugging or a rape."

"Make it a mugging." After a pause, Louise added, "But I don't want Ballard seriously injured. Just enough to get what we need."

"Broken bones?"

"That's fine."

"How about DiMano?"

Louise grimaced. "DiMano." She shrugged. "Whatever is needed. And make sure whoever you send thinks that the errand is for Theo."

Lucas nodded and started for the door.

"Lucas?"

He turned.

"Send someone expendable."

15

———

I t was near midnight when Andy eased the hotel room door open. Owen lay propped up in one of the two beds, wearing the navy flannel pajamas decorated with small white elephants that Andy had given him a few Christmases ago. The voluminous pajama top hung loose on Owen's now thinner frame.

Andy glanced toward the closed door to the adjoining room. "Have the ladies turned in for the night?"

Owen set aside the medical journal he had been reading. "Just a little while ago."

Andy nodded and let the door close behind him. He crossed the room and opened the mini bar fridge. "Want a beer?"

"I already brushed my teeth. Plus, anything from the mini bar is going to cost an arm and a leg."

"True." Andy closed the refrigerator door without removing a beer and dropped into one of the two chairs at the table.

"How were drinks with your colleague?" asked Owen.

"Fine."

"Anyone I know?"

"I doubt it."

"Where did you go?"

"Someplace on the boardwalk."

"You guys could have had your drinks here."

"I didn't want to run into Lizzy and have the guy asking questions."

"Ah, good point."

"How did she do?"

"She said she had a good evening. I hope she gets enough that she can find a nice place to live. Prices around Philly are so high. Maybe she could find a place a little further from the city …"

"She wants to pay you back for all the money you've sunk into keeping her safe."

Owen frowned. "I'd rather have her thinking about finding somewhere safe. I don't want to worry about her getting mugged."

"It would probably turn out worse for the mugger than for Lizzy."

"Unless he had a gun."

"True."

They were silent for a few moments, then Owen said, "Lizzy was all dressed up."

"Red dress, high heels?" asked Andy. "That's what she was wearing when I went to the casino with her in Arizona."

"High heels but a blue dress," said Owen. "I've never seen her in high heels before." After a moment, he added, "She looks so grown up."

"Yeah. I guess that's the point. At least she's not wearing that kind of stuff all the time—just when she needs to pass for twenty-one."

"It is disconcerting. When we left her in Arizona, I still thought of her as a child. Now … she may not be legal to gamble, but she's an adult."

"Ready to make her own life decisions."

"Yes."

Andy laughed quietly. "Although that's not exactly new."

Owen gave a rueful smile. "True." He heaved a sigh. "Lizzy wants to stay another night. Any chance you could stay here with her?"

A half minute ticked by in silence, and when Andy spoke, his voice was low. "When we left her in Arizona, I thought of her as a kid, too. I don't know if that made it easier or harder to leave her with Castillo, although I felt better about that when Olivia Riva showed up, and it was clear Castillo had feelings for her. And I have to admit he's taken good care of Lizzy." He lapsed into silence again, then continued, his voice even softer. "When I went to visit her, I thought she was the same old Lizzy ... until she showed up in that dress." He laughed without humor. "Although it wasn't just the dress—it was the way she held herself, her confidence. She really had grown up. I—" He cleared his throat. "I had never thought of her that way before."

"As an adult?"

"As a woman."

Owen's eyebrows climbed. "But ... she ... you ..."

Andy scowled. "Yes, I know. She's seventeen. I'm more than twice her age. I'm not telling you I'm *proud* of my reaction. I'm —" He cleared his throat. "I'm ashamed of it. She may be mature, but she *is* still a kid."

After a moment, Owen said, "Ah." After a beat, he asked, "Does she know? That you think about her that way?"

Andy dropped his head back against the chair. "I hope not."

"That's why you left before she got the injection—before she could read minds."

"Yes."

"Did you really have drinks with a colleague?"

"No. It was just an excuse. I just walked up and down the boardwalk."

"All evening?"

Andy shrugged.

"But you were with her when she went to the casino in Phoenix. She must have taken the drug then."

"Yeah, but she told me that she generally can't read the minds of people who actively don't want her to do that—who put up mental barriers—so I spent the whole freaking night running through mnemonics from med school."

"Like what?"

Andy snorted. "Well, I started with, *Some Lovers Try Positions That They Can't Handle—*"

"Carpal bones," interjected Owen.

"Right. But obviously not helpful under the circumstances. So then I switched to, *On old Olympus's towering top, a Finn and German viewed some hops.*"

"Cranial nerves."

"Bro," Andy said, exasperated, "this isn't a quiz."

Owen blushed. "Right. Sorry."

"When that guy hassled her at the casino, I told the security guard she was my daughter."

"That was commendable."

"It wasn't much of a stretch." Andy scrubbed his hand down his face. "The whole thing is humiliating. At least she's your goddaughter and not your—our—actual niece. Although maybe if she was, I wouldn't feel this way."

"She *is* a lovely young lady," Owen said, his voice bleak.

"*Young* being the key word."

"Yes."

Another half minute ticked by, then Andy said, "Beer? My treat."

Owen pushed back the covers and swung his legs off the bed. "Yeah, why not."

16

The next morning, Lizzy and Ruby found Owen and Andy at the table in their room, which was covered with an assortment of cups, a McDonald's bag, and wrappers from four Egg McMuffins.

"Doctor McNally," Ruby said to Owen in a tart tone, "I don't think McDonald's is on the approved list."

Owen held up his hands. "I didn't order it—Andy brought it."

"'Bad influence' is practically my unofficial job title," said Andy. He gestured to a bag and beverage holder on the dresser. "There are McMuffins for you guys, and some coffee and juice."

Ruby shook her head and started cleaning the detritus of Owen and Andy's breakfast off the table.

Andy stood. "I can do that."

"All right," said Ruby, stepping back from the table and taking the McMuffin that Lizzy held out to her. "Will we be staying another day? Lizzy would like to have another evening in Atlantic City."

Lizzy nodded, her mouth already full of McMuffin.

"It's certainly fine for Lizzy to stay until tomorrow," Owen said, "but Andy needs to get back to Philly today. Ruby, if you're willing to stay, then I can go back to Philly with Andy, and he can take me to my appointment."

"I wouldn't mind staying," said Ruby. "Atlantic City is interesting."

Lizzy was about to mount yet another argument about the fact that she didn't need to be babysat but changed her mind. Not only did she not believe another argument would be successful, but it would be nice to have Ruby as company.

Ruby continued. "Lizzy can drop me off tomorrow—not Doctor McNally's house but somewhere close by—as long as I can get a ride to Lansdowne." She turned to Lizzy. "I imagine you'll need to keep the Caravan for a bit."

Lizzy blushed. "If it's okay, that would be great. I promise as soon as I can I'll get a car of my own."

"It's no problem—the older Doctor McNally is letting me use his car."

Owen and Andy finished their coffees, then they packed up.

When they left, Lizzy and Ruby adjourned to their room.

"When do you want to go back to the casino?" Ruby asked.

"Probably not until this evening. It'll be busier then, and easier for me to blend in. We could check out the boardwalk until then." She brightened. "We can shop for fun clothes."

They drove to the boardwalk and parked near its northern end, then walked south. The buildings were an odd mixture of old-time elegance and modern kitsch, the shops and hotels providing a near-continuous audio backdrop of Springsteen songs. They played a round of mini golf, which Ruby won, and bought a sleeve of french fries, which resulted in pursuit by a well-fed squirrel. They checked out the shops, where Ruby bought a blue sunhat, and Lizzy found a yellow sundress with purple and pink flowers, and a pair of yellow flip flops decorated with purple flowers. Her search for flats she could wear to the casino in place of her high heels was unsuccessful.

They walked part-way back on the beach, especially pleasant on the unseasonably warm May day, then took an electric tram the rest of the way to their starting point.

As the sun dipped toward the horizon, they returned to the Fortuna, changed into their dressier clothes, and headed for the casino.

After Lizzy had scoped out the situation, had given herself the injection, and was seated at a table, she realized that the latest supply of the juice was even less concentrated than the previous one had been. She sighed—she was really going to have to have a talk with Uncle Owen.

After losing several hands, Lizzy cashed out her chips and led Ruby to the lobby.

"I think I need to give myself another injection," she whispered to Ruby.

Ruby raised an eyebrow. "Is that wise?"

"I'm sure it's fine." She normally limited herself to not more than one injection per day, but the concentration seemed so low that it didn't seem like much of a risk. She continued before Ruby could make an argument to the contrary. "But I don't want to go back to the same table." Lizzy got out her phone and brought up the map app. "There's another casino practically next door—Lucky Shores."

Ruby peered at the phone. "What's that empty space between here and there?"

Lizzy switched to the satellite view. "A field. Look, there are some paths across it. Probably people go back and forth between the casinos all the time."

They went outside and headed toward Lucky Shores. Although the high heels were exactly the wrong kind of footwear for walking through sand, Lizzy didn't want to take them off and risk treading on a piece of shell or broken glass.

When they reached Lucky Shores, and Lizzy had scoped out the casino, she retired to the restroom, gave herself the second injection, then joined a game of Texas hold 'em. However, her ability to eavesdrop on her fellow players faded as quickly as it had at the Fortuna. Feeling increasingly irritated with Owen, she cashed out her chips. Her aching feet didn't improve her mood.

When they got outside, Ruby looked skeptically across the now-dark parcel of land. "Maybe we should go around."

Lizzy groaned. "It would be twice the distance, and my feet are killing me." She got out her phone and tapped. "Plus, I don't think the road is really meant for pedestrians."

"We could get a cab."

Lizzy looked toward the taxi stand, where two dozen young men—based on the raucous shouts, she guessed it was a huge bachelor party—were waiting for rides. "It will take forever. Do you have a ride share app?"

"A what?"

Lizzy sighed. She herself didn't have an app because she didn't have the credit card it would require. "Let's just walk."

Lizzy had planned on lighting their way with her flashlight app, but once they reached the path, they found there was enough ambient light from the buildings on either side of the parcel to light their way.

They were about half-way across the lot when Lizzy heard the pad of footsteps in the sand behind them and a shout from Ruby, then her head exploded in pain.

Lizzy dropped to her knees, one hand clamped to the back of her head, where she could feel a warm pulse of blood. Vaguely, through the din in her head, she heard Ruby yelling.

Something jerked against her torso, and she landed on her butt. She looked up to see a man looming over her, and she realized that he had grabbed her cross-body bag, whose strap was still looped over her body. As he zipped the bag open, Ruby scrambled to her feet, drew back her purse, and landed a blow on his shoulder.

The man swept an arm behind him, the dim light catching something metallic on his hand, and caught Ruby in the face. Ruby reeled backward and went sprawling, her glasses flying into the seagrass bordering the path.

"Hey!" Lizzy raised her voice, but a lifetime of training herself to avoid attracting attention kept it short of a full-throated yell. She dropped her hand from her head and tried to push herself to her feet but was overcome by a wave of dizziness and fell back.

The man pulled the cash from Lizzy's bag, sending her phone and the case containing the drug vial tumbling to the ground. Trying to keep her eyes on their attacker, who was shoving the roll of cash into his pocket, Lizzy groped in the sand, driven by a confused sense of urgency about the importance of not allowing those items to fall into someone else's hands. Her fingers closed on the phone, and she looked up to see the man withdrawing his hand from his pocket. Lizzy suspected that the blow to her head was making her hallucinate, because he was holding what looked like a handkerchief. He reached for Lizzy's head.

Lizzy tried to swat his hands away. "Leave me alone!" she gasped.

He clamped the handkerchief over the wound on the back of her head, his other hand on her forehead to provide counter pressure.

She felt the sluggish stirrings of the squeeze percolating in her brain, but with very little power behind it. She also felt the man's thoughts tickling at her mind, but they were gibberish. She felt poised in some no-man's-land between the ability to squeeze her attacker and the ability to hear his thoughts, with neither functional enough to help her.

Ruby scuttled on her hands and knees toward Lizzy and the attacker, then rose to her knees, drew back her purse, and landed a well-aimed blow at the back of the attacker's knees.

He went down, still holding the now blood-soaked handkerchief.

Ruby set up to swing her purse again, aiming for his head.

The man scrambled to his feet. He drew back his hand, aiming at Ruby, and Lizzy saw what was on his hand: brass knuckles.

"No!" she screamed.

The last remnants of the man's thoughts fell away, replaced by a slight coalescing of the squeeze. Her mind reached out and slapped his.

He groaned and doubled over, one hand pressed to a temple, one hand supporting himself on his knee.

Ruby levered herself upright, circled behind him, planted her foot on his butt, and shoved. He toppled forward, barely extending his hands to break his fall.

Ruby knelt beside Lizzy, keeping her eye on the man, who was still on the ground and groaning softly. "Are you okay?" she asked, her voice nasal, blood flowing from her nose.

Lizzy nodded. "Are you?"

"I'm fine." Ruby grabbed her arm and tried to haul Lizzy up. "Let's go."

"The case with the juice—it's on the ground somewhere. We can't leave it."

From the direction of Lucky Shores, Lizzy heard a raised voice—*Hey, what's going on?*—and saw the strobe of a flashlight beam, although it seemed too far away to pick them out among the tufts of seagrass. Having someone find them now would surely result in an interview with the Atlantic City police, and any encounter with the police was to be avoided. She swept her hands frantically across the ground, hoping the case hadn't been kicked away into the grass.

Ruby bent and snatched something off the sand. "I've got it." She thrust the case into Lizzy's hand and grabbed Lizzy's arm again.

"But he's got my money ..." Lizzy pulled her arm from Ruby's grip and started to crawl toward their attacker. He was now on his hands and knees but was making progress toward getting upright.

"You can get more money another night," said Ruby. "We need to go." She grabbed the wrap from where it had fallen and dragged Lizzy to her feet.

They moved as quickly as they could down the sandy path toward the Fortuna, Lizzy stuffing the case containing the drug vial and her phone into her evening bag.

Ruby handed her the wrap. "Hold that on your head," she whispered.

"Is he following us?" Lizzy whispered back as she pressed the wrap to her wound.

Ruby, still holding Lizzy's arm with one hand and using her other sleeve to wipe away the blood from her nose, glanced back. "I can't see much without my glasses."

Lizzy looked back. "I think he's getting up."

"Can you squeeze him from here?"

"No—not from this far away."

They turned back to the Fortuna and hurried on as best they could through the sand. More than once, a wave of dizziness hit Lizzy, and she stayed on her feet only because of Ruby's hand on her arm.

"Where are we going?" Lizzy asked, trying to marshal her thoughts. "To our room?"

"We can't walk through the hotel lobby looking like this," said Ruby. "We'll go back to the van."

When they reached the Fortuna, they took a circuitous route to the parking garage, detouring when they saw people or heard voices approaching. There was no sign of their attacker.

When they reached the Caravan, Lizzy opened the back door and practically fell into the cargo area. Ruby climbed in more gingerly and pulled the door closed.

"Do you have any towels or washcloths?" Ruby asked.

Lizzy pointed to a plastic tote. "In there."

Lizzy propped herself up against the side of the van, still holding her wrap against the back of her head. "What about your nose?"

Ruby dabbed her nose with the back of her hand. "It's stopped bleeding—it's just a matter of getting it cleaned up."

"Is it broken?"

"No doubt."

Ruby found some washcloths, wet one with water from a plastic gallon container, and began scrubbing blood off her mouth and chin.

Lizzy gave a sympathetic wince. "Doesn't that hurt?"

"Not particularly." Ruby pulled an empty plastic grocery bag from the tote and stuffed the washcloth inside, then handed a clean cloth to Lizzy. "Use that. It will work better than the wrap."

Lizzy swapped the wrap for the washcloth.

"I need to check out your head. I need more light."

"You can use my phone, but pull the curtains shut first so the light doesn't attract attention."

When Lizzy and Philip had been on the road, she had rigged removable curtains to screen the cargo area. Ruby got the curtains in place, then shone the light on the back of Lizzy's head. "I think it's going to need stitches."

Lizzy shuddered. "I don't know how that's going to happen. We can't go to an ER without them asking questions."

"I don't think we can drive at all. You certainly can't drive after getting hit in the head, and I can't drive without my glasses." She clicked off the light and handed the phone back to Lizzy. "We'll call the younger Doctor McNally and ask for his advice."

"How about Uncle Owen?"

Ruby arched an eyebrow. "I don't want to describe your injury to him and risk having him pass out."

With the phone on speaker, Andy talked them through an assessment of Lizzy's head wound: did she feel nauseated? Was she having any trouble seeing or hearing? He decided, clearly reluctantly, that the risks of waiting for treatment until he got to Atlantic City were lower than the risks of having to identify herself to the authorities.

"I feel better knowing Ruby's there to keep an eye on you," he said.

"Should I try to keep her awake?" asked Ruby.

"The advice to avoid sleep after a concussion is a little outdated—it's more a matter of making sure if she falls asleep, she doesn't vomit. I'll be there as soon as I can—and, of course, if you start feeling worse, you'll need to find a way to get to an ER, regardless of the risks."

When they ended the call, Ruby said, "We don't know that the attack was anything but a plain old mugging, but just in case it's not, you should probably let Mr. Castillo know about it. While you do that, I'll see if I can find anything online about it." She got out her phone. "Do they have police blotters online?"

"Maybe check social media," Lizzy suggested.

When Lizzy got through to Philip, she described what had happened.

"What did the guy look like?" he asked.

"White. Blond. Maybe six feet. Not big, but strong. Pretty young—maybe twenties. Better dressed than I would have expected from a mugger."

"Could you read his thoughts at all?"

"Not much—the drug had almost worn off. What I heard didn't make any sense."

"Is it possible it was a foreign language? Like Swedish?"

She sat up, regretted it, and lowered herself back against the side of the van. "You think Theo Viklund sent someone to Atlantic City to mug me and steal my poker winnings?"

Ruby glanced up from her phone, eyebrows raised.

Philip said, "I'm pretty sure your poker winnings wouldn't be enough to tempt him to risk anything that would attract the authorities' attention."

"But if Theo did send that guy, why did he hit me on the head and then try to stop the bleeding?" She considered for a moment. "Maybe he didn't mean to hit me that hard and was surprised I was bleeding so much."

Philip laughed ruefully. "Lizzy, you always think the best of people."

"Okay ... maybe he wanted to disguise the fact that an attack had taken place and didn't want me bleeding on the ground. Ruby's checking online to see if there are any reports of the mugging."

"Nothing yet," said Ruby.

"How was the guy who attacked you when you left him?" asked Philip.

"It was hard to tell because it was dark," said Lizzy, "but I think he was on his feet."

"Any chance he followed you?"

"I don't think so. We were watching out for him."

"Assuming Andy can patch you guys up, what are you going to do now?"

"I'm not sure, but I'll call you when I know."

"I wonder if we came back East too soon."

"Jeez, Philip," she said, wincing as her head set up a pounding again, "what would you suggest? That we hide out in some survivalist off-the-grid hut in Idaho for the next decade?"

She regretted the outburst as soon as it was out of her mouth ... but she had just seen Owen and Ruby for the first time in months and she couldn't stand the thought of another prolonged separation.

"Off-the-grid in Idaho would be low on my preference list,

too," he said, his voice soothing. "We'll think of something that will keep you safe ... *and* keep Owen, Andy, and Ruby safe as well."

Tears pricked her eyes. "I know it's not just about me. We need to keep you safe, too. And Olivia."

"We'll do our best to keep everyone safe. Call me back if you want to discuss options."

"I will. Thanks, Philip."

18

<hr>

Lizzy and Ruby huddled miserably in the back of the Caravan as they waited for Andy to arrive. Lizzy realized how out of it she must have been to think they could walk through the hotel lobby without attracting attention. Her dress and wrap were both blood-stained, her evening bag's strap almost torn through, its beading ruined. Ruby had fastened the washcloth to Lizzy's head with her dress's belt and was now alternating between looking unsuccessfully for news of the attack online and blotting her swelling and still-bleeding nose.

After confirming that the vial of the juice was undamaged, Lizzy transferred the case from her evening bag to her duffel, then, unsure of what to do with the bag itself, tucked that into the duffel as well. As the temperature dropped, she struggled into a zip-front sweatshirt and passed Ruby a cotton throw to wrap around her shoulders.

When they finally heard a car pull up next to the Caravan, Lizzy pulled back one of the curtains and peeked out.

"It's Andy." Then she added, her voice brightening, "And Uncle Owen is with him!"

She opened the door as Owen levered himself out of the passenger seat of Andy's low-slung sports coupe, and Andy pulled his medical bag from the trunk.

"Pumpkin," Owen said as he lumbered over to the van. "Are you all right?"

"Yes, I'm fine."

"Let's get in the van," said Andy. "I don't want someone coming by and wondering what's up—or monitoring us on CCTV. Owen and Ruby can sit on the couch, and Lizzy and I can sit on the floor."

Owen and Andy were both well over six feet tall, and although Owen had lost a lot of weight since his heart attack and the stabbing, he was still sizable. Once they all got in, with Owen and Ruby perched on the tiny couch that folded out into a bed, there was little room to maneuver.

"Owen," said Andy, "you check out Ruby's nose, and I'll check Lizzy's head."

Lizzy suspected that Andy proposed this division of labor because, after Ruby's vigorous ministrations, her nose was much less bloody than her own head.

As Owen gently pressed the area around Ruby's nose, Andy took a penlight out of his bag and moved the beam across Lizzy's eyes, then asked her to follow it without moving her head. "So far so good," he said. He put the penlight back in his bag and took out a headlamp, which he slipped onto his head.

"Let's see the cut."

Lizzy glanced at Owen, who immediately looked queasy. She tried to arrange herself to maximize Andy's view of the wound and minimize Owen's. "What's the verdict on Ruby?"

"Fractured," said Owen.

"There's no reason Ruby can't get checked out at a hospital," Andy said as he eased the washcloth off Lizzy's head and examined the wound. "Ruby, I'll take you to Mercy tomorrow. We'll think of some explanation that doesn't implicate Owen in domestic abuse."

"Ruby, *I'll* take you somewhere tomorrow," said Owen. "It's the least I can do after all the chauffeuring you've been doing getting me to doctors' appointments."

"Neither of you will take me anywhere tomorrow," said Ruby. "There's nothing a doctor is going to do that I can't do myself with a couple of bags of frozen peas and an aspirin."

After a moment, Owen said. "Actually, I think that's true."

"This doesn't look too bad, kiddo," Andy said to Lizzy. "It shouldn't take more than a couple of stitches."

"Are you going to have to shave my hair off?" she asked.

"I'll work around it."

She dropped her voice, although it was obvious that everyone in the van would be able to hear her. "Is it going to hurt?"

"Nope. I have lidocaine."

"Can you clean the wound?" asked Owen.

"Yup. I have betadine."

"Sutures?"

"Four-oh Monocryl."

"Saline?" asked Owen.

"Yup."

"Bandages?"

"And tape."

Owen peered into Andy's bag. "You're very well supplied."

Andy smiled. "Bro, you hang around with your goddaughter long enough, you know you better be equipped for emergencies."

Lizzy returned his smile ruefully.

As Andy stitched up the wound, Lizzy conveyed the conversation she had had with Philip. "What if the guy that attacked us on the boardwalk really is associated with Theo or Louise?" She glanced toward the curtained windows. "What if someone is watching the Caravan right now?"

"If they wanted to hurt you more than they already did," Andy said, "they've had plenty of time to do it." After a moment, he added, "Unless the guy who attacked you is out of commission."

"Last we saw him, he was on his feet."

"Did you hold back on the squeeze, Pumpkin?" asked Owen.

"Not intentionally—I wasn't thinking that straight. And I was coming down off the juice. Which reminds me ... Uncle Owen, you really need to bump the concentration back up a little in the next batch."

He sighed. "All right. Do you have any of the last batch left?"

"Yes. I can probably use it up—it's better than nothing."

They were silent while Andy finished stitching the wound. As he packed up his bag, he said, "I think we've administered all the medical aid that's possible in the back of a Caravan. I propose that Ruby and Owen take the van to Lansdowne and Lizzy come to Philly with me. I know we've been avoiding that, but if Mortensen or Viklund *are* behind the attack, then they know where Lizzy is, and an apartment building with a security guard in the lobby is probably safer than a hotel with a sleepy night clerk."

"But Lizzy will need the van," said Ruby. "If you take Lizzy to your apartment in the van, she can leave as soon as she gets the okay to drive. The senior Doctor McNally can drive us back to Lansdowne in your car, and we'll get it back to you tomorrow."

Andy snapped his bag shut. "Okay. But first, I'm going to check the odometer on the Lexus to make sure you two don't decide to take it for a little joyride." Lizzy's snort of laughter at the visual of Owen and Ruby cruising some small-town strip with the cherry-red coupe's top down elicited a grin from Andy. "And I'll pop up to your hotel room to pick up your stuff."

Lizzy's expression sobered. "What if someone's watching the room?"

"I'm ready for them," said Andy. He pulled back the flap of his jacket to reveal a gun in a shoulder holster.

"You're carrying a gun?" Owen squawked.

"I think the fact that someone brained Lizzy and broke Ruby's nose goes to show that some personal protection is a good idea."

"You don't need to get my bag," said Lizzy, although she regretted leaving behind the new sundress and flip flops, and cringed to think of what it would cost to replace even her modest supply of possessions. "Let's leave it. There's nothing that important in it."

"I agree," said Ruby.

"Still," said Andy, "it's a loose end. It's best not to leave any loose ends."

19

At three in the morning, the streets surrounding Andy's Center City apartment building were nearly deserted. He parked the Caravan in the ground-floor garage, got Lizzy's duffel and his medical bag out of the back, then hurried to where Lizzy was climbing out of the van. He offered her his arm. "You might be a little unsteady on your feet."

"I'm feeling fine so far," she said, "although I wouldn't mind swapping these shoes for something without heels."

Once she had replaced the sandals with the flowered flip-flops, she zipped up her sweatshirt to cover the blood on her dress and pulled up the hood to cover her hair. "Not very fashionable, I'm afraid."

"Nonsense—you're going to start a new trend."

They took the elevator up a floor, to a spacious lobby overseen by a reception desk staffed by a uniformed security guard.

The guard stood and nodded a greeting as Andy and Lizzy crossed the lobby. "Doctor McNally. Miss."

"Hey, Sherman, how're you doing?" said Andy.

"Top notch—thanks."

Lizzy felt Sherman's eyes following them, realizing that her outfit probably made her look even younger than seventeen. When the elevator door slid shut behind them, she said, "I don't think Sherman approves."

"It's not Sherman's job to approve. It's Sherman's job to keep the building safe."

They stepped out on the top floor, then followed a short, artfully lit hallway to the last door. Andy punched a code into a keypad, opened the door, and stepped aside to let Lizzy enter.

As he muted a beeping alarm, Lizzy looked around the apartment. The vibe was elegant but comfortable. The couch looked like it had cost more than the Caravan was worth, but its fawn-colored leather also looked like it would be a great place to settle in with a book. The art on the walls was modern but not jarring. "Nice place."

"Thanks. Want anything to eat? Or drink?" After a moment, he added, "Like fruit juice or soy milk?"

"Not right now, thanks. But I would like to get cleaned up."

He dropped his medical bag by the front door, then gestured her to follow him. "Right this way."

Carrying her duffel bag, he led her down a hallway and flipped on the light in one of the rooms. It looked more like a spa than a bathroom. The pale gray towels were so fluffy, Lizzy thought she could spread them on the tiled floor as a decent mattress.

"Do you have towels that aren't quite so nice?" she asked. "I'm afraid I might get blood on them."

"Not to worry—there are more where those came from." He set her bag on the floor. "Need anything else?"

"I don't think so."

"You should keep the stitches dry for the next day or two. There are some toiletry supplies I picked up in hotels in the vanity—there's probably a shower cap in there."

"Thanks, Andy."

"Sure thing, kiddo."

He stepped back and closed the door.

She took a long, hot shower, letting the jets pound the tightness out of her shoulders. When she finally emerged and patted herself dry, she was relieved that the towel appeared to be stain-free. She put on a T-shirt, sweatshirt, sweatpants, and flip flops.

She found Andy in the small but sparklingly clean kitchen, whipping a bowl of eggs.

"How are you feeling?" he asked.

"Much better after the shower."

"Let me take a look at the stitches," he said, setting the bowl aside. He examined her head. "Gorgeous. My talents are wasted in the ER—I should be doing all my work in the field." He went to the sink and washed his hands. "Want some scrambled eggs?"

"Sure, that sounds great."

He poured the eggs into a pan already warming on the stove and popped down bread already staged in the toaster. Two glasses of orange juice sat on the kitchen island, and coffee steamed into the carafe on the counter.

"Coffee?" he asked.

"No, thanks."

"I might have tea—want that?"

"No, I'm good. Actually, I'm thinking that I might get some sleep before I go—is that okay?"

"I'm counting on it—I'd feel better if you get some rest before you leave. I need to head out in a couple of minutes, but I made up the fold-out couch in the room next to the bathroom."

"Where are you going?"

"Shift at Bryn Mawr."

"Oh, jeez, Andy," she groaned, "you have to go to work after all this? I'm so sorry."

"Not a problem. When I was a resident, I held the title for the best performance on the least sleep."

She knew he meant it as a joke, so she mustered a smile, but she felt guilty for adding to the tally of sleepless nights she had caused him.

When the coffee was ready, Andy poured some into a mug and the remainder into a thermos.

"Okay if I use the van?" he asked as he portioned the eggs and toast out onto two plates.

"Of course."

"I should be able to sneak out after a couple of hours and come back to see how you're doing," he continued. "And if you're still looking unconcussed, you can hit the road." He jabbed a forkful of eggs. "What will you do? Where do you plan to go?"

"I have some ideas, but I only want to tell you guys on a need-to-know basis."

"Yeah, I guess that makes sense. But stay in touch."

"I will. And, Andy, thanks for coming to the rescue." She sighed. "Thanks for *always* coming to the rescue."

He smiled, his eyes on his plate. "Anything to keep Owen from getting all the credit."

As soon as Andy had scooped the last bit of egg off his plate with his last piece of toast, he glanced at his phone, then grabbed the thermos. "I'll clean this up when I get home. And if you start to feel weird in any way, call me immediately."

He showed her how to turn the alarm on and off, then hurried down the hall to the elevator.

Lizzy set the alarm, then finished her breakfast, rinsed the dishes, and loaded them into the dishwasher. Then she went looking for her bed.

The room next to the bathroom was a combination office and media room, but Andy had made up its fold-out couch. Retrieving the shower cap from the bathroom, she put it back on to protect the pillowcase. She kicked off her flip flops but didn't bother removing her sweatshirt and sweatpants before climbing into bed.

She barely had the blanket pulled up around her shoulders before she was asleep.

20

———————

Lizzy woke to the beep of the security alarm being deactivated, another beep as it was reactivated, and a tuneful humming that could only have been Andy. She checked the time on her phone: almost noon.

She climbed out of bed and, calling a greeting to Andy and receiving a cheery response, considered her meager wardrobe options. She was bored with the clothes she had been wearing since she had gone into hiding in Arizona. She decided to wear the new yellow, pink, and purple sundress, even though it wasn't really appropriate for the cool spring weather. After slipping on the dress, she shrugged back into the sweatshirt and slipped on the flower-trimmed flip flops.

She found Andy in the kitchen, brewing another pot of coffee.

After checking the stitches again and quizzing Lizzy about how she was feeling, he said, "You seem shipshape. And I kept an eye out on the way to and from the hospital. I didn't see anything suspicious."

"That's good. I think I'll head out, unless you still need the van."

"No, I'm good. Owen and Ruby are going to be dropping off the Lexus in a little bit. Want anything before you hit the road? Lunch?"

Although she was tempted to take Andy up on his offer, not so much for the meal but so she could see Owen and Ruby again, she shook her head. "Thanks, but I think I'll leave while the coast seems clear. Do we need to plan to meet up in a couple of days so you can take the stitches out?"

"No, they'll dissolve on their own."

Lizzy collected her belongings, and Andy carried her duffel bag through the lobby and down to the garage. When they reached the Caravan, he put Lizzy's bag in back and opened the driver's door for her. "Be careful, kiddo. And if you need anything, let me know."

"I will. Thanks, Andy."

She gave him a quick hug, then climbed into the driver's seat. He helped direct her out of the space, which was tight, and she rolled down the window and waved before pulling out of the garage.

She had implied to Andy that she had a more well-thought-out plan than she actually did. She had a better idea of where she *didn't* want to go than where she *did*. Despite the money-making potential of Atlantic City's casinos, she didn't want to return there. There were casinos in the Philadelphia area, and she'd explore those when things settled down. But, setting aside the proximity of Andy, Owen, and Ruby, even Philadelphia itself wasn't a welcome destination.

She had killed Lucia Hazlitt on an Amtrak train under 30th Street Station. She had killed Louise Mortensen's husband, Gerard Bonnay, in a Center City skyscraper. Louise and Gerard's enforcer, George Millard, had killed Lizzy's father in an alley near the William Penn University campus and had tried to kill

Owen at Penn U. Hospital. No, Philadelphia held too many unpleasant memories for Lizzy.

Plus, she felt more confident when she was on familiar ground, and that would be Chester County, where she had lived for most of her childhood. Owen and Ruby and Andy wouldn't be too far away, and even Philip would be relatively close in D.C. She'd get a motel room there to use as a base for investigating options for a more permanent living arrangement. She had enough to pay for a few nights—she could sleep in the Caravan when the money ran out.

She pulled over and tapped *West Chester* into her GPS app.

Once out of Center City, Lizzy deviated from the app's route and began a series of nonsensical turns, keeping an eye on the rearview mirror for anyone following her. She saw no one.

Then, remembering how George Millard had managed to follow her and Owen so effortlessly when they were in Arizona, she pulled over again and checked the wheel wells for a tracking device. Nothing looked out of place, but she wasn't sure what she was looking for.

She got out her phone and tapped Philip's number. After giving him a quick update of her status, she said, "I'm trying to check the Caravan for a tracker. What should I be looking for?"

"Someone could stick a tracker on any metal surface. Hell, they could stick a tracker on any surface, metal or not, if they had a way to secure it. I don't know of any way to be absolutely sure there isn't a tracker on the van. Just keep an eye out for anyone who seems unduly interested in you."

"Okay."

"How's your head?"

"Sore, but otherwise fine."

"How are *you*?"

She sighed. "Disappointed that I've been back on the East

Coast for barely a day, and I've already run into trouble. How are things going down there?"

"Olivia really likes her job. She says she feels like she's done more good in the time she's been here than she did in the last couple of years in Arizona."

"Will she want to stay?"

"Seems possible."

"Would you want to stay?"

After a pause, he said, "I have to say that the D.C. metro area is not my idea of heaven."

She waited to see if he would say more, but he was silent.

"Come up here," she said suddenly. "You could get a place in Delaware, and take the train from Wilmington right into D.C."

His laugh sounded a little sad. "I'm guessing that would be an expensive commute."

"Maybe I can earn enough money playing poker—"

"Hey, I'm trying to figure out a way to make some money so that I don't need to rely on handouts from Olivia. I really don't want to be in your debt as well."

She grimaced. "I know how that feels. Sorry—I should have known better than to suggest that."

"No apology necessary. And don't worry about me. Worry about getting yourself settled. You worked hard to get back to Pennsylvania. I want to see it work out for you."

They ended the call, and Lizzy reopened the GPS app and tapped in the name of the destination she had decided on: the Gateway Motel on 322 south of West Chester. She remembered it because it was mostly hidden behind some straggly landscaping, and whenever she and her father had passed it, he would comment that he couldn't imagine anyone staying in a place if they couldn't at least get a glimpse of it from the road. He must have underestimated other travelers' daring, since it stayed open year after year.

Before she reached the motel, she stopped at another haunt from her childhood: Jimmy John's Pipin' Hot Sandwiches— *Famous for Frankfurters*. She got two hot dogs, eating them in the Caravan, then continued on to her destination.

She could understand the benefit to the motel of not being easily seen from the road: the parking lot was potholed, the originally white siding was blotched with mildew, and the roof covering the walkway that ran in front of the rooms sagged between its supporting posts. But the rates were the lowest in the area, and it looked like a place that would be more likely to take cash than a chain hotel would.

She was feeling tired again, even after the relatively short drive from Center City. She figured she'd give it one night and, if it lived down to her first impression, she'd find a different place in the morning.

She parked next to a white Nissan Quest, a near twin of the Caravan, and went into the office.

A red-haired woman, thin to the point of emaciation, was fussing with a bouquet of silk flowers in a vase, an empty Michaels craft store bag on the desk beside her. "Help you?" she asked, not unfriendly.

"I'd like a room for the night."

The woman looked past her out the window that overlooked the parking lot. "Just you?"

"Yes."

The woman returned her gaze to Lizzy. "How old are you?"

"Twenty-one."

The woman raised a skeptical eyebrow.

Lizzy got out her fake license and showed it to her.

"Oh. You just look younger."

"I get that a lot."

The woman quoted a price a few dollars higher than the rate

listed online, but Lizzy was too tired to argue. She handed over the cash for one night.

The woman took Lizzy's money, then handed her a key with a diamond-shaped plastic key fob. "Eleven."

Lizzy trudged down the concrete walkway to 11 and let herself in.

It was pretty much what she had expected. Flimsy furniture, dinged walls, worn shag carpet. She checked out the bathroom—she was not staying if the bathroom was dirty—but it looked clean enough. It would do for at least one night.

She retrieved her duffel bag from the Caravan and unpacked her few items into the dresser, only one of whose drawers opened, and that one barely half a foot. Even if she just stayed one night, she was tired of living out of the duffel. And with so few clothes, it hardly took any time. She stuffed the bag under the bed.

She kicked off her flip flops and took off the sweatshirt, then pulled back the slippery polyester coverlet, fluffed the flattened pillows, lay down, and fell into a deep sleep.

21

_____

W hen Lizzy awoke, momentarily disoriented by her unfamiliar surroundings, it was dinnertime, and she was famished.

She considered venturing out for food, but despite having slept for hours, she was still tired—no doubt the emotional and physical effects of the attack. She ordered pizza, then called Andy and then Owen and Ruby. None of them had noticed anything usual or suspicious since their return from Atlantic City.

She spent the evening watching TV—she had access to a TV so infrequently that it was a novelty. As the evening, and her room, became chillier, she added leggings to her outfit.

Her long nap meant that even as midnight neared, she wasn't sleepy, and the idea of venturing out was starting to have some appeal as an alternative to listening to the argument that had been rising and falling for the last hour in the next room.

"As soon as you have a paycheck coming in," growled the man's voice, "you can spend it on whatever the hell you want. As long as you're spending _my_ money, you spend it on what I say."

"It's not like I spent the money on myself, Derrick," the

woman said, her tone appeasing, "I was trying to make the office look nicer."

"It's a waste of money—nobody spends any time in the office."

"*I* spend time in the office," said the woman, now angry. "And I don't have a paycheck coming in because I'm working for you for free."

"Well, Fran, did you ever think that's because it's all you're goddamned qualified to do?"

Lizzy shifted uneasily. Maybe instead of going for a drive, she should just check out and find another motel.

"And whose fault is that?" yelled Fran. "I'd go back to school if you—"

Derrick cut her off with a nasty laugh. "You? Back in school?" His voice rose to a trembly falsetto. "I have my saddle shoes and knee-highs on—I'm going to be the teacher's pet."

"Bastard!"

Lizzy heard the sound of a slap. Then there was a scuffling sound, a grunt, and a loud thump, and the wall against which Lizzy's back rested vibrated. She sat forward, alarmed. That could only have been a person hitting the wall.

She expected another volley of shouting, but instead became aware of the softer but more upsetting sound of Fran crying. She could hear Derrick's voice—apparently standing close to Fran—and although his words were indistinguishable, his tone was malevolent.

Lizzy jumped up from the bed, in an agony of indecision. Should she intercede? Unless Derrick had a gun, she didn't have much to fear from him for herself. Then her thoughts flashed to the attack in Atlantic City. She had dealt their attacker that mental slap, but there must have been enough of the steroid drug in her system to reduce its strength. When they fled, he was not only alive but on his feet.

But the effects of the drug should have worn off by now. And she was already angrier with the man in the next room than she had been with the man in Atlantic City—at least until he drew back his brass-knuckled fist to hit Ruby a second time. For most of the attack, her predominant emotions had been alarm and confusion.

Then she heard some hissed comment from Derrick—the words too low for her to make out—and Fran's tearful, pleading response: "Please, Derrick, stop it …"

Lizzy ran to her door, jerked it open, and hurried the few steps to the door of the neighboring room. She pressed her ear to the door. Fran was still crying, her few unintelligible words almost a whisper.

Lizzy jumped at Derrick's thundered response. "I thought I told you—!"

Lizzy heard a little shriek from Fran, and imagined a hand raised, ready to fall.

Lizzy pounded on the door. "Hey!"

Everything inside the room fell silent.

"Stop it!" She wished her voice didn't sound so obviously like that of a teenage girl.

She heard a single short command from Derrick, then heavy steps crossing the room.

She prayed he didn't have a gun.

The door opened.

Derrick was thin and not much taller than Lizzy, but his body had that corded hardness that suggested that he punched above his weight. Lizzy was relieved to see that his hands were empty.

"The fuck do you want?" he snarled.

Fran, the woman who had checked Lizzy in, was sitting on the bed, trying to make herself small. Lizzy guessed she had climbed onto the bed from the floor.

From the doorway, Lizzy asked the woman, "Are you okay?"

The woman nodded, eyes skittering between Lizzy and Derrick.

"The fuck …" the man muttered. He started to close the door.

Lizzy put out her foot to block it. "Do you want to leave?" she asked Fran.

The woman's eyes widened.

"Mind your own goddamn business," said Derrick. He tried to push Lizzy's foot out of the way, but she had it planted firmly.

"Fran, if you want to leave, you can," Lizzy said. "I'll make sure he doesn't hurt you."

Her apparent calmness seemed to rattle both of them. They exchanged a look.

"But if you want to leave, you need to do it now," Lizzy continued. She added, with an attempt at toughness, "I don't feel like standing here all night."

Fran rose slowly from the bed and took a step toward the door.

"Don't you dare," Derrick said over his shoulder.

Lizzy reached her hand out toward Fran. "Come on out here."

Fran took another hesitant step toward the door.

Derrick dropped his hand from the door and turned toward Fran. "I mean it, woman. Don't you dare."

Lizzy beckoned Fran forward. "Come on. I'll drive you somewhere."

Derrick wheeled on Lizzy. "Like hell you will." Evidently realizing that moving Lizzy's entire body was going to be easier than trying to move her foot, he shoved her on the shoulder.

She stumbled back and reached out to grab something to recover her balance. Her fingers closed over the doorframe just as Derrick swung the door shut.

Lizzy squawked, more from surprise than immediate pain, as the door bounced open again.

"Holy Christ," he muttered, trying again to shut the door.

But by now Lizzy had removed her fingers from the doorframe and gotten her foot planted back at the threshold. "Come on!" she called to Fran.

Lizzy sensed the door of the next room along the walkway opening and someone sticking their head out. "What's going on?" came a quavery voice. "Do I need to call the cops?"

"Fran, if you're coming," Lizzy gasped, breathless from adrenaline, "you have to do it now."

"I said get the fuck out!" Derrick bellowed, then turned back to Fran. "And you sit the fuck down!"

Lizzy's unwillingness to squeeze the man was diminishing with every passing utterance.

"That's it—I'm calling the cops," said the neighbor, slamming the door shut.

From further down the row of rooms, Lizzy heard another voice. "Hold it down out there—some of us are trying to sleep!"

Fran took another step toward the door, then her gaze shifted past Lizzy and her eyes widened.

Lizzy felt vise-like fingers close on her shoulder from behind, and she was jerked out of the doorway.

She reeled back, and her head banged into one of the posts holding up the walkway roof.

Pain shot from her head directly to her gut, and she was afraid she was going to vomit. She staggered and grabbed the post, managing to stay upright, dimly aware of blood trickling down her scalp and neck.

"Dammit, Dwayne," Fran gasped. "What did you do to her?"

"Just pulled her away from the goddamned door," said the new arrival, interposing himself between Lizzy and the door, as if it would take two men to keep Lizzy out of the room. They looked so much alike, they had to be brothers.

"The guy next door is calling the cops," Lizzy said through gritted teeth, hand clamped over the back of her head.

Dwayne stepped away from the open door and banged on the door of the neighboring room. "Stevie!"

"Yes?" Came the querulous voice from behind the door.

"You didn't actually call the cops, did you?"

"No."

"Don't."

"Okay, Dwayne."

Dwayne smiled nastily at Lizzy.

"I'll complain to the manager," Lizzy said.

"Stevie is the manager."

"I'll complain to the owner."

Dwayne crossed his arms in a posture Lizzy guessed men adopted to make their biceps look bigger. "I'm the owner."

Fran had her arms crossed, too, but it was obviously in an effort to look smaller, not larger.

Tiring of the conversation, Dwayne pointed to Lizzy's room. "Pack up and get out. And if the cops show up, I have the license plate of your van. I'll find you."

"I doubt you could do that," she muttered as she turned toward her room, supporting herself with a hand on the wall.

He dropped his arms and took a step toward her. "What did you say?"

Lizzy turned back toward him, her arms falling to her sides. She felt a drop of blood slip off the end of her finger and could almost hear it plop onto the concrete walkway. She took a step toward him, her face a foot from his. "I said I doubt you could do that," she repeated, her voice as steady as she could manage. "Dwayne."

"Sweetie," Fran said from the doorway, her voice pleading, "don't ..."

Lizzy guessed Fran wouldn't be calling Dwayne *sweetie*, so the warning must have been for her.

But the woman didn't know that if the situation deteriorated further, it would end worse for Dwayne than for Lizzy—or so Lizzy hoped.

And Dwayne looked, if not scared, at least taken aback by Lizzy's retort.

Several seconds ticked by, Lizzy's heartbeat thundering in her ears.

When Dwayne finally spoke, his tone was of someone addressing an equal, not threatening an inferior. "You'd do well to leave now."

"My thought exactly." She stepped back and looked toward where Fran stood in the doorway.

The woman's eyes were wide, her expression like someone who has watched a fellow traveler cross a swaying bridge over a yawning chasm and is starting to wonder if she might be able to cross it, too.

Lizzy wanted to caution Fran, to explain that it was far easier to stand up to an unarmed bully if you believed you could likely drop him with a thought. But she couldn't think of anything she could say that wouldn't make the situation worse for both Fran and herself.

With blood now flowing down her scalp and neck, she made her way to her room and locked the door behind her. A bout of dizziness hit her, and she would have gladly traded the squeeze for the ability to teleport out of this horrible place instead of having to drive.

She went to the bathroom, grabbed a washcloth, and pressed it to her head. Then, one-handed, she wrenched open the dresser drawer and pulled items out and threw them into her duffel bag. She returned to the bathroom and pulled a couple more washcloths from the rack and stuffed those in the bag, as well. She grabbed the bag, went to the door, and stepped outside.

Dwayne was watching her from the door of the neighboring room. "I didn't do that to your head. Don't try telling the police I did. Wasn't my fault you lost your balance."

"Yeah, you're a real knight in shining armor," said Lizzy, trying to decide if she wanted to put down the duffel bag long enough to pull the motel room door closed behind her.

"And why don't you mind your own goddamned business," Derrick called from inside his room.

"Why don't you keep your goddamned hands to yourself," she called back.

Leaving the motel room door open, she tossed the duffel bag into the back of the Caravan and climbed into the driver's seat, locking the doors behind her.

One hand still pressing the now-sodden cloth to her head, she managed to back out of the space, get to the exit, and turn onto the nearly deserted highway.

22

Lizzy tried to think of where she could go to regroup. She had heard that Cracker Barrels didn't mind vehicles parking overnight, and she was trying to remember if there was one nearby, when she saw the lights of a Dodge dealership. A number of vehicles, including a few Caravans, were parked near the side of the building housing the service bays—another one wouldn't stand out. She pulled into the parking lot and drove to the furthest empty space, then climbed into the back and took stock of her condition.

She no longer felt dizzy, but the cut on her head was throbbing, and with each throb, she could feel the washcloth get a little more saturated. She pulled it away from her head and felt a trickle down her scalp. Now she did feel dizzy, and she was glad she was sitting down and that the dim light filtering in from outside didn't give her a clearer view of the condition of the cloth. She stuffed it into the trash bag, got another one out of her duffel, and pressed it to her head. She thought she'd feel better lying down, but keeping her head elevated was probably a good idea.

The second washcloth soon felt sticky with blood. On top of

the pain from the torn stitches, she was starting to feel some panic that the bleeding wasn't stopping. She couldn't think what else to try. Even if she could think of some medicine or product she could get at a pharmacy that would help stop the bleeding, she not only didn't feel up to trying to find one that would still be open, but also could hardly walk in with a blood-soaked cloth pressed to her head.

Any normal teenager could have just called 911 and asked for an ambulance to come get her and take her somewhere they would take care of her.

Any normal teenager wouldn't be huddled in the back of a banged-up Dodge Caravan nursing a wound inflicted in a vacant lot in Atlantic City and reopened by a bully at some fleabag motel.

She began to cry, and she could tell her sobs were increasing the flow of blood. She stuffed the washcloth into the trash bag and pressed another one to her head. She needed to call someone to help her—yet again—and the obvious choice was Andy. But she shouldn't be crying when she made the call—that would make him panic. Well, not *panic*, he wasn't a panicker. But it would make him think it was more serious than it was.

Although, she thought, crying harder now, what did she know? Maybe it *was* more serious than she thought. How much blood could she lose before it was a problem?

She fumbled her phone out of her pocket and hit Andy's name in her Favorites list, her trembling finger leaving a smear of blood on the screen.

The call rang a few times, and she was trying to organize her thoughts enough to decide what to do if he didn't answer, when he picked up. "Hello?" He sounded a little out of breath.

She drew a deep breath, trying to steady her voice. "Andy, it's Lizzy. I ..." She swallowed back a sob.

"Lizzy, what's wrong?" He was instantly on the alert.

She heard a woman's voice in the background. "Who's Lizzy?"

"My brother's goddaughter," said Andy, his voice aimed away from the phone.

"Oh, jeez, Andy," said Lizzy. "I'm sorry—"

"It's okay." She heard noises that she guessed were Andy moving away from whoever had asked who Lizzy was, and a soft thunk of a door closing. "What happened?"

"I banged my head and tore the stitches, and I can't get the bleeding to stop."

"Are you somewhere safe?"

"Yes. I'm in the Caravan."

"What have you tried to stop the bleeding so far?"

"I've been pressing a washcloth to it, but I've gone through three of them, and it's still bleeding."

"How long ago did it happen?"

"Maybe fifteen minutes?"

"Do you feel dizzy or nauseous?"

"Not now. What if I can't stop the bleeding?" She could hear her voice spinning up.

"I know it's upsetting, but it's probably not serious. Head wounds, even superficial ones, bleed a lot. Are you sitting up?"

"Yes."

"That's good. Don't lie down—that will make it bleed more."

"That's what I thought."

"Good girl. Tell me where you are, and I'll come and check it out."

"A Dodge dealer on 202, a little bit south of West Chester."

"Okay, I should be there in less than an hour."

"I'm sorry that I have to keep asking you for help, Andy."

"You know it's no problem, kiddo." He laughed ruefully. "Although that's easy for me to say. You're the one who's getting the tough end of the situation."

23

———

A ndy returned to the bedroom, a confection of pink and white.

"Sorry, Stace—change of plans," he said, pulling on his pants. He had managed to snag his briefs on the way out of the bedroom and get them on while talking with Lizzy.

"What happened to Lizzy?" asked Stacy, sitting up, the sheet dropping to her waist.

He wandered around the room, dressing as he located items of clothing. "She had a little accident."

"A car accident?"

"Yeah."

Stacy crossed her arms under her breasts. "Couldn't your brother help her out?"

"He's recovering from a heart attack."

"Oh." said Stacy, looking contrite. She pulled the sheet up to cover her breasts. "I'm sorry to hear that."

"He's on the mend, but it's best for him not to be too stressed."

"Sure, I understand." She watched as he finished dressing,

then asked, "Are you coming back?" She smiled. "We have unfinished business."

He leaned across the bed and kissed her. "If I possibly can, I will. But don't wait up."

"Still on for dinner tomorrow?"

"Absolutely. You pick the place."

"Nectar? I've been wanting to try it."

"Sounds great." He kissed her again. "Sleep tight."

She lay back on the pillow and pulled the sheet over her shoulder. "Give my best to Lizzy. I hope the accident wasn't too bad."

Andy grabbed his jacket off the living room couch and let himself out of Stacy's apartment. As he crossed the parking lot to his car, he considered his options.

He must have assumed that even Lizzy wouldn't need stitching up again quite so soon, because he had left his medical bag at home. Stacy's apartment was in West Grove, and a drive to Center City to pick up the bag and then to West Chester would take close to two hours.

However, Stacy's apartment was only about ten minutes from Mercy Hospital and its nicely equipped ER. He had met Stacy, an ER nurse, during one of the overnight shifts he picked up at Mercy as a way to supplement his income from his regular job at Bryn Mawr Hospital, since he had been helping Owen out with Lizzy-related expenses. He could drive to Mercy, pick up some supplies, and be in West Chester a little over half an hour later.

When he reached the hospital, he pulled into one of the staff parking spaces near the ER. It seemed like a quiet night, with relatively few vehicles in the lot. He sighed—it would probably have been easier to get what he needed if it were busy.

He found Isabel and Carlos hanging out at the nurses' station, chatting.

"Hey, Andy," said Isabel. "Are you working tonight? I thought you and Stacy had plans."

"We did, but my brother's goddaughter was in a car accident and got a little cut. She has a phobia about hospitals, and I told her I'd take care of it. Mind if I snag some sutures and a needle? Maybe some lidocaine? I'll replace it."

"Sure, go ahead," Isabel said. "Hope she's okay."

"Thanks."

Andy collected the materials, stuffed them in his pockets, then hurried back to the parking lot. He was almost to the Lexus when he saw the clamp on the front driver's side wheel.

"Shit!" He scanned the parking lot. It could hardly be a coincidence that this had happened while he was collecting supplies to restitch Lizzy's head. He wished he had gotten more information from her about the circumstances that had led to the wound reopening. Could someone have followed them from Atlantic City and then followed him from his apartment to Bryn Mawr, to the restaurant where he and Stacy had had dinner, to Stacy's apartment, and then to Mercy?

He always tried to remember to keep an eye out for tails these days, but on the ride from Stacy's place, he had been worried about Lizzy and couldn't guarantee he had kept a careful watch. And if someone wanted to keep him from driving away from the hospital, they'd no doubt be waiting in the dark to take advantage of the situation.

He'd go back to the ER and ask if he could borrow someone's car. He'd get to West Chester, keeping a more careful eye out for tails this time, and stitch Lizzy up. Then they could call Owen and Ruby and plan next steps.

As he started toward the entrance, a van rounded the corner of the building and rolled toward him. It stopped in one of the dark areas between the pools of illumination from the parking lot lights, but before it did, Andy could read the sign on its side: *AJ's Auto Repair*.

He picked up his pace.

His phone buzzed and, not slowing, he pulled it from his pocket and checked the ID: *Lizzy*.

He hit Accept. "Lizzy, I think someone's following me—"

"This isn't Lizzy," a man said, just as Andy realized that he had Owen's goddaughter entered in his contacts list not as *Lizzy* but as *LB*.

Andy stopped walking. The man's accent was Swedish, if he wasn't mistaken. At least he now had a pretty good idea of who had booted his car.

"She's here in the van with me," continued the man.

"I want to talk to her."

"I don't want to take the duct tape off her mouth. Pulling it off can be painful—no need to do it more than is necessary. Walk slowly to the van, or something unpleasant—more unpleasant than removal of a strip of tape—will happen to Miss Ballard."

Andy stared at the van, idling a few dozen yards away. "I think something unpleasant might happen to *me* as well as Miss Ballard if I get in. I like my chances better out here."

"You've taken bigger risks for Miss Ballard's wellbeing than getting in a van. If you cooperate, you'll both be released in a short time, none the worse for wear."

"And who's guaranteeing that?"

"Theo Viklund. You know his name?"

"Maybe." Andy knew Viklund's name from Philip, but he had no way of knowing if admitting that was a good idea or a bad one. Andy tried to sort through the options, which appeared exceedingly limited.

"Walk toward the van, Doctor McNally," said the man.

Andy started toward the van, walking as slowly as he felt he could get away with, hoping that in the few extra seconds it bought him, he'd come up with a clever plan to extract both himself and Lizzy from the situation.

When he was about ten yards away, the voice said, "Stop there. Take your jacket off and throw it toward the van."

Andy could see the backlit profile of the driver, and Andy was pretty sure the driver wasn't the one speaking on the phone. There must be more than one man in the van. Andy did as he was told.

"No gun, Doctor McNally? I'm surprised."

Andy had left the gun, as well as his medical bag, at his apartment, figuring that removing his jacket to reveal a weapon wasn't the best way to set a romantic tone for the evening with Stacy. "It didn't go with my outfit."

He heard a soft chuckle. "It does interfere with the drape of a jacket. Toss your phone onto the jacket."

Andy tossed his phone. No clever plan was coming to him.

The back door of the van slid open—the interior was dark—and a pair of handcuffs clattered onto the asphalt a few feet in front of him.

The man's voice came from the cargo area. "Put on the handcuffs, hands in back."

Andy hesitated and heard a sound come from the back of the van that could have been any number of things ... including a fist striking flesh.

"Just give me one goddamned second!"

"I'm not a patient man, Doctor McNally."

The options for a clever escape were narrowing by the moment.

Andy picked up the cuffs. He slipped one cuff over his left wrist and ratcheted it shut. He briefly considered leaving it loose, but what might they do to Lizzy if they thought he was trying to circumvent their instructions? He snugged down the cuff, then, hands behind his back, slipped on the other one. With one hand cuffed, and unable to see what he was doing, it was harder to tighten the second. He hoped they realized that leaving this one looser was not a choice. After all, they sounded like pros—they probably understood the mechanics of handcuffs all too well.

The van rolled toward him, and he peered through the open back door, trying to make out Lizzy's form. The van stopped, the back door even with where he stood. It was empty, except for a brawny blond man in a sport coat, a phone in one hand, a gun, pointed at Andy, in the other.

The man gestured with the gun. "Get in the van."

"I thought I heard you hit her," Andy said, his voice leaden.

The man thumped his fist into the back of the front passenger seat, making the noise Andy had heard. "She's with colleagues who would be none too pleased if you were to do anything rash."

"Me? Rash? I'm nothing if not cooperative."

"Let's test that claim. Sit in the door, feet on the pavement."

Andy did as instructed. The man in the cargo area was standing right behind him, and Andy thought he could probably knock him over by throwing himself backwards. He had seen that the driver had his seatbelt on, so it would take him a second or two to get out of the car. Andy could make a run for the ER entrance … but he had to assume that they had Lizzy—

From behind him, he heard a crackling sound, a pop, and then every muscle in his body seized and his skin felt as if a swarm of hornets had been loosed on it. He wanted to scream, but the muscles in his jaw wouldn't unclench. The agony persisted, second after second—or was it minute after minute?

When it finally stopped, he collapsed forward, barely registering the sting of his cheek scraping painfully across the pavement.

"*Oj då* ," muttered the man in the back of the van. "Get him in here and tie his legs," he said as the driver climbed out of the van. "We need to get back to the compound."

24

———

When Lizzy awoke, morning light was leaking through the curtains that protected the back of the Caravan from prying eyes.

When her arm had gotten tired holding the washcloth to her head, she had positioned herself so she could lean her head against the side of the van to hold the cloth in place. Now she probed the cloth with her fingers and decided that the van wall had done a better job of stanching the blood than her hand had done. Unfortunately, blood had now firmly adhered the washcloth to the back of her head.

She wondered for a moment whether she had fallen asleep or passed out from blood loss, but when she examined the other used cloths and assessed the extent of the bloodstains, she realized she had probably lost less blood than she had feared.

It was only then that her brain cleared enough to wonder where Andy was. She checked the time on her phone: a little before seven. She had called him around midnight, and he had said he was less than an hour away.

She raised herself stiffly to her knees—her sleeping position might have stopped the flow of blood, but it hadn't done any favors for the rest of her body—parted the curtains separating the back of the van from the front seats and scanned the parking lot.

Outside the service area, a man in coveralls was walking down a row of cars, comparing the license plates to a clipboard or tablet in his hand—no doubt looking for the next car due in the service bays. She needed to move the Caravan soon, before someone realized that there wasn't an entry for it in the list.

She got out her phone and tapped Andy's number. The call rang to voicemail.

"Andy, it's Lizzy. Just wondering where you are."

She ended the call and considered her next dilemma. She no longer felt she needed immediate medical assistance, but she still wanted Andy to take a look at the wound. And she needed to get herself cleaned up.

She could get a motel room—ideally one nicer than the Gateway—but it was so early in the day that she was afraid they'd charge her extra, and she had spent so much time in the Caravan during the drive from Arizona that she didn't feel like killing time in it until check-in time.

She'd drive back toward Andy's Center City apartment. If he was home, she could take a shower there. If he wasn't home ... she'd decide on next steps then.

She needed something to cover the washcloth and the blood in her hair. She dug through the duffel bag, looking for a base-ball cap that she had picked up during the drive from Arizona.

Not only could she not find the baseball cap, but she realized she was also missing a few toiletries and her evening bag. She must have left them in the dresser in the motel room. Not that it mattered—the toiletries would be easy and cheap to replace, and the attack in Atlantic City had probably damaged the bag beyond repair.

She searched through a couple of plastic totes until she

found one that contained a pink stocking cap, which she pulled on over the washcloth.

She tapped the name of Andy's apartment building into her GPS, slipped into the driver's seat, and started up the Caravan.

The coverall-clad man looked up, surprised at the sound of an engine turning over. Lizzy gave him a friendly wave as she rolled past him. He raised a hand in greeting, then shrugged and continued his scan of the vehicles in the lot.

As she drove, she realized she should probably alert Owen that Andy was not answering his phone—and, perhaps more importantly, that he hadn't shown up after she had called him the previous night. But that would mean not only worrying him about Andy, but also about her, because she'd have to tell him why she had called Andy.

Perhaps it was the lingering effects of the repeated blows to the head—or just one too many of the blows that life seemed to hand out to her all too often—but she was stumped as to what to do.

After a few more miles of consideration, she decided she'd call Ruby. She knew Ruby would keep a secret from Owen if she thought it was the best thing for him, and Ruby was someone whose help Lizzy had learned to appreciate when she was in a pinch. She pulled into a shopping center parking lot.

She was gazing out the window, considering how she could relay the information to Ruby without Ruby's responses alarming Owen, when her phone rang: Andy. She puffed out a relieved breath and tapped *Accept*. "Andy—"

"I'm afraid not," replied Louise Mortensen.

The last time Lizzy had seen Louise, she was driving Owen's SUV away from the burning Pocopson mansion.

The last time Lizzy had had any direct—if virtual—interaction with her, Louise had been encouraging her husband,

Gerard, to shoot Lizzy, and then watched as a terrorized Lizzy squeezed Gerard to death.

"Where's Andy?" Lizzy asked, her voice dull with dread.

"He's right here," said Louise. When she spoke again, Lizzy could tell she had switched the phone to speaker. "Say hello to Lizzy, Doctor McNally,"

"Hello, Lizzy," said Andy, his voice strained but otherwise fairly normal sounding.

"Andy, what happened?" Lizzy asked.

"Tell her what happened," said Louise.

"Two guys grabbed me when I stopped by Mercy," said Andy. "I got called for a moonlighting gig, but it turned out they didn't need me after all."

Lizzy realized Andy must be trying to convey to her that Louise didn't know the real reason for his midnight outing. He must have gone to Mercy to get supplies to treat her reopened head would.

"Are you okay?" she asked.

"Tell her what your physical condition is," said Louise.

"I'm fine," said Andy shortly.

"Where are you?" Lizzy asked.

"I don't know. They brought me here in a van. There were two—"

"That's enough," Louise interrupted. "Lizzy, I'll call you back shortly," she said and ended the call.

Lizzy gripped her phone, her knuckles white. If she had been stumped by her situation before the call, she was completely at a loss now.

A couple of minutes ticked by, then her phone rang again with a call from Andy's number.

She answered. "Why did you take Andy?"

"Because I need you to apply your skills," said Louise, "your apparently expanding set of skills—to help me resolve a situation."

"What do you mean, 'expanding skills'?"

"I've watched you play poker. I suspect you did as well as you did because you could read the other players' minds."

"You've been following me?"

"Obviously."

"Did you send the person who mugged me?"

"Yes."

"Why? You said you need me to help you. Why would you have someone attack me?"

"I wanted a blood sample."

"Is that why the mugger used the handkerchief on me?"

"Yes."

"And what did you find out from the blood sample?"

"I found traces of a steroid drug, similar to what I gave Mitchell to enhance his abilities."

"What makes you think I need a drug to read minds?"

"Because during the time you stayed with me and Gerard in Pocopson, there was never any indication of clairvoyance."

"And why are you getting in touch with me now?" Her voice hardened. "Why did you kidnap Andy?"

"Because I need you to read someone's mind for me."

"That's it?"

"At the moment, yes."

"At the moment?"

"Lizzy, I have your friend Andrew McNally here, and I have people at my disposal who wouldn't hesitate to punish him for any hesitance you display in complying with what I think is a quite modest requirement for his release."

"Why should I believe you'll release him?"

"Because you don't have any choice."

Lizzy's head was hammering, and she squinted her eyes shut. "Okay. Fine."

"I need you to come to where I'm holding Doctor McNally. And I need you to bring Philip Castillo with you."

Lizzy snapped her head up. "Philip? Why?"

"Because he was supposed to have performed a task for one of Theo's colleagues, and that task is still pending."

"What is he supposed to do?"

"That's none of your concern. But his presence is the other requirement of Doctor McNally's release."

"So you have one of us, and you want two more of us to just walk into ... wherever you are."

"Yes."

Lizzy tried to marshal her whirling thoughts.

After a few moments, Louise said, "Lizzy, do I need to go back to the room where we're holding Doctor McNally and have one of his guards hurt him?"

"No!" Lizzy drew a deep breath. "No. I'll come."

"With Castillo."

"I don't know whether Philip will agree to come with me."

Louise laughed humorlessly. "Has your influence over Mr. Castillo lessened since you talked him into coming to Pocopson, breaking into my home, and shooting my assistant?"

Lizzy waited for Louise to make some comment about Philip escorting her on her poker-playing outings. When she didn't, it occurred to Lizzy that Louise might have only seen her in Atlantic City, when she was accompanied by Ruby, not in the Arizona casinos, when Philip had been her escort.

"I haven't talked to him in a while," she ventured. "We had a falling out."

"I doubt that," said Louise briskly. "Contact him, tell him the requirements for Doctor McNally's release, and be ready for further instructions. And perhaps it should go without saying, but I will say it anyway: do not discuss this phone call with Owen McNally or Ruby DiMano."

"I won't."

"When you have Castillo with you, I'll have someone pick you up at the Gateway Motel." Louise's tone was smug. "I'll be in touch." She ended the call.

Lizzy dropped her hand into her lap and let her head fall back against the seat.

She was both upset and relieved that Louise's terms meant calling Philip—upset because she hated to get him involved, relieved that she wouldn't be facing the situation alone. The only other bright spot in an otherwise awful situation was that Louise seemed to think Lizzy was still at the motel. Lizzy wasn't sure how she could use that, but she was willing to grab any tiny advantage she could.

Heaving a deep breath, she tapped Philip's name in her Contacts list.

"Hey, Lizzy, what's up?" he answered. She could hear traffic noise in the background, as if he was walking on a busy street.

She sighed. "Nothing good."

She told him about Louise's call, including that fact that Louise evidently thought Lizzy was still at the motel, but not about her reopened head wound.

"She thinks you owe some friend of Theo's a favor," she concluded.

"Viklund told me he'd get me into Williams as a janitor so I could take care of Hanrick myself—I think he knew I regretted asking you to kill him for me—and in exchange, I'd need to help him out with something. He made it clear that helping his buddy was a requirement, not a request."

"But it sounds like Louise doesn't know where you are. You could probably just hide out in D.C. ... or even go back West if you think that's safer ..." Her voice trailed off.

"If you're going to Louise's den, then I'm going with you. I want to keep Andy safe as much as you do."

Her eyes stung with tears. "Philip, I'm so sorry I keep dragging you into these situations—"

"Lizzy, the only thing you did was come to me back in Sedona looking for advice. Everything else that has happened with Viklund and Hanrick—that's all on me."

She swallowed a lump in her throat. "I know it's not as simple as that ... but I appreciate you saying it."

"Next time you vacation in Red Rock country, you'll be better off spending your money on a Pink Jeep tour instead of a visit to a psychic counselor," he said, a smile in his voice.

She gave a watery laugh.

"Speaking of vehicles," he continued, "do you want me to see if I can get a train up there?"

She tapped Bethesda into her map app. "No, I can come pick you up. That'll probably be faster—and we can strategize on the drive back. If I leave now, I'll be there in about two-and-a-half hours. Where should I pick you up—your apartment?"

"I'm actually near Olivia's office—got a lead on a possible job. You might as well pick me up here." He named an intersection.

"Okay, see you soon."

She ended the call and started up the van, steeling herself for the drive. She didn't like driving even under the best circumstances, and these were definitely not the best circumstances.

She hoped she didn't doom Andy by cracking up the van on the way to Bethesda.

25

———

Louise walked briskly down the central hallway toward the back of the house, the shorter Maja puffing a bit as she hurried next to her. At their heels trotted Fredrik, one of the younger members of the security staff. Although perhaps *trotted* wasn't quite the right word—there was a hitch in his step, thanks to his encounter with Ballard in Atlantic City. Louise had wanted someone to accompany her to her meeting with Billy Chapel, but despite the fact that Fredrik was armed and that the guards at the front gate had confirmed that Chapel was not, Fredrik looked more scared than scary. She wanted to chalk it up to him being the staffer Lucas had deemed most expendable. She suspected it was because Fredrik, like Lucas, was aware of Chapel's reputation.

"If I can't get him to leave," Louise said to Maja, "we'll need somewhere to put him."

"He'll expect a suite, and we only have two."

"Clear my things out of my suite and put him there." Louise planned to put Ballard and Castillo in the other suite.

"Yes, Doctor Mortensen."

They reached the hallway that led to the conservatory, and

Louise said, "I'll let you go and make the arrangements, Maja. Fredrik and I can take it from here."

Maja nodded and hurried off.

Louise turned to Fredrik. "Remember, you're not to say anything."

"Yes, Doctor Mortensen."

"And I'll be introducing myself as Louise Vivant."

"Yes, Doctor Mortensen."

She wondered if she should review the other instructions she had given him, but she didn't want to keep Chapel waiting any longer. She led Fredrik down the corridor and stepped into the conservatory.

Despite the research she had done online, Chapel looked younger than she had expected—mid-to-late thirties. More noteworthy than his age was his physical presence. The word that sprang to mind was *broad*: he had a broad nose set in a broad face. His neck was barely narrower than his broad jaw, which sloped down to broad shoulders that stretched the seams of his platinum-sheened leather jacket. His hands were stuffed into the pockets of his black jeans, his feet clad in black work boots. He would have looked at home in some British pub, buying rounds for the lads and deconstructing the latest rugby match. He could hardly have been less like Theo Viklund, or like Louise's idea of the kind of person Theo would have done business with.

She crossed the room, hand extended. "Mr. Chapel, I'm Louise Vivant."

He kept his hands in his pockets and examined her as one might a zoo exhibit. "I'm here to see Theo, not the hired help." He might have looked like a rugby player, but he sounded more like the coach of some football team just south of the Mason-Dixon Line.

She dropped her hand. "I'm not the hired help. And I'm the

only person who can provide a connection to Theo, at least for the time being. If you'd like me to take a message to him, I'll do that, but I'm going to reiterate what I've already conveyed to you: Theo knows you're here. He regrets that you came here despite the warnings that he's seeing no one. If seeing Theo is your only purpose in coming here, then I suggest you leave."

Chapel threw back his head and laughed. When the laughter died down, he shook his head. "I like your style, Bon."

"Bon?"

"Bon Vivant." He smirked at her. "Don't tell me I'm the first person to come up with that nickname."

"As a matter of fact—"

He shook his head. "Yup, you're a card. I wish we had met in different circumstances."

She scowled. "I'm sure it would have been delightful."

"Let's patch things up over a drink," he said. Louise opened her mouth to disabuse him of the idea that she'd be sharing cocktails with him, but he raised a hand and continued. "But not right now." His mouth stretched wide in a yawn. "Right now, I'm going to have a smoke and take a nap. You can have your errand boy there," he jerked his head toward Fredrik, "take me to wherever I'm staying while you work things out with Theo."

Louise couldn't recall a time when she had been so utterly at a loss for how to respond to a situation.

"Actually," Chapel continued, "since I'm guessing your boy is carrying, maybe you shouldn't send me away with *him*." He waggled his eyebrows. "You wouldn't want him to end up empty-handed, and me with a gun."

Louise glanced at Fredrik, who had flushed a deep red.

She turned back to Chapel. "Won't your driver—and your other men—be concerned if you don't come out?"

"I'll stay in touch with them."

"There's no cell phone reception at the compound." She

wondered if Chapel knew that, except for the phones of select staff, the signals were blocked.

"Oh, my boys expect me to be in here for a while. I'll walk up to the gate to check in with them a couple of times a day." He grinned. "And if I don't show up, they'll come in to check on me." He yawned again. "Is Maja still around? Maja and I go way back. Maybe she can show me to my digs."

Louise thought that Fredrik would probably be of more use going to fetch Maja than standing here like a chastised schoolboy. She turned to the young man. "Please go get Maja and ask her to come to the conservatory."

Fredrik proved that he could, in fact, be more damaging present than absent when he said, "Yes, Doctor Mortensen." Realizing his mistake, his face reddened further, and he hurried out of the conservatory.

"Doctor Mortensen, eh?" said Chapel, examining his fingernails. "*Vivant* must be your middle name."

Louise crossed her arms and maintained a stony silence.

"So, Doctor Louise Vivant Mortensen, are you a medical doctor?"

"Yes."

"Treating Theo for his depression?"

"No."

When she said no more, Chapel shrugged. "Still, doctor-patient confidentiality, am I right?" He dropped onto one of the chairs at the cafe table in the middle of the conservatory, stretched out his legs, and began whistling an off-key melody whose sour notes seemed more intentional than accidental.

Maja hurried in a minute later.

"Hey, Maja!" said Chapel with a grin. "How's it hanging?"

"Fine, Herr Chapel," said Maja, not meeting his eyes.

"Mr. Chapel is tired from his trip and would like to rest," said Louise. "Can you take him to his quarters?"

"Of course, ma'am," said Maja.

Chapel pushed himself up from the chair and crossed to where Louise stood, approaching a few inches closer than was comfortable. "I said I was going to take a nap, Doctor Louise Vivant Mortensen, not that I was tired. I'm never tired." He was smiling, but the smile didn't reach his eyes.

"We'll send some food to your suite," she said, resisting the urge to take a step back.

"Don't bother. I'll get something from my boys at the gate when I go out for my check-in. But send some champagne—some of that Perrier-Jouet." Louise suspected that his pronunciation—*PAIR-ee-er JOO-et*—was less an accidental mispronunciation than a dig at his hosts' pretensions. "Maybe the idea of sharing a bottle or two with an old friend will bring Theo out of hiding." He stared into her eyes a moment longer, then crossed the conservatory to where Maja stood by the door. When he reached the door, he turned back. "Oh, and send Philip Castillo to my suite when he gets here." He stepped into the hallway, followed by Maja, and Louise heard his off-tune whistle fade down the hall.

Louise got out her phone and hit Lucas's number.

"Yes?" he answered.

"Chapel is here."

"*Fy fan.* Did he bring anyone?"

"The guard at the front gate said they showed up in three SUVs. " After a pause, she added, "Fredrik called me *Doctor Mortensen* in front of Chapel."

"Idiot," growled Lucas.

"Is he the best we have at the compound at the moment?"

"The *best* men were the ones who knew the most about Viklund and his business," snapped Lucas. "The ones you wanted sent away."

She drew a deep breath. "Of course. I only meant to convey

that I'll feel better when you're back here and able to direct the remaining security staff in person. Is there anything of interest going on there?"

"The van's still at the motel, but no sign of Castillo—although since we haven't seen him with Ballard yet, I'm not surprised. He might still be in Arizona for all we know."

"Yes." She twisted her wedding ring on her finger. "Chapel says he's going to stay at the compound until he can talk with Theo and meet with Castillo. I know we agreed to monitor the motel to see if Castillo showed up, but now that I've met Chapel, I don't want to wait that long. Let's bring Ballard in and hope that speeds up getting Castillo here as well."

"I'm across the street from the motel. I'll get her now."

"Do you need help? Remember what happened to Fredrik in Atlantic City."

"I'm well aware of what happened to Fredrik—I was videoing it. And I guess I can handle a teenage girl on my own."

"Not just any teenage girl."

There was a pause, then Lucas said, "She can't do the stroke thing if she's knocked out, right?"

"Correct—as long as she's unaware of what's coming and doesn't have time to react. I also suspect that her power is not effective over any distance—more than a dozen feet or so."

"Unless you want her dead, I'll have to be up close, but I'll take her by surprise and find a way to put her out of commission for the ride back to the compound."

Before Louise could ask what that way might be, Lucas ended the call.

She wondered how quickly he could get Ballard from the West Chester hotel to the compound, especially driving McNally's Lexus.

She got out her phone and tapped Maja's number.

"Yes, Doctor Mortensen?"

Louise knew that if Maja was referring to her as *Doctor Mortensen*, she couldn't be near Chapel. Maja was not one to slip up the way Fredrik had. "Is Mr. Chapel settled in?"

"Yes. And a bottle of Perrier-Jouet is on its way to the suite." After a pause, she added, "The *first* bottle."

"Has he refused to eat at the compound in the past?"

"He would eat, but only if Herr Viklund served himself from the same dish first."

Considering Theo had died from poisoned tea Louise had prepared for him, she thought it a wise precaution.

"You were able to remove my things from the suite? I realize we didn't give you very much time."

"Yes, Elsa collected them. There wasn't much to collect."

It was true—Louise had never asked Maja to supplement the few dresses that had been provided when Louise first arrived at the compound.

"Where would you like us to put your things?" Maja asked.

"In the bunker, I suppose—although we don't want Elsa going in there."

"I'll take care of it."

"Thank you, Maja. And don't spend too much time getting things settled there—I'm hoping it will be a temporary arrangement."

"Yes, Doctor Mortensen."

Louise ended the call. While waiting for Lucas's return call, she wandered the conservatory, spending a few minutes absently pulling dead leaves from the plants before acknowledging they needed more than casual attention. Maintaining the conservatory was one of the many things that had fallen by the wayside as they reduced the staff.

She was considering occupying herself in the lab when her phone rang.

"She's not there," Lucas said when she answered.

"Not there? What happened?"

"She had some problems with management last night and left. When it got light this morning, it looked like her van was still there, but it's just a similar one."

"But the tracker Fredrik put in her purse—"

"She left the purse behind."

"On purpose?"

"It's possible. Although it sounds like she left in a hurry. I think it was an accident."

Louise restrained herself from berating him. She could tell by his tone that he was as angry at himself as she was.

"Call her back," he continued, his voice hard. "Tell her to go back to the motel. Use McNally to make sure she complies. There are a couple of men at the compound who wouldn't mind making an example of him. Send her a video."

Louise suppressed a shudder. "We'll do that if needed, but I don't want to antagonize her unnecessarily. She'll be more trouble than help if she arrives here angry." Without waiting for him to respond, she continued. "If she's not at the motel, we need to establish a new meeting point. If she's driving the van, she can't be too far from the Philadelphia area."

"If you want her back at the compound fast," said Lucas, obviously still irritated, "we could pick her up in the helicopter."

Louise raised an eyebrow. "We have a helicopter?"

"Yes. There's a helipad a few hundred yards from the house. But where will we pick her up? An airport is problematic—too many eyes, too many security cameras. It should be somewhere out of the way, but with plenty of open ground for landing."

"It seems like a challenging set of criteria—" she began, then stopped. She allowed herself a small smile. "Actually, I know just the place."

26

———

Lizzy hated multi-lane highways, although it was not actually the driving on the highway as much as the merging onto it that she hated. She managed to get to Bethesda without incident, but she was having some difficulty navigating the streets while also keeping an eye out for Philip. Maybe she was confused about the pickup location ... or about the instructions the GPS app kept delivering in a silky monotone a few seconds after she needed them.

She was stopped at a red light, examining buildings that she was pretty sure she had passed a few minutes earlier, when she jumped at a knock on the passenger-side window.

Philip waved from the other side of the glass.

She hit the unlock button just as the light turned green and the car behind her honked.

Philip jumped in and pulled the door closed as Lizzy pulled away.

"Thanks for flagging me down," she said. "How many times did I drive by you before I got stopped by the light?"

"Just twice."

The light they were approaching turned yellow and Lizzy hit the brakes, eliciting another honk from the car behind her.

"Want me to drive?" he asked.

"Yeah, that would be good," she said gratefully.

They jumped out of the van and swapped seats.

"Where to?" he asked.

"Let's go back toward West Chester. If Louise thought I was at a crappy motel near there, that's probably where she planned to meet us or pick us up." She tapped the destination into her map app and propped the phone on the dashboard.

The light changed and Philip pulled away. "If Mortensen thought you were still at the motel, it means she didn't have a tracker on the van. Maybe someone followed you to the motel."

"Maybe, but I thought of another explanation. When the guy attacked me in Atlantic City, he got the money out of my bag, but the strap was still looped around me. I thought it was weird that he didn't just pull the bag off me and run away with it. I think stealing the money was just a cover—I think he was also putting something in my bag or sticking something to it. When I left the motel, I was in a hurry and I forgot a couple of things, including the bag. But it was pretty shot, so it wasn't worth going back for. If Louise thinks I'm still at the motel, it might be because there was a tracker in the bag." After a moment, she added, "Now that I think about it, there was a van that looked a lot like this one in the parking lot. If someone followed the tracker to the motel, they might think that van is mine."

Philip nodded and glanced over, then did a double take. "Why do you have blood on your dress?"

"I banged my head, and it opened up the cut again. That's why I'm wearing a winter hat in May."

He knit his brows. "How did you do that?"

Lizzy described what had happened: the altercation in the neighboring room, the argument with Derrick, the arrival of

Dwayne, and the shove that had sent her into the porch support. She twisted her fingers in her lap. "I feel like I did Fran more harm than good. Not only did I make Derrick madder that he was already—and get Dwayne involved—but I made it seem like it was no big deal to stand up to them." She frowned out the window. "Easy for me to do, considering. But what if she decides she can do it too, and she isn't armed with a weapon to fight back? I was thinking back to Marcus in Phoenix. I just let him walk away, and he's probably doing the exact same thing to some other girl as he did to me, and she has to just go along with it. I should have just squeezed those guys a little, like I did to the guy in Atlantic City."

He raised an eyebrow. "You really think you have that level of control over it?"

She sighed. "No. I think Atlantic City turned out like it did because I was coming off the juice."

"You did the best thing you could have done in the circumstances. You can't save everyone."

"I guess." Anxious to change the topic, Lizzy said, "Why do you think Theo Viklund is letting Louise be the one to contact us? I don't really have any personal issues with him, like I do with Louise, so I might be more willing to cooperate with him than with her."

"I get the feeling he likes having staff take care of things for him." After a moment, he added, voice hard, "And he doesn't have Rey to run his errands for him anymore."

Lizzy snorted. "You think Louise is Theo's errand girl?"

After a moment, he said, "I shouldn't have called what Rey did for Theo 'errands.' I imagine he was grooming her to take a bigger role in his business. Maybe he's decided Mortensen might move into that role after Rey died." They drove in silence for a few minutes, then Philip asked, "Since you need to choose your weapon for when we meet up with Mortensen or her associates, which are you going to choose—the squeeze or the juice?"

Lizzy chewed her thumbnail. "I don't know. It would be nice to get a read on what people are thinking about the situation before I start squeezing them." She dropped her hand and sighed. "I doubt Louise is going to take the chance of being in a room with me, and as far as I know, I can't mind-read or squeeze long-distance. And Uncle Owen lowered the concentration of the drug, so even under the best circumstances, I can't eavesdrop on people's thoughts as much as I usually can." She turned to Philip. "Which do you think I should be able to do, at least at first?"

"I think you have to decide."

She marshaled a smile. "You can have a vote. It will make a difference to you as well."

"I'm comfortable with whatever you choose."

Lizzy appreciated Philip's vote of confidence, especially when she considered some of the dangerous situations she had led him into. But she wished he was willing to voice an opinion about their plan of action.

"I think if I can, I'll take the juice. Maybe Theo will be willing to meet with us in person, and I'd rather be able to see what he's thinking than squeeze him right off the bat. Plus, if he doesn't do anything to make me angry or scared, I probably wouldn't be able to squeeze him in any case."

"How much of it do you have with you?"

"Not a lot. Maybe two more doses."

"Let's hope we can get in and out fast."

Another few miles passed in silence, then Lizzy asked, "What did you tell Olivia?" When Philip didn't answer immediately, she said hurriedly, "You don't have to tell me—it's none of my business."

"No, you should probably know," he summoned a smile,

"just in case we need to match stories. I told her a buddy from Williams had gotten a place in a rehab facility down South, but his family needed help transporting him there. I figured that would cover me for a couple of days."

Lizzy was itching to ask Philip more about why he had lied to Olivia, but it was true that it was none of her business. "Another reason to want to get in and out fast."

They were silent for most of the rest of the drive.

They had turned off 95 onto 202 when Lizzy's phone rang. She snatched it off the dashboard: *Andy*. She hit Accept and put the call on speaker. "Yes?"

"Have you contacted Castillo?" asked Louise.

"Yes."

"Is he with you?"

Lizzy glanced over at Philip.

He shook his head.

"No," Lizzy said.

"Humor me if I speak as if he is with you and is listening in on the call," said Louise.

Philip shrugged.

"Sure," Lizzy said to Louise. "Humor me if I answer you as if he's not."

Philip smiled.

"I'm calling to give you the location where my representatives will meet you. The people I send had nothing to do with McNally's abduction. I wouldn't want you thinking you could wreak revenge on them."

"Fine."

"They'll pick you up and bring you to where Doctor McNally is. And just to ensure we're in agreement, arriving with anyone other than Castillo will result in an unfortunate outcome for Doctor McNally."

"I understand. Where are we meeting them?"

"The Pocopson house."

Lizzy looked over at Philip, who didn't bother hiding his grimace. The location held no attraction for either of them—Louise's enforcer, George Millard, had shot Philip in the mansion's basement, and Lizzy and Philip had almost burned to death when Louise locked them in.

"Fine," said Lizzy.

"I'll expect you in an hour," said Louise, and she ended the call.

27

A s Lizzy and Philip approached Pocopson, she thought back to her first trip to Gerard and Louise's home. That drive had been in the middle of a cold winter night, with little of the Chester County countryside visible except for the stone walls lining the two-lane road, visible in the headlight beams when the road curved. Now, on this sunny spring afternoon, they drove through natural tunnels formed by the trees bordering the road and emerged into vistas of rolling hills and grazing horses. The landscape was a far cry from the stark beauty of Arizona, but Lizzy had always thought these views were some of the prettiest she had ever seen.

She was far from being in the right frame of mind to enjoy them now.

Lizzy pointed when she saw the stone pillars topped with ornate metal lamps that marked the drive to Louise's house. "There it is."

They turned off the road and followed the curving drive, the land on either side not noticeably neglected despite the months since anyone had lived on the property. But when they neared the top of the drive, they saw the first signs of the destruction that had taken place: one of the decorative stone lions that flanked the drive had been knocked off its pedestal, perhaps by a firetruck responding to the blaze. And as they passed the remaining lion, the full extent of the devastation became apparent. The stone planter that had stood in the middle of the circular drive now lay in fragments across the pavement, the branches of the surrounding trees were blackened and leafless, and the house they had previously shaded was a charred skeleton.

Philip pulled the van to the edge of the drive, and they climbed out.

"Man, there really is nothing left," she said, scanning the scene. She pulled her duffel bag out of the back of the van, then glanced back down the drive. "I wonder how long they're going to make us wait."

The words were barely out of her mouth when she heard the thump of blades beating the air and, a moment later, a black helicopter with gold trim appeared over the trees surrounding the property and descended toward an open area behind the remains of the house.

Philip shaded his eyes against the midafternoon sun. "That seems more like Viklund's style than Mortensen's."

As the helicopter neared, they could see the pilot, headset over a baseball cap, eyes hidden behind mirrored sunglasses. As he turned to line up for a landing, Lizzy could see a young woman in the passenger seat. Definitely not Louise.

When the skids had settled onto the grass, the woman climbed out of the helicopter. Her blond hair was smoothed back in a ponytail, and as she approached them, holding down her full skirt, Lizzy could see that the delicate floral pattern of her dress brought out the blue of her eyes. She would have looked at home on a fashion shoot in the streets of Stockholm.

When she reached them, she nodded to Philip. "Hello, Mr.

Castillo," she said, raising her voice to be heard over the chop of the blades. "It's good to see you again." Her accent would have been just as at home in Stockholm as her looks.

"Hello, Elsa," said Philip. "Fancy meeting you here."

Lizzy tried to keep from raising her eyebrows. She thought Philip had told her everything about his time at Theo Viklund's compound, but she hadn't heard about Elsa.

Elsa turned to Lizzy. "Miss Ballard, I'm pleased to meet you. I'll be accompanying the two of you to your destination." She nodded at the duffel bag. "You won't need to bring anything. We will supply anything you need."

"I need something from the bag. I ..." Lizzy considered how to pose the dilemma to Elsa. "I won't be able to do any favors for Louise without it."

"Doctor Mortensen says you may bring any medications you need. That is all."

Thinking that Elsa probably wouldn't have referred to the juice as a "medication" if she had known its purpose, Lizzy unzipped the duffel bag and removed the case containing the vial and syringes.

Elsa held out her hand. "I'll take care of it for you."

Lizzy reluctantly handed over the case.

Elsa pulled a small cloth bag from a pocket of her dress and slipped the case into it. "And I will need the contents of your pockets, including your mobile phones."

This was hardly a surprise, but still an unpleasant development. They both handed over their phones, and Philip gave Elsa his wallet.

When Lizzy dug the key to the van out of her pocket, Elsa said, "You can put that in the duffel bag and put the bag in the vehicle, but leave it unlocked."

After Lizzy had delivered the duffel bag to the Caravan, Elsa performed various other checks: searching the pockets of Lizzy's sweatshirt, having Philip lift his pants legs and Lizzy hold her sundress close to her body—no doubt so any weapons hidden underneath would be apparent. During all this, the pilot watched them from the helicopter, and Lizzy noted that Elsa positioned herself so that she wasn't directly between Lizzy and Philip on one side and the pilot on the other. No doubt the pilot was armed and ready to intercede if needed.

"If you are carrying a weapon that my search didn't reveal," said Elsa, "it would be best for all of us if you discarded it now."

"We're not carrying weapons," said Philip.

Elsa gestured to Lizzy's stocking cap. "I understand you've been injured. We will provide facilities for you to clean your head." She gestured toward the helicopter. "After you."

She directed Lizzy and Philip to the second row of seats, then climbed back into the front passenger seat.

The helicopter lifted from the ground, and even the alarming circumstances didn't completely eliminate Lizzy's excitement at her first helicopter ride, and the thrill of watching the rapidly expanding view of the area.

At first, she could track their location by familiar landmarks—buildings she thought were the conservatories at Longwood Gardens, a runway and hangars she guessed was Avondale Airport—but soon she had lost her bearings and could only tell that they were heading west, which would be in the direction of Theo Viklund's compound. She tried to pay attention to the pilot's radio calls, but the noise made it difficult to hear without a headset, and the words and phrases she could pick out were in an aeronautical lingo that she couldn't understand. However, she could hear enough to note that the pilot had the same Swedish accent as Elsa.

Lizzy had trouble estimating how long they had been airborne—more than half an hour, less than an hour—when they began their descent toward a wooded area next to a large pond or small lake from which streams snaked into the trees. As they got closer to the ground, Lizzy spotted a paved clearing. She scanned the surrounding area and wondered if they would be driven to their ultimate destination from this seemingly desolate spot.

The helicopter's skids settled, and Elsa climbed out and opened the back doors for them, then motioned them to follow her.

A golf cart was parked near the landing pad, at the entrance to a path that had been hidden by the leaves and spring buds of tree branches arching overhead. At Elsa's instructions, Lizzy climbed into the front passenger seat and Philip sat in back. Elsa got into the driver's seat, and they rolled down the path.

Lizzy glanced back to where the helicopter's rotors were slowing. "No guard for us?" Lizzy asked. "Louise and Theo aren't afraid we'll try to overpower you?"

"Why would you?" replied Elsa. "You're here because of Doctor McNally, no? How would overpowering me help you?"

Lizzy considered that, under other circumstances, she might have argued that they could use Elsa as a bargaining chip in an exchange for Andy. However, based on what she knew about Louise, and what she gathered from Philip about Theo, they didn't seem like the kind of people who would be too worried about the fate of one of the staff.

Lizzy was wondering how long their drive through the woods would last when she realized they were approaching a low but sizable building. Its windows were mirrored and its structure, which on one side disappeared into the rolling ground, was brushed metal. Raised banks topped with bushes masked the entrance. Other than a flagstone-paved area outside the entrance, she imagined it would be well camouflaged in satellite photos, if she ever had the chance to search for their destination online.

Elsa pulled to a stop at the door and the three climbed out of the cart.

"When are we going to see Andy?" asked Lizzy.

"Very soon. In the meantime, I'll take you to your suite. Please follow me."

They stepped into a utilitarian-looking corridor that became progressively more elegant as they continued—tile giving way to plush carpet, a branching corridor leading to what looked like a conservatory, an open door revealing an elaborately paneled dining room—until eventually they entered a large entrance hall. Elsa led them to the right, and they followed another hallway up a slight incline, past windows overlooking the wooded grounds. When they reached the end of the hallway, Elsa opened a door and preceded them into a room.

The thick Persian rugs and leather club chairs facing a gas fireplace looked like they could have been borrowed from a posh private club. Two of the walls were floor-to-ceiling windows, giving a view into the upper branches of the surrounding trees.

Elsa indicated doors leading off the main room. "You'll find kitchen, bath, and bedroom through those doors, and some snacks in the refrigerator. I'm afraid we don't have any two-bedroom guest suites," she gestured to a screened area at one end of the living room, "but we've set up a separate sleeping area for Mr. Castillo. I hope it's acceptable."

"It's fine," said Philip.

"How long do you expect us to be here?" asked Lizzy, trying to keep her tone matter of fact.

"You'll have to discuss the terms of your stay with Doctor Mortensen." Without giving Lizzy a chance to ask any more questions, Elsa gestured toward an antique table against one wall. "You will hear a chime when Doctor Mortensen is calling on the video conference line. I can't tell you exactly when, but, Miss Ballard, you'll have time to shower if you'd like." She pointed to a mobile phone on a side table near the door. "There's no cell phone reception, but if you need anything, just press zero and I'll come right away. And please don't leave the room without being invited to do so." She went to the door, dropped a minuscule curtsy, then stepped out and eased the door closed behind her. They heard the click of a lock engaging.

"It's good to see you, Mr. Castillo," said Lizzy, in as close an approximation of Elsa's accent as she could manage.

Philip rolled his eyes. "Theo Viklund offers his guests what he thinks will appeal to them. He's only sometimes right."

28

Louise and Lucas sat at the dining table in the bunker, watching on Lucas's iPad as Lizzy gingerly removed the pink stocking cap and Philip examined the cloth covering the back of her head, listening as he murmured an apology when she winced at his light touch. Lucas had returned to the compound a short time earlier, driving Andrew McNally's Lexus. Now they were regrouping over an early dinner in the bunker.

"We can't very well introduce her to Billy Chapel while she's bleeding from a head wound," said Louise as Maja topped up her cup of coffee. "Thank you, Maja."

"Certainly, Dr. Mortensen," said Maja, filling Lucas's cup.

"*Tack*," said Lucas.

"What if we use the dispensary for her meeting with McNally?" Louise asked Lucas. "He could stitch her up while they talk."

Lucas shrugged. "I suppose it would be okay, as long as we don't let McNally get hold of something he could use as a weapon."

On the screen, Lizzy disappeared into the bathroom, while

Philip first examined the mobile phone Elsa had left—no doubt confirming her claim that there was no cell service—then began prowling around the living room.

"I'll lay out the supplies he would need," said Louise. "Unless he tries to throttle someone with suture thread, it shouldn't be a problem." She turned to Maja, who was stacking the last of the plates on the trolley. "We'll also need to get her clean clothes to wear. Perhaps something of Elsa's?"

"Miss Ballard is taller and more slender than Elsa," said Maja.

"Any other candidates among the remaining female staff?"

"None that are Miss Ballard's size. But she is about the same size as Rey Viklund. Rey kept a wardrobe here."

"Excellent solution, Maja. Thank you." Louise gazed at the screen for a few moments, then asked, "Did Rey Viklund have any siblings?"

"No."

"Would Chapel know that?"

"I'm not sure, but I don't think so. Will there be anything else, Dr. Mortensen?"

"No, thank you. The meal was lovely."

Maja bobbed her head. "Thank you." The chef had been gone for weeks, and Maja was now preparing the meals for those remaining at the compound, on top of her other household responsibilities. "I'll ask Elsa to find something among Rey's things for Miss Ballard to wear."

When Maja had wheeled the trolley out of the bunker, Lucas asked, "Why were you asking about whether Rey had siblings?"

"I wonder if we could pass Ballard off as Rey's younger sister, visiting the compound in the wake of Rey's death?"

He considered. "Perhaps."

"It might even lend credence to our story about Theo going into seclusion. If we tell Chapel that Theo won't even see his own niece, maybe he'll be less upset about Theo not seeing him."

"It's possible." He sipped his coffee, not taking his eyes off the video display, which now showed Philip Castillo standing at the window, hands stuffed into his pockets, surveying the grounds. "What has Chapel been doing to pass the time?"

She raised an eyebrow. "Drinking champagne. He won't eat anything—says he'll get something to eat when he goes to the front gate to check in with his men." She took a sip of coffee. "Chapel wants to see Castillo, but first I'd like Ballard to try to find out what he's thinking. We'll need to figure out a reason to bring Ballard and Chapel together, once her wound is stitched up. McNally is secure in the lab apartment?"

"Yes. Rinnert was none too happy to have the apartment next to him being used as a cell."

"I'm not overly concerned about how happy Edmund is."

"Having a guard there to keep an eye on McNally means he's keeping an eye on Edmund, too."

"Not Fredrik, I hope."

Lucas scowled. "No. I kicked Fredrik back to patrolling the grounds. At least he isn't likely to run into Chapel."

They watched the video feed in silence for a few moments, then Louise said, "Having the helicopter was convenient. Are there any other resources at our disposal that I should know about?"

"No."

"Why didn't you mention it earlier?"

"Why? Planning to go somewhere?"

"Not immediately, but it's an option for when we decide to leave the compound for good, correct?"

He nodded. "Yes, I think it's the best option."

"And speaking of leaving the compound for good, what's the progress on my identity documents?"

"In process. The good ones take some time."

"Not too much time, I hope."

"No. They'll be ready and waiting for you in Philadelphia when they're needed."

Louise set aside her napkin, stood, and smoothed her dress. "I'll get the supplies set up for McNally and Ballard."

Lucas swallowed the last of his coffee and stood as well. "I'll find someone to keep an eye on them while they're in the dispensary."

As they left the bunker, Louise thought back to her unsettling interaction with Billy Chapel in the conservatory. There were things she wanted to do that required the resources at the compound, including better understanding Ballard's expanding set of abilities. But once she had accomplished those things, and once her documents were ready, she would be only too happy to be helicoptered out of the compound, leaving Chapel and his men to clear the wine cellar of any champagne that might remain.

29

Lizzy had planned to hop in the shower just long enough to make herself presentable, but she lingered, confident that Philip would let her know if Elsa came to take them to Andy. She decided to try to rinse the blood out of her hair, despite Andy's caution to keep the stitches dry, and hoped the hot jets would also massage the tension out of her neck and shoulders. When they had achieved the first, and when she had given up on the hope that they would achieve the second, she turned off the water and touched the back of her head. Her fingers came away stained with a fresh trickle of blood. Wincing, she pressed a fluffy white washcloth to the wound and slipped the pink stocking cap over it.

She was patting herself dry when there was a light knock on the door and Elsa called, "Miss Ballard, I have some clothes for you."

Lizzy slipped on the terrycloth robe hanging from a brass hook next to the shower and opened the door.

Elsa stood outside holding a stack of clothes. "Once I know how these fit, I'll bring you more." She nodded to where Lizzy's clothes lay in a heap on the floor. "Would you like your clothes to be laundered, or should I dispose of them?"

"I really don't want to be here long enough for you to wash my clothes."

Elsa blushed. "I'm sorry, I don't have any information about how long you will be here."

"Fine. Then I guess you might as well see if you can get the bloodstains out."

"Very good." Elsa slipped past Lizzy, set the stack of clean clothes on the vanity, and gathered up Lizzy's dirty clothes. She hurried out of the bathroom and closed the door behind her.

Lizzy sorted through the clothes: a pair of skinny jeans, a loose-fitting turquoise V-neck T-shirt, turquoise suede loafers, and a soft leather jacket. It was an outfit more appropriate for a twenty-something than a teenager, but the clothes were pretty and obviously expensive. And although the jeans were made for someone slightly shorter and curvier than Lizzy, and the sleeves on the jacket didn't quite cover her wrists, the fit, even of the loafers, was pretty good. When she was dressed, she assessed herself in the mirror. The otherwise fashionable outfit lost something in combination with the pink stocking cap.

When she stepped into the living room, she found Elsa hovering next to the door to the hallway and Philip standing near the window, hands stuffed in the pockets of his jeans.

"Louise wants to talk to me," he said to Lizzy.

"Just you?"

"Yes," said Elsa, "just Mr. Castillo. Someone else will come for him soon. In the meantime, Miss Ballard, I'm to take you to see Doctor McNally. You will meet in the dispensary, so not only will you get to see him, but he will be able to restitch the cut to your head." She shifted nervously. "Doctor Mortensen says to tell you that if anything should happen to me while I escort you to see Doctor McNally, he and Mr. Castillo will pay the price."

"Why do Philip and I have to be apart? Why can't he come with me?"

Elsa twisted her fingers in front of her. "Doctor Mortensen says it's because she's seen the trouble the two of you can make when you work together."

"Can't argue with that," said Philip laconically.

"I guess not," said Lizzy, loathe to be separated from Philip.

He crossed the room to where she stood and raised his fist, which she bumped with hers.

"See you soon," he said.

Lizzy followed Elsa back down the sloping hallway to the entrance hall, then toward the back of the house. They made a few turns, then Elsa stopped outside a closed door. Without meeting Lizzy's eyes, she said, "Doctor McNally suffered a few minor injuries when he was brought to the compound. Doctor Mortensen asked me to let you know so you weren't surprised by them."

Lizzy wondered what Elsa knew about the consequences of giving Lizzy Ballard an unpleasant surprise. "Okay, you've warned me," she said, her voice stony.

Elsa knocked lightly on the door, then pushed it open and stepped aside. "I'll bring you back to your suite in ten minutes."

"What if ten minutes isn't enough?"

"I've been told to take you back to your suite in ten minutes."

After a beat, Lizzy nodded, then stepped inside.

After the opulent décor of the suite, the stripped-down functionality of the room was striking. A utilitarian screen blocked her view of most of the contents of the room, except for a gray metal desk to one side and a gurney on the other. Next to the desk stood a large blond man, arms crossed, a gun in one hand.

Next to the gurney stood Andy.

She rushed across the room and threw her arms around his

neck. "Oh my God, are you okay?" she asked, then jumped back. "*Are* you okay? Are you injured? Did I hurt you?"

He smiled. "No, you didn't hurt me and, yes, I'm fine."

"But your face—" she said, gesturing to raw scrapes running down one cheek. "Did they do that to you?"

"No, it was all completely self-inflicted. I fell."

"Did they push you?"

"No. They tased me. Actually, the way they positioned me, I think I was supposed to fall backwards into the van, but I fell forward onto the pavement."

"They tased you??"

"Yes. Not that I'm going to ask for seconds, but it was probably better than the alternatives." He gestured to her pink stocking cap. "Cut still giving you trouble?"

Her hand drifted self-consciously up to the cap. "It won't stop bleeding." In the scheme of things, it was the least of her troubles, but she heard the quaver in her voice.

Andy gestured to the items on a stainless-steel tray next to the gurney. "Our host thinks of everything." He patted the gurney. "Why don't you hop up here and I'll take a look."

"Elsa says we have ten minutes," said Lizzy, climbing onto the gurney and carefully removing the cap. "Probably only nine minutes now."

Andy eased the washcloth, which had already begun to stick to the wound, off her head. "Then what happens?"

"I don't know." She glanced at the guard, standing well out of reach even of Andy's long arms. "I think Louise wants me to do a favor for her, then she says she'll let us all go."

"'All'?"

"Philip's here, too."

"Philip, eh?"

"That's enough about that," said the guard in the inevitable Swedish accent.

As Andy worked on her head, Lizzy tried to think of something she could tell him—either overtly or in some sort of coded message—that would pass muster with the guard. She couldn't think of anything. If Andy's conversation—mainly related to places he was thinking of going on his next vacation—contained a coded message, she couldn't tell what it was. She suspected his soothing patter was intended mainly to calm her down.

Andy had set aside the needle and was examining the finished sutures when the door opened, and Elsa stepped in. "It's time to go back to your suite, Miss Ballard."

"Your *suite*?" said Andy, raising his eyebrows melodramatically. "Swanky."

Lizzy tried for a laugh and jumped off the gurney. "What's that quote about a gilded cage?"

Both their expressions sobered.

"Where are *you* staying?" she asked.

"That's enough about that," said the man again.

Lizzy smiled wanly at Andy. "I'll do whatever Louise needs, and then we'll be out of here."

But she didn't sound convincing, even to her own ears.

30

L ouise stood in the conservatory, hands clasped behind her back, looking through the grimy windows at the rapidly darkening landscape. The transition from the indoors to outdoors was becoming less marked with each day, the conservatory plantings now nearly as ungroomed as the wooded ground on the other side of the glass. She turned when she heard the squeak of the door from the hallway opening.

Philip Castillo stepped in, followed by Lucas.

Louise hadn't seen Castillo since passing Ballard and Mitchell Pieda loading his unconscious form into a car as she drove away from Pocopson. She had certainly never expected to see him again.

"Mr. Castillo," she said.

"Doctor Mortensen," he replied.

She gestured toward a cafe table and two chairs. "Please have a seat."

Louise and Philip sat, Lucas taking up a position a few feet behind Philip.

"I understand this isn't your first visit to Theo Viklund's compound," she said.

"No. But at least I got a little sabbatical from Theo's hospitality. How about you?"

"As you can imagine, leaving the compound would be risky for me, in view of the authorities' interest in me in the wake of the fire."

"The fire you tried to trap Lizzy and me in."

"After you shot my assistant ..."

His mouth quirked up. "He started it."

"... and after Elizabeth killed him."

"She finished what he started."

They stared at each other for a moment, expressionless, then Philip said, "So, Theo wanted me back here?"

"Yes."

"Will he be explaining the reason to me?"

"Not directly. Rey's death affected him deeply, and he has gone into seclusion. Theo has asked me to serve as his second-in-command."

"I'm not sure whether to offer congratulations or condolences."

"I'm happy to be able to be of use to Theo. After all, he kept me out of the hands of the authorities, just as he did with you."

"Yeah. Lucky us."

"What do you know about Rey's death?" asked Louise.

"Very little."

"You weren't responsible?"

"No."

"Do you know who was?"

Philip's eyes narrowed, and he gazed at her for a few beats. "Yes."

Louise tried not to let her surprise show. "Who?"

"Ask Theo. He can probably guess, and if you're his second-in-command, I'm sure he'd be happy to tell you."

"He won't talk about Rey with anyone. But if he doesn't know who Rey's killer is, and if you told him, I suspect he would be grateful for the information. And anxious to act on it to avenge Rey's death."

"Tell him he doesn't have to worry about it."

Louise waited, but Philip was silent. Eventually, she said, "I'll let him know. I'm sure he'll be gratified."

"Gratified enough to let Lizzy and McNally and me go?"

"No, not *that* gratified." She crossed her legs. "I'll save you the insult of small talk and get right to why we asked you and Ballard to come here. I don't expect you to believe me—at least not immediately—but my purposes are better served by telling you the truth." She clasped her hands in her lap. "A former colleague of Theo's has arrived at the compound, despite the fact that I've explained to him that Theo is not seeing anyone. We don't know what this colleague's intentions are, and I suspect that, based on Elizabeth's performance at the poker tables, she could let us know."

"What do you mean?"

"Please, Mr. Castillo. You don't really expect me to believe that Elizabeth Ballard has discovered a completely natural and non-drug-enabled ability to win consistently at cards." She re-crossed her legs. "It seems clear that Lizzy got the steroid drug that I made for Mitchell Pieda, and that it enables her to read minds. Based on my analysis of the blood sample brought to me from Atlantic City by one of Theo's security staff, one of the McNally brothers must have formulated more of the drug."

"And, assuming all that's true, you want her to read this colleague's mind?"

"Yes."

"And then kill him with a stroke?"

Louise waved a hand. "If she can tell us what he's thinking, it's likely we could find a way to deal with it that wouldn't require anyone to die."

"Finding ways to keep people from dying doesn't seem to be high on your priority list."

"I might say the same about you."

"I think I'm a little more selective about the people I'm willing to see get hurt—or to hurt myself."

"Our criteria aren't so different."

He raised his eyebrows. "Lizzy's mother?"

"I didn't hurt her—Elizabeth herself was responsible for her mother's death."

His expression darkened. "Lizzy's father?"

Louise's lips tightened. "I do what I need to do to reach the desired goal. I don't go out of my way to cause unnecessary harm."

"I can't help thinking that putting Lizzy together with this mysterious colleague—"

"His name is Billy Chapel. Do you know him?"

"No. You don't think putting Lizzy together with Billy Chapel might lead to some unnecessary harm—on one side or the other?"

"We'll provide a cover story for her."

"Like what?"

"We'll tell him Ballard is Rey Viklund's younger sister."

"Yeah," he said, his tone bitter, "I can't imagine how that could go wrong."

"He can't harm her. You don't imagine Theo would allow someone—even a colleague—to come into the compound armed, do you?"

"No, I suppose not." He crossed his arms. "But if it's Lizzy's cooperation you want, she's the person you need to be speaking to."

"I intend to speak to her."

"So what do you want from me?"

"Theo promised Mr. Chapel that you would help him with something."

"It could be," said Philip. "Theo was helping me out with an issue, and it was clear he expected me to help him out with something in return, but I don't know what it was or who it was for."

"It was for Chapel. Theo didn't give me details—he doesn't want me to have to get involved—but Chapel evidently needs someone who isn't quite as blond-haired and blue-eyed as the rest of Theo's staff."

Philip scowled. "Great."

"Chapel is at the compound not only to speak with Theo, but to meet you as well."

"And you expect me to discharge whatever favor Theo promised this guy, without even knowing what that is?"

"Not necessarily. For now, I merely expect you to let Chapel *think* that you're willing to do whatever he wants you to do, or at least to discuss it."

"And how long would I have to play along?"

"Not long. Once Ballard can tell us what Chapel is planning, I believe we'll have the information we need to get him to leave the compound."

"To leave it with me in tow?"

"I'm sure we can find a way to avoid that outcome."

"And you want us to believe that's it? Lizzy tells you what Chapel is thinking, and I pretend to go along with his plans, and then we all get to leave here. With Andy."

"Yes."

"After she killed your sidekick, George."

"Yes."

"And your husband."

Louise felt a muscle twitch in her jaw, and she forced her

facial muscles to relax. "I have more immediate goals than getting revenge on Elizabeth Ballard."

"I think you're lying."

"I don't blame you. But to be frank, I don't care whether you think I'm lying or not. All I need you to believe is that unpleasant things will happen to you, Elizabeth, and Doctor McNally if you don't cooperate."

"Like what?"

She nodded to Lucas, who gestured to someone outside the conservatory's glass door.

A moment later, Andrew McNally stepped through the door, his hands behind his back, followed by a member of the security staff. McNally's expression was strained. Louise regretted that McNally had injured his face when he was abducted, since it would no doubt undermine Castillo's belief in Louise's concern for their well-being. She was gratified that Castillo's expression didn't change.

"In answer to your question," Louise said to Philip, "let's not have to find out."

"As long as all I'm supposed to do is pretend to go along with whatever Theo's buddy's plan for me is, and not actually follow through on whatever Theo promised, I can sign up for that."

Louise appreciated that Philip didn't mention Chapel's name in front of McNally. "I assume Theo's *colleague* will want his meeting with you to take place somewhere he expects not to be overheard, since he might reasonably expect his suite to be bugged, and I want to hear what he has to say to you. We need you to wear a wire."

"If you think this guy would expect his suite to be bugged, don't you think he'd expect me to be wired? Seems like things could go badly for me if he somehow found out what I was doing."

Louise's eyes flickered to Lucas, who nodded to the man standing behind McNally.

The man stepped forward, grabbed McNally's arm, spun him around, and drove his fist into his face.

McNally let out a yelp of surprise as well as pain. He staggered but regained his balance as blood began to trickle from the cut that had opened over his eye.

Philip's gaze didn't shift from Louise. "I was just pointing out a consideration. No need to have your goon weigh in."

Louise pulled something from her pocket. "He might suspect you're wired, but I assure you he won't find the device." She opened her hand to display what appeared to be the waist button for a pair of jeans, almost indistinguishable from the one on Philip's jeans.

He glanced at it, then met her eyes again. "Very clever." After a brief pause, he said, "All right."

"Maja will swap your actual button for this one," said Louise, "then she'll take you to see Theo's colleague."

"What about Lizzy—?"

Lucas nodded again and the guard drove his fist into McNally's nose.

This time McNally didn't make a sound, but he did drop to his knees. His choked cough sent a spray of blood onto the conservatory's brick floor.

Philip's head jerked toward McNally, then turned back to Louise, his expression dark. "Goddamn, can you reserve using him as a punching bag for when I actually disregard one of your instructions?"

Louise forced herself to keep her temper in check—she thought Lucas had agreed to her position that inflicting one injury on McNally would be sufficient for their purposes. "Lucas apparently thought it best to give you one more reminder about the importance of keeping your mind on your assignment—not on Miss Ballard."

Lucas nodded to the guard, who pulled McNally to his feet and, steadying the injured man, hustled him out the door. As they exited the conservatory, Maja entered, averting her eyes from McNally's bloodied face.

Not waiting for Philip to respond, Louise stood and crossed the conservatory to the door, followed by Lucas. At the end of the corridor, they turned left, toward the bunker.

"Was the second punch really necessary?" she hissed.

"Castillo wasn't being as cooperative as I would have liked. A broken nose is a small price to pay for keeping our visitors in line."

"Someone else's broken nose."

Lucas looked surprised. "Of course." They walked in silence for a few moments and had almost reached the bunker, when Lucas said, "Chapel must know by this time that he isn't going to see Viklund, and I'm guessing he suspects the reason. Once he's got Castillo, the next time he goes to the front gate, he might take him along ... and might just keep on walking."

"That would be the best outcome for everyone concerned," Louise said tartly.

"Yeah." After a moment, Lucas added, "Everyone except Castillo."

31

Louise and Lucas stood in the bunker, listening via Lucas's phone's speaker to the footsteps as Philip Castillo and Maja walked down the hall to Billy Chapel's suite, then a light knock on the door and the faint sound of Chapel's *Come!*

There was the rustle of movement, the click of a door closing, then Maja's voice. "Mr. Chapel, this is Philip Castillo."

"Pleased to meet you, Phil." Chapel's voice was clearer now. "Can I call you Phil?"

"I'd rather you didn't," said Philip.

A booming laugh from Billy. "Sorry—what do you expect from a guy who goes by *Billy*? Can I pour you some champagne? It's good stuff—at least I assume it is, since Theo Viklund wouldn't serve anything else to his guests."

"No, thanks."

"Yeah, I'm not much of a champagne lover myself, but I love seeing the expression on little Elsa's face when I ask for another bottle. You know Elsa?"

"Yes."

"Sweet thing, isn't she?"

"Yes."

Another laugh. "You know, I've spent so much time in this room swilling bubbly, I'm in the mood to stretch my legs. Plus, it's time I go down to the front gate to let my guys know I'm still among the living."

"Perhaps Mr. Castillo can accompany you," said Maja.

"Good idea," said Chapel heartily. There were more footsteps—Louise imagined Maja leading Chapel and Castillo back down the corridor—then Chapel's voice again, echoey in the entrance hall. "I'll take it from here, Maja."

"Yes, Herr Chapel. I will meet you back here when you return."

A moment later, the background noise became more expansive, with two pairs of steps on the flagstone terrace and then on the drive.

There was no conversation for a minute. Then, when the two men had no doubt covered enough distance that a bend in the drive would have taken them out of view of the house, the footsteps stopped—first one set, then the other.

"Wearing a wire?" asked Billy.

"No."

"Care to prove it?"

"I don't see how I could. You don't think Theo Viklund would need to have actual wires taped to my body or a transmitter tucked in my pocket, do you?"

"You could strip down—leave your clothes behind."

"After you."

Billy's laugh boomed over the speaker. "I like you, Phil. Not sure what my boys would think if we got to the gate, both of us naked as jaybirds. We'll just make sure it doesn't matter if someone's listening in." The footsteps resumed. "Have you gotten to talk to Theo?"

"No."

"Think he's still around?"

"I don't have any reason to think he's not."

"I don't have any reason to think he *is*. I'll believe it when I see him." When Philip was silent, Billy continued. "You knew Rey?"

"Yes."

"What you think of her?"

"Sweet."

Another burst of laughter. "You know, Phil, I generally find one-word answers annoying, especially when I'm trying to get some information, but you have a way with the ones you use."

"What information are you trying to get?"

"I'd like to get to know you a little better."

"A little better than what?"

"Better than I do now, based just on what Viklund's told me."

"And what has he told you? Just so I don't waste your time giving you information you already have."

The footsteps stopped.

"I know you were in prison at the Williams Correctional Facility in Arizona for murder," said Chapel. "I know that while you were in, you had some trouble with some psychopath named Tobe Hanrick. I know Viklund promised to get you into Williams as a janitor to kill Hanrick, and that you wanted to do it yourself, not have one of Viklund's guys do it for you. I know he sent Rey with you to Arizona as your minder. And I know Hanrick and Rey ended up dead in your old stomping grounds not long after you showed up." There was a pause, then Billy continued, his tone less jolly. "Did I get any of that wrong?"

"No."

"Did you kill Rey?"

Louise found herself holding her breath as she waited for Philip's response.

"No. I wasn't interested in being minded, so I found a way to get away from Rey, but she was alive—and none the worse for wear—when I left her."

"And Hanrick?"

"Yes. I killed Hanrick."

"I understand his throat was slit."

"Yes."

"Was it all you hoped for? Killing him?"

A pause. "Yes."

"You want a job?"

Another pause. "Not particularly."

"Actually, I shouldn't make it sound like it's an option, because the only reason you got to Arizona and were able to kill Hanrick is because Viklund let you do it, and the only reason he let you do it is because I needed someone out there to do a favor for me. And not one of his lily-white henchmen. Theo didn't mention that little detail to you?"

"He said he wanted me to do a favor for a friend of his in exchange for help killing Hanrick. He didn't say who the friend was."

"That was me."

"Okay."

"Curious what the favor was?"

"Sure."

"There are deals to be made on the Indian land."

There was a pause, and when Philip spoke, his voice had an edge. "Oh?"

"Don't play dumb—you must know what I'm talking about. They're your people—am I right?"

"I don't have 'people.'"

"You know what I mean. Those Indians are sitting on a shit-load of resources, but they're not taking advantage of them. I figure if they're not using them, I will, but I don't have the resources to send out there to scout around, and obviously anyone Theo could send would stick out like a sore thumb on the res. But you ... you're probably already tight with some of them. Am I right?"

"No, you're not right."

Billy sighed theatrically. "Okay, sure, whatever you say. But tight or not, you could find out shit—shit that might be useful to me."

"And that's the job you're offering me? Hang out on the res and collect information?"

"That was the original plan—" Louise could imagine Billy waving his hand dismissively. "—but I have a better idea now." After a pause, he said, "That's your cue to say, 'What's that, Billy?'"

"What's that, Billy?"

"I'm always on the lookout for someone who doesn't balk at slitting a man's throat."

"You're offering me a job slitting throats?"

"Maybe ... but not necessarily. It might turn out you have other skills I could use. Maybe skills you don't even know about yourself."

"And you're offering me this job based on a résumé you got from Theo Viklund and a five-minute conversation?"

"Oh, there'd be a probationary period, but I have a feeling you'd pass that test."

"And what if I failed the test?"

"Phil, old buddy, if I were you, I'd do my best not to fail."

Louise shuddered at the menace in his voice. She was grateful she wasn't the one walking alone with Billy Chapel.

When he spoke again, his voice had resumed its more cheerful—although in some ways no less menacing—tone. "And I pay well—you can ask any of my guys when we get to the gate. You do a good job for me, I do a good job for you."

"And when do I need to give you my answer?"

"Right now."

"Not much time to make such a life-altering decision."

"If I thought you needed time to make a decision, I wouldn't be offering you the job."

After a moment, Castillo said, "If Viklund's not going to meet with *you*, he's not going to meet with *me*, but I'd feel better if Mortensen would give me some assurance that I've discharged my responsibility to the head of the organization. An assurance from Viklund, of course."

"Oh, I'm pretty sure Theo won't stand in the way. But as you say, we can't ask him ourselves, so we better check with Louise." Billy's voice rose slightly. "Hey, Louise! What do you think? Will old Theo be okay with Phil leaving with me when I head out?"

Louise's eyes snapped up and met Lucas's. Lucas muttered what must have been a Swedish profanity, although he didn't look completely surprised.

"Just send that pretty little Elsa to my suite to let me know," continued Chapel. "And tell her to bring some more of that fancy champagne." The footsteps resumed. "Phil and I are almost at the gate. Since he's one of the team now, I think I'll have him swap clothes with one of my guys." He gave a rough laugh. "Although I don't necessarily want my guy wearing Phil's clothes. I'm sure you understand, Louise."

32

Louise and Lucas listened on Lucas's phone, set to speaker, as Chapel called a greeting to his men at the gate, then joked with them about whose clothes would be the best fit for Castillo.

"What am *I* supposed to wear, Billy?" asked the man whom Chapel had evidently chosen as the clothing donor, the other men guffawing at his dilemma.

"Wear a goddamn tarp for all I care," said Chapel. "There should be one in the back of one of the SUVs."

There were some rustling sounds that must have been Castillo removing his clothes, with some background conversation of Billy complaining about the sandwich his men had provided him. Then Chapel's voice: "Throw his old clothes in the woods down the road."

Louise heard the sound of feet hitting pavement in a regular rhythm, and increasingly heavier breathing, followed by what sounded like static, then silence.

Lucas scowled. "They probably stuffed the clothes in that drainage ditch."

Louise crossed her arms. "Chapel knew the whole time that we were listening to him."

"He didn't get where he is without being a suspicious son of a bitch."

"He's not only suspicious of Castillo wearing a microphone and of us listening in, but he obviously doesn't believe our explanation of what has happened to Theo." She raised an eyebrow. "Although he doesn't sound too concerned about the idea of Theo being dead."

"The longer we try to keep the story going about Theo hiding out in the bunker, the more unbelievable it sounds."

"I'm aware of that," she snapped.

Lucas was silent for a moment, then said, "I assume the comment Castillo made about wanting an assurance that he has discharged his responsibility means he wants to be sure that him leaving with Chapel doesn't jeopardize Ballard and McNally."

Louise uncrossed her arms and twisted her wedding ring. "I suppose so." She grimaced. "I'd almost be willing to forego having Ballard read Chapel's mind if they would all just leave. Why *does* Chapel keep coming back to the house?"

Lucas rubbed his hand across his crewcut. "If he believes Viklund's alive—which I doubt—I suppose he could be waiting to see if he makes an appearance. The more likely explanation is that he assumes Viklund's dead and figures the more time he spends here, the more useful information he can get to take advantage of the situation."

"And how might he take advantage of it?

Lucas shrugged. "Viklund's death creates a power vacuum. We don't plan to fill it—at least long-term. I'm sure Chapel would be happy to step in."

"But would that be enough for him? Would he come after us? Where would he look? Maybe more importantly, where *wouldn't* he look? We need to know what he's thinking—and what he's planning. And I want to test Ballard's mind-reading ability. We can't pass up the opportunity to accomplish both those goals at once."

Lucas looked skeptical. "How will we know if she's telling us the truth about what information she gets from Chapel?"

"Because she knows we'll find her friends and punish them for any lies she tells us."

"*Find* her friends? So you really want to let McNally go?"

"Yes—and Ballard. But we can find Andrew McNally again if we need to. As well as Owen McNally and Ruby DiMano, if we need even more leverage."

He crossed his arms. "I think you're not willing to do what needs to be done when it comes to the girl."

She drew a deep breath. "I'm willing to do what needs to be done, but I'm not willing to sacrifice the most successful result of my experiments on a whim."

"Ballard killed your husband."

"He was firing a gun at her."

"And you don't care?"

"Of course I care," she said through gritted teeth. "But I am trying not to let my personal considerations interfere with pursuing the most productive path."

They glared at each other wordlessly for a few beats, then Louise said, trying for an even tone, "We'll deal with Ballard—and do whatever is necessary—when the time comes."

"Fine." He picked up his phone from the table. "I'm going to go watch for Chapel and Castillo to come back from the front gate." He scowled. "And check the champagne supply." He left the bunker, closing the door a little harder than was necessary.

Louise dropped into the desk chair and leaned her head back. Was Lucas right—was Louise putting them at jeopardy to protect Ballard? Perhaps. But what were the odds she'd have a chance to replicate whatever combination of circumstances had resulted in the girl's extraordinary abilities? Depressingly low.

The question was, how far could she pressure the young woman—mentally or physically—before such pressure backfired? Could she force Lizzy to cooperate with her in the same way Chapel had apparently forced Castillo to cooperate with him? It was hardly the same thing. Nothing she saw in Philip Castillo suggested that he regretted the murders he had committed. Ballard was a killer, too, but not a cold-blooded one. Louise knew that Lizzy was haunted by the deaths she had caused, perhaps even including Gerard's.

But what an asset Ballard would be. Having an ally with the ability to read minds and to kill in a way that could so easily pass as a natural cause was a nice weapon indeed. How was she to achieve that, if not through Ballard? Even if she were willing to wait years for the result of a modified pregnancy to mature to adulthood, as she had with Ballard, she doubted she would ever again be able to assemble the equivalent of her Vivantem research lab. She was even less likely to have access to women like those who had come to the fertility clinic for treatment, and who had become Louise's unwitting test subjects.

But what she did have, she mused, was a lab in which she could formulate more of the steroid drug that had enabled Ballard to read minds and had boosted Mitchell Pieda's ability to cause strokes. She needed to turn her attention to exploring how such a drug might be modified to produce the desired effects in a subject who was not a result of the experiments she had run at Vivantem.

Pondering what modifications might be needed, and more out of habit than from any expectation that she would be able to do anything productive, Louise removed Theo's hand from the refrigerator. She was able to unlock the computer on her third attempt. Not surprisingly, there were no new messages—Billy

Chapel hardly needed to threaten her via email when he could do it in person—and she had no better luck than on previous days in accessing Theo's untapped accounts.

As she put the now noticeably spongy hand back in its container, she thought of another asset she had: Edmund Rinnert, whose expertise in electrophysiology was the only reason they could continue to access the computer. Might electricity be another option for creating the abilities she sought?

33

When Lizzy arrived back at the suite after her visit with Andy in the dispensary, Philip wasn't there.

When Elsa arrived a little later with dinner—a thick vegetable soup, crusty bread, cheese, and fruit—Lizzy asked her where he was, but Elsa claimed to have no information. Lizzy briefly wished she could take a dose of the juice to see if she could learn more from Elsa, but she suspected that if Louise didn't want Lizzy to know what was going on with Philip, she wouldn't send a person with that information to the suite.

Lizzy picked half-heartedly at the food, but she had no appetite.

She wandered the suite, testing the doors leading outside and to the hallway and, not surprisingly, finding them both locked. She was somewhat surprised to find knives in the kitchenette. However, with Andy and now Philip both available as leverage to ensure her cooperation, the value of having a weapon was even more questionable than the value of taking Elsa as a hostage when she drove them from the helipad to the house.

She returned to the living room and dropped onto the

couch. Hugging a silk-fringed throw pillow, she gazed morosely out at the now-dark woods.

She must have drifted into an uneasy sleep because she was startled awake by a chiming sound. It took her a moment to remember Elsa's instruction about the sound indicating an incoming video call. She jumped up from the couch and saw that what she had thought was a painting over the suite's antique desk now displayed a video feed: Louise Mortensen. She crossed to the desk and sank down in the chair.

"I trust you're reasonably comfortable in your quarters," said Louise.

"Where is Philip?"

"He's perfectly fine—and you'll be seeing him soon. Elsa will be arriving in a moment with the drug she took from you in Pocopson. After you've injected yourself, she'll take you to the suite where Theo's colleague, Billy Chapel, is staying. You just need to read his mind and tell us what he's planning."

"*Just* read his mind," Lizzy muttered.

"Yes. Is that a problem?"

Lizzy was torn between a desire to lower Louise's expectations of her mind-reading ability, especially on the lower concentration of the drug that Owen had given her, and the idea that it might be beneficial for Louise to think her abilities were greater than they really were. She opted for the second. "No, it's not a problem."

"You'll tell Chapel that you're Rey Viklund's younger sister, Elisabet. You know who Rey was?"

"Yes."

"And you know what happened to her?"

"Yes." Lizzy suspected she knew more than Louise did— Philip had explained about how his friend Wayne Watchman had knocked out Rey with a tranquilizer so Philip could escape her supervision, and how Tobe Hanrick's lackey, Clemson, had accidentally killed Rey while questioning her.

"Rey didn't actually have a sister," said Louise, "but we have no reason to think Chapel knows that. Can you imitate a Swedish accent?"

"No."

"Try."

"I can't imitate a Swedish accent," said Lizzy, her attempt bearing out her claim.

Louise winced. "You're Rey's sister who grew up in the United States."

"Do I need to know anything else about this fictional sister?"

Louise provided Lizzy with some backstory. "If he asks you anything beyond that, just make it up."

"What do you want to know from him?" asked Lizzy.

"Why he's here and what his plans are. The security staff has ensured that he didn't bring a weapon into the compound, and we'll monitor your interaction with him and intercede if anything goes wrong."

"I can't imagine that something *won't* go wrong, considering this whole messed-up situation." Her anger was clear in her tone.

An emotion flashed over Louise's face—Irritation? Embarrassment?—but was quickly replaced by her usual unreadable expression. "I didn't want to show you this, but ..." Louise's face disappeared, replaced by an image of Andy.

He was seated in a chair in the middle of what looked like a large cell, his hands behind him, no doubt tied. But the worst part of the picture was his face. A bloody piece of gauze was taped over one eyebrow, one eye was ringed in an angry red, and his nose was swollen to twice its normal size.

Lizzy jerked upright in the chair. "What did you do to him?" she yelled. "And why? We've been cooperating!"

"You've been cooperating, but Mr. Castillo has not, and Dr. McNally bore the brunt of Theo's displeasure."

"What did Philip do? And where is he?"

"You'll see him soon enough." The image of Andy was replaced by Louise's face. "I'm sure it's upsetting to see, but McNally isn't badly injured. A minor cut and a broken nose. If you cooperate—if you provide the information we need from Mr. Chapel—he won't be any more badly injured that that. How long after the injection will the drug take effect?"

Lizzy swallowed down the bile rising in her throat. "Not long. A few minutes."

"Very good."

"But you need to let me know—where is Philip?"

The monitor went black.

Lizzy jumped up from the desk and ran to the door to the hall. She tried turning the knob—still locked—and pounded on it. "Let me out!"

"Miss Ballard," she heard Elsa's voice from the other side of the door, "please step back so I can come in."

Lizzy backed up a dozen feet. The lock disengaged, the door opened, and Elsa stepped in, holding the drug case in one hand and a baseball hat in the other. Behind her, positioned just before the corridor curved out of view, stood a young blond man. He reached under the flap of his jacket, no doubt to draw a weapon, but when Lizzy didn't advance out of the suite, dropped his hand again. Lizzy guessed the security staff had been warned to try to avoid doing anything overtly threatening to her.

"Where is Philip?" Lizzy yelled.

Elsa, looking alarmed, took a step back. "I don't know."

Lizzy glared at her, breathing hard, and then turned and stomped back to the suite's living room.

Elsa eased the door shut. "I have the vial you gave me in

Pocopson," she said timidly. "Do you want me to give you the injection?"

"No, I don't want you to give me the injection," said Lizzy, her voice trembling. "I want—" She drew a deep breath. She doubted poor Elsa had any more control over the situation than Lizzy did. "I'll do it myself."

Elsa crossed to the dining table, taking a path that kept her as far as possible from Lizzy, and put the case and the hat—the same turquoise as Lizzy's T-shirt and shoes—on it. "You'll need to cover your head so that Mr. Chapel doesn't see the stitches. You left the pink cap in the dispensary." She hurried back toward the door. "I'll wait outside, just come out when you're ready." She slipped into the hallway.

Lizzy tried to slow her breathing, hoping the pounding of her heart would lessen. She wasn't going to do Andy—or Philip —any good if she let herself panic.

When her heartbeat had slowed to a more normal rate, she opened the case and took out the vial and a syringe. She estimated that the vial contained two doses. Under other circumstances, she might have been tempted to take a partial dose to stretch her supply, but she didn't want to do anything that might jeopardize her ability to discharge her assignment. She briefly considered taking a double dose to compensate for Owen's lower concentration but decided against that as well—she was afraid that it would be just as likely to jumble her thoughts as to improve her ability.

She removed her jacket, rolled up the sleeve of her T-shirt, and injected herself in her bicep. After packing the vial and syringe back in the case, she put on the jacket and the cap. Then she went to the window and looked out across the wooded ground until she thought the drug would have had time to take effect. She went to the door to the hallway and opened it.

Elsa stood just outside, and the guard a little further down the hall.

"I'm ready," said Lizzy.

Elsa extended her hand, and Lizzy put the case into it.

As Lizzy followed Elsa toward the entrance hall, she sensed a whirl of nervousness in Elsa's thoughts, but nothing more. Was it because Louise had been careful to send a representative who had no information that would be of use to Lizzy, or was it because the lower concentration of the drug was interfering with her eavesdropping ability? Her stomach clenched at the possibility that she might not be able to discharge her assignment, and at the thought of what that might mean for Andy.

They crossed the entrance hall and entered another corridor. It was almost identical to the one that led to her suite, the only difference being that Lizzy's corridor sloped up, whereas this one sloped down. As a way to gauge the extent to which the juice had kicked in, she tried scanning Elsa's thoughts, but got nothing more concrete than she had before. She briefly considered asking for the case so she could inject herself with the remaining dose, but they had reached the end of the corridor, and Elsa knocked lightly on the door. To a shouted *Come!* from the room, Elsa opened the door and stepped inside. Lizzy followed.

A brawny man wearing a shiny leather jacket over an all-black outfit pushed himself off the couch, taking care not to spill any of the champagne in the glass he held. This, she guessed, was Billy Chapel.

Another man, dark-haired, sat with his back to her. As he stood, she noticed that his clothes looked like a cheaper and flashier version of the first man's clothes. She experienced a twinge of irritation that Louise hadn't warned her that she would be meeting with more than one person. Until the man turned to face her.

It was Philip.

34

"Well, well, well," said Billy Chapel with a grin, "This must be the visitor Louise told me to expect."

Elsa led Lizzy into the suite. "Yes, this is Rey Viklund's sister, Elisabet."

"Come on over here, Elisabet, and join me and my friend for a glass of champagne."

As Chapel bent to pull the bottle from a silver ice bucket, Philip marshaled a rueful smile for Lizzy, and she tried to sort through the jumble of thoughts—all from her own mind—about what might be going on.

"Phil," said Chapel, "run into the kitchen and get another glass."

Philip picked up the full glass from the table next to the chair where he had been sitting. "She can have mine."

"That's mighty white of you, Phil," Chapel said. "No offense." He topped up his own glass. "That'll be all, Elsie," he said without looking up.

Elsa flushed and hurried out of the room.

Lizzy crossed the suite, and Philip handed her his glass.

"Phil," said Chapel, "there's fizzy water and some other stuff in the fridge—help yourself."

"I'm fine," said Philip.

Chapel shrugged. "Suit yourself." He turned to Lizzy and lifted his glass in a toast. "Cheers!"

"I don't drink," she said.

"Jesus Christ," he exclaimed with a laugh, "I'm surrounded by tee-totalers! I had an aunt who was a tee-totaler—you couldn't crack open a beer without getting a bunch of bible verse thrown at you about how you were going to burn in hell." He sat down on the couch and patted the cushion next to him. "Have a seat."

Lizzy lowered herself onto a chair next to the couch.

Philip resumed his seat.

Chapel shook his head. "You don't drink with me. You don't sit with me. You're not making me feel very welcome, Elisabet."

Lizzy put down her glass and folded her hands in her lap. "I'm sorry you feel that way, but this is a difficult time for my family." She was frantically trying to scan Philip's thoughts but could sense nothing.

"Yeah, the Viklunds are going through a rough patch for sure." Chapel took a sip of champagne. "How come you don't have an accent?"

"I grew up in the United States."

"Why's that?"

"My father arranged it," Lizzy improvised. She looked down at her hands. "He never really wanted a second daughter."

She had wanted to break eye contact with Chapel not only because this information seemed like something that Elisabet Viklund would be uncomfortable sharing, but also because she thought avoiding the distraction of his gaze might help her access Philip's thoughts. All she could sense was tension, like a mongoose ready to spring into action if a cobra struck … but she wouldn't have needed to read his mind to know that.

Chapel sat back and rested an arm along the back of the couch. "What do you miss most about Sweden?"

She shrugged and met his gaze again. "I don't remember much about it. I was very young when I came here to live with my aunt."

"And where did you grow up?" asked Chapel.

"Parkesburg. It's in Pennsylvania, west of Philadelphia." It seemed easier to bake some truth into her story—less likely for Chapel to be able to trip her up.

"Go into Philly much?"

"No, not much."

"Why not?"

She frowned. "Why do you care?"

He laughed. "Just making small talk, Lizzy."

She suppressed a start, and she noticed Philip masking his own reaction by shifting in his chair and crossing his legs. Then she remembered Chapel calling Elsa *Elsie*. He must have a habit of calling young women by such nicknames.

But it wasn't doing her any good to try to read Philip's thoughts, and she might have seen that coming if she had been paying more attention to Chapel. She shifted her mental focus to him.

His thoughts were barely more readable than Philip's and, she thought, for a similar reason. Both of them were men who had secrets to keep and reasons for erecting mental barriers. But she did sense some suspicion—or maybe just skepticism— about what she was saying, as if she was looking past his joking facade and perceiving a sneer behind it.

"Are you familiar with Philadelphia, Mr. Chapel?" she asked.

"Mr. Chapel? Come on, I'm not *that* old." He shrugged. "I've been there a few times. Liked the cheesesteaks. We could go together." He kept his eyes on her as he took a sip of champagne. "You could show me around. Seems like your uncle doesn't need you here, since he's not seeing anyone."

"I'm hoping he'll bounce back quickly." She looked down at her hands again. "I'd like to think it would be helpful for him to have family to talk to. Louise hasn't been able to convince him yet, but she says she'll keep trying."

"You ever think Mortensen might be lying about your uncle?"

Lizzy looked up, trying again to scan Chapel's thoughts. "No. Why would she lie about Uncle Theo?"

He shrugged. "If no one can talk to him, no one can give him a chance to contradict her claim that he put her in charge."

So maybe this was where that sense of suspicion or skepticism was coming from—his belief that Louise was lying about Theo Viklund's situation. She'd like to know more about that herself, but she reminded herself that she was here on an assignment from Louise—to figure out why Billy Chapel had come to the compound—and that Andy's well-being depended on her providing Louise with an answer.

She wasn't getting anything from Chapel by being coy, and she didn't know how much longer the effects of the drug would last. It was time to be more overt. "Why did you come here?"

"Because Theo and I were working on a deal, and then suddenly he's ghosting me."

"Because of Rey's death—"

He waved a hand. "Yeah, let's not rehash that, okay? I'm getting bored with that story."

He took a sip of champagne, and Lizzy snuck a look at Philip, who gave a barely perceptible shrug.

She looked back to Chapel. "What was the deal you were

working with him on?" Maybe if she got him to think about his plan, his thoughts would be more accessible to her.

"Like you asked me, why do *you* care?"

She shrugged. "Rey helped Uncle Theo with his business. I thought that maybe when he felt well enough to go back to work, *I* could help him. It would be useful for me to know more about what he does, and I can't ask him ... at least not at the moment."

She risked a glance toward Philip. His stony expression made it clear he didn't approve of her conversational gambit. She looked back at Chapel and tried once again to scan his thoughts.

Now that psychic sneer had morphed into something even more unpleasant: a knowing grin, as if the cobra had spotted a rabbit hopping unconcernedly across its path.

Chapel leaned forward and topped up his glass, although Lizzy noticed that he had actually drunk very little of the champagne. "Were you and your sister close?"

"Not really. As I said, I moved here when I was quite young, and Rey stayed in Sweden."

"But she ended up in the U.S., too—am I right?"

Lizzy was getting even less from Chapel now than she had earlier—like a door swinging closed and the dim shaft of light from the other side narrowing second by second.

"Yes."

"What brought her here?"

"She went to law school at Georgetown." She had gotten that bit of information from her prep session with Louise.

"Where did she live while she was there?"

"I don't know. I never visited her."

"Why not?"

Lizzy twined her fingers together to keep them from shaking, frantically scanning for any hint of what Chapel was thinking.

A few seconds ticked by, and Chapel repeated the question. "Why not?"

"Billy," said Philip, "I don't see why—"

"Shut up, Phil," said Chapel, without taking his eyes off Lizzy.

Lizzy was getting nothing—nothing at all. Billy Chapel had slammed his mental door shut and she was confronted with total darkness.

She wasn't going to get the information Louise wanted—and Andy would pay the price—but she thought that if she could get out of the suite before the conversation deteriorated any more, it might at least help Philip.

She unlaced her fingers and stood. "I didn't come here for you to grill me about my relationship with my father and my sister."

"Why *did* you come here?"

"I told you—to see if I could help you and Uncle Theo with whatever Rey had been helping you with."

"Your sister Rey?"

Lizzy anticipated what was coming, and fear hit her like a punch to the gut.

"Rey Viklund didn't have a sister," continued Chapel. "I remember Theo telling me over dinner one night about how Rey's mother had been killed in a car accident when Rey was just a few months old, and how sad he was that Rey would never have a little brother or sister."

Philip stood. "Billy—"

Chapel slammed his glass down on the table, spraying champagne across the table and the front of Lizzy's pants, and pushed himself to his feet. "I swear to God, Castillo, if you say another word without being asked, I'll bend your finger back until it snaps."

Philip, his expression dark with anger, took a step toward Chapel.

"Stop it!" Lizzy yelled. "Just stop it!" She drew a deep, hitching breath. "You might be a guest of Uncle Theo's, but I'm not going to stand here listening to you tell lies about my family and threatening—" She waved a hand at Philip. "—whoever this guy is."

There was complete silence for a few beats. Then, to her knee-weakening relief, Chapel laughed.

"Sure," he said, shaking his head. "Sure, Liz. Didn't mean to upset you." He pulled a handkerchief from his pocket and wiped his eyes, then folded the handkerchief with what seemed like excessive care and tucked it back into his pocket. When he looked up at Lizzy, he was no longer smiling. "But you just run along and tell Louise—or whoever is giving you your marching orders—that I don't like being lied to."

Lizzy looked from Chapel to Philip and back. She wondered for a wild moment whether she could find a way to stay in the suite until the steroid drug wore off, because she felt sure she could squeeze this awful man for what he had threatened to do to Philip. But she realized that anything she did to prolong her presence in the suite was more likely to make the situation worse for Philip—and herself—than to improve it.

"How about him?" She said, gesturing to Philip. Ignoring the single, emphatic shake of his head, she continued. "Uncle Theo won't like it if someone who's here as his guest is ... you know ..."

"Taught a lesson?" Chapel reached down, pulled the champagne bottle from the ice bucket, and sloshed some more into his glass. "Fine. I'll do any lesson-teaching that's needed after we leave."

Lizzy tried not to look toward Philip. "'We'?"

Chapel nodded toward Philip. "Me and my new guy." The

cruel smile crept back onto his face. "Why—you got a problem with that?"

"No, why would I have a problem?" She hated the tremble in her voice. Steeling herself, she ventured one more question. "And when will you be leaving?"

Chapel grinned at her. "I haven't quite decided yet. I'm still having some fun here."

35

———

Lizzy fought back tears as she followed Elsa back to her suite. What could possibly have happened between the time she had left Philip in the suite when Elsa took her to the dispensary to see Andy and when she had found Philip drinking—okay, not drinking but being served—champagne with Billy Chapel?

But champagne or not, Lizzy couldn't believe that Philip had willingly joined forces with a man who had threatened to break his finger. Louise must have assigned Philip a role in her machinations against Chapel, just as she had assigned Lizzy a role. And Philip must be cooperating for the same reasons Lizzy was —threats against Andy, or against Lizzy herself.

When they reached Lizzy's suite, Elsa gestured toward the desk. "Doctor Mortensen will speak with you shortly." She twisted her fingers together at her waist. "Is there anything I can get for you?"

Lizzy pulled off the turquoise baseball hat and threw it on the floor. "I doubt it," Lizzy said, her throat tight.

Elsa bobbed a little curtsy and hurried from the room.

A moment later, Lizzy heard a chime and Louise's face appeared on the monitor.

Lizzy crossed the room and, hands planted on the desktop, leaned toward the monitor. "What is Philip doing with Billy Chapel? And why is Chapel saying that when he leaves the compound, he'll be taking Philip with him?"

"Theo had an agreement with Philip," said Louise calmly. "He let Philip leave the compound and helped him achieve some goal that Philip had, and in return Philip was to do a favor for Chapel."

"A favor that involved Chapel threatening to break Philip's finger?"

"I have no idea what the agreement was among the three of them."

"You don't? You can't ask Theo?"

"No. As I've told you—"

"He's dead, isn't he? That's what Chapel thinks, and I'm starting to think that, too. You killed Theo and now you're pretending he's still alive so you can take over."

Louise narrowed her eyes and examined Lizzy for a moment, then said, "Theo is still alive and in charge—and he's not likely to share with me the details of a deal he made with Chapel and Castillo. Besides," she continued before Lizzy could respond, "even if Castillo didn't share the details with you explicitly, you should have been able to glean some information about the situation from him when you were in the suite."

"I can't read his mind!"

"No?"

Lizzy's heart was pounding. What price would she—or Philip or Andy—pay for that indiscretion? "No. Some people I just can't read, and Philip is one of them."

"Interesting. Who else's mind can't you read?"

"Some of the players at the casinos."

"Why not?"

Lizzy frantically tried to sort through the possible costs and benefits of telling Louise the truth. "If someone knows I can do it, sometimes they can block me."

"Castillo intentionally blocked you from reading his thoughts?"

"I don't know. Sometimes, I suppose. Sometimes I just can't read people, even if they don't know that I'm trying to do it."

Louise's expression became stony. "And what about Billy Chapel?"

"He's one of those people." Her words were spilling out now. "I couldn't get anything except some sense that he was suspicious about something. And then I just kept digging myself in deeper and deeper with the story about me being Rey Viklund's sister, and I could tell he was glad, that he was enjoying it." She knew she couldn't hold her tears back much longer.

Louise leaned toward the camera. "You got nothing? No sense of why he was here or when he planned to leave?"

"No," wailed Lizzy, the tears finally falling. "I tried. I tried to get him to think about it so I could get some information for you. You must have been listening in, right? I tried."

Through her tears, Lizzy could see that Louise looked displeased but not entirely surprised.

"What are you going to do to Andy?" Lizzy sobbed.

"I'll have to consult with Theo," Louise said, and her image disappeared from the screen.

36

———

Louise swung her chair away from the monitor and toward where Lucas sat out of range of the bunker's videoconference camera.

"That was a waste," he said.

"It wasn't a waste," she snapped. "It certainly wasn't what we wanted, but every piece of data is useful. We know now that Ballard can't read everyone's mind."

"Do you believe her?"

Louise thought back to the ill-advised pass Mitchell Pieda had made at her, just days after Gerard's death. He certainly wouldn't have done that if he had been able to read her mind. "Yes, I believe her."

Lucas ran his fingers over his crewcut. "Fine—you think she was telling the truth, and you have a useful piece of information. But she still didn't discharge the assignment you gave her. There have to be consequences."

"I don't see why. If she can't read his mind, she can't read his mind."

"It's not a matter of whether or not she can read his mind," said Lucas, exasperated. "It's a matter of proving to her that if we make a threat, we'll act on it. Otherwise, she's likely to start pushing the boundaries, seeing what else she can do without any consequences."

Louise sighed and rubbed her neck. "It's late and I'm tired. Let's discuss it in the morning."

"You don't have the stomach for this," Lucas muttered.

She dropped her hand and met his gaze. "What?"

He crossed his arms. "You don't have the stomach for this. If we make a threat, we have to follow through on it—immediately. Anything else is a sign of weakness. Weakness is what gets you killed."

She stood. "Hasty action can have the same effect."

He stood as well. They glared at each other for a few moments, then Lucas sighed. "I'll take care of it."

"What does that mean?"

"Evidently you don't want to know."

"McNally can't be killed. An investigation into his disappearance would cause more problems for us than we already have. And I have full confidence that he—and Ballard and Castillo— have sufficient incentive not to go running to the authorities when we let them go."

"I agree. And do you know why I agree? Because we can pose a *credible* threat if they do that."

Louise regarded him, her eyes narrowed. Finally, she said, "Fine. This is your area of expertise. You do what you feel is appropriate. But Ballard's not to be hurt."

"You're too attached to the girl."

"I'm not *attached* to her." She took a step toward Lucas and said, laying emphasis on every word, "She can read people's thoughts, and she can kill with the power of her mind." She gave that a beat, then said, "Is that a resource you'd want to do away with based on a hasty decision?"

"She doesn't do us any good if she won't cooperate."

"Let's not count out the possibility of her cooperating. We just haven't found the right incentive—or the right circumstances—yet. But I, for one, am willing to wait and watch for opportunities."

Lucas regarded her for a few moments, then said. "I'm willing to let you have your way when it comes to deciding what to do with Ballard. And you let me have my way when it comes to deciding what to do with McNally."

She gave a brisk nod. "Very well."

"What are we going to do about Chapel?"

"I have some ideas. I'll need to go to the lab to explore them."

"When?"

Louise pinched the bridge of her nose. "Maybe tomorrow."

He waited a moment, evidently expecting more of an explanation. When she was silent, he said, his tone sour, "Well, let me know when you want to share your plans. I have things to take care of."

"McNally?"

"*I'm* not taking care of McNally. I need to make sure Chapel gets to his check-in with his men." Lucas left without further comment.

Louise went to the desk and sat, thinking she might make another attempt at accessing the untapped accounts, but she was too frustrated—and too antsy—to try. She got out her phone and dialed Maja.

"Yes, Doctor Mortensen?"

"Maja, I skipped dinner—could you bring something simple to the bunker? Soup and a salad is fine."

"Certainly."

Louise disconnected, then clicked over to the browser on Theo's computer and scanned listlessly through a few of the more reputable international news sites, but her mind wasn't on the content.

In less than half an hour, the door to the hallway opened and Maja wheeled in a cart, which held a soup bowl, a Caesar salad, and a bottle of Perrier.

Louise stood and went to the dining table, onto which Maja was moving the dishes and silverware. "Thank you, Maja." She sat. "Do you have the sleep aid for Edmund that I gave you?"

"Yes."

"I think tonight would be a good night for him to have it. Could you take it to him in the lab?"

"Of course."

"I'd recommend doing that now. It might be best if Edmund were to sleep extra soundly tonight."

"Certainly, Doctor Mortensen."

Maja wheeled the cart out of the bunker, and Louise picked at the food—she suspected the soup was Campbell's—and mulled over everything that had happened since Chapel had arrived just that morning. She had just finished the salad when her phone buzzed: Maja.

"Yes?" she answered. She heard yelling in the background— Edmund—and the growl of a quieter voice—probably one of the security staff. She stood, alarmed, her napkin gripped in her hand. "What in the world is going on?"

"Dr. Rinnert is quite upset," said Maja, sounding uncharacteristically upset herself. "There are some things going on in the lab that he's unhappy about."

Louise heard Edmund's voice in the background. "Unhappy? How the fuck do you expect me to feel?"

Louise's confusion stilled into an angry calmness. "Do these things have to do with Doctor McNally?"

"Yes," said Maja. "There has been some ... activity in Doctor McNally's apartment."

"Is everything under control?"

Maja said something in Swedish, her voice aimed away

from the phone. Louise heard a response, also in Swedish, then Maja said, "Emil says everything is under control." Her voice was flat.

"Is Lucas there?"

"I believe he's accompanying Herr Chapel and Herr Castillo to the front gate for a check-in."

So Lucas had delegated responsibility for meting out McNally's punishment—after all, he was the supervisor, and they were the staff.

She tossed her napkin onto the table. "I'll be right there."

She ended the call and hurried out of the bunker.

When she arrived at the lab, Edmund sat, hunchbacked, on a stool at one of the lab tables, Maja was standing to one side with her arms crossed, and one of the security staff—Emil, she supposed—was lounging on a chair just outside the door that led off the lab to the apartments.

Emil stood and stretched himself to his full height. Louise had a passing curiosity about whether he had to duck to pass under door lintels.

"What's going on?" she asked.

"Lucas said McNally needed a little lesson," he said with a satisfied smile.

Louise noticed that there was a spot of what might be blood on his shirt.

"And I had to sit in my apartment and listen to it!" Edmund burst out. "I am not staying in that goddamned apartment one more night!"

"Edmund, calm down—"

"I will not calm down! The rest of you are all living in luxury at the house, and I am stuck out here in this glorified outbuilding having to listen to—" He waved his hand toward the door to the apartments. "—that!"

Emil shrugged. "We didn't make a lot of noise."

Edmund jumped to his feet, sending his chair clattering to the floor. "It's not the volume I'm talking about!"

"Quiet down there, Doctor Rinnert," Emil said, flexing his hands. "Or else—"

"Or else nothing!" snapped Louise.

Emil raised his eyebrows in surprise.

"Maja, please make up a room for Edmund in the house."

"Yes, Doctor Mortensen," said Maja.

"Emil, please accompany Edmund to the conservatory, where he can wait while his room is made up."

Emil jerked his head toward the door to the apartments. "I'm not to leave McNally unguarded."

"I'll clear it with Lucas."

Emil considered for a moment, then shrugged. "The door to McNally's apartment is locked. I guess he can't do any harm in his current state."

Louise turned back to Edmund. "Edmund, go to the house and get a good night's rest. We can talk about long-term plans in the morning."

Edmund looked uncertainly between Louise and Emil, then got to his feet and sidled toward the door that led outside.

Emil lifted his jacket from the back of the chair and pulled it on—the fabric strained at the shoulders—then gestured toward the door. "After you, Doctor Rinnert."

Edmund was out the door almost before Emil had completed the sentence.

Maja started after him but turned at Louise's voice.

"Maja, you have Edmund's sleep aid?"

Maja patted the pocket of her cardigan.

"He was obviously quite upset," said Louise. "Even more reason for him to take it tonight."

"Of course, Doctor Mortensen."

Maja slipped out after Edmund.

"Emil, you'd better hurry up," Louise said. "You don't want to lose them in the dark."

Emil nodded curtly and followed Edmund and Maja out the door.

Louise got her phone out of her pocket and tapped a button.

"Yes?" Lucas answered.

"I thought you weren't going to do anything to McNally tonight," she said, her voice tight with anger.

"I said *I* wasn't going to do anything to him tonight—I had to babysit Chapel and Castillo for their trip to the front gate. I didn't say *no one* was going to do anything to him tonight. Like I said, prompt action is key."

"I'm in the lab. Edmund was quite upset by what you had the security staff do to McNally, and I sent him back to the house with Emil and Maja."

"Do you think that's wise? It was convenient to have an excuse to keep one of the security staff in the lab—he could keep an eye on both McNally and Rinnert."

"I don't want to be dealing with Edmund's hysterics on top of everything else. And I can hardly blame him for resenting that he's living in quarters whose twin we're using as a prison cell. Once we get Chapel out of the compound, we can decide what to do with Edmund long-term."

Lucas sighed. "Fine."

She glanced toward the door to the apartments. "What *did* you do to McNally—or have Emil do to him?"

"Broke a couple of fingers."

A snatch of conversation floated through Louise's mind: *I'll bend your finger back until it snaps.*

"Inspired by Mr. Chapel?"

She could almost see the shrug. "Seemed like a good idea. Painful but not serious."

"Is McNally tied up?"

"Yes."

"Where's the key to the apartment?"

"Why do you want to know?"

"Because I want to check on him."

"Seems like an unnecessary risk."

"If your staff is competent at tying up a man, I'm sure I don't have anything to worry about."

As soon as she said it, she had half-hearted second thoughts about the wisdom of questioning the competence of Lucas's staff, but when he spoke, his voice was uninflected. "Okay, fine. The key's on the counter near the door to the apartments."

"Thank you."

Louise ended the call and returned the phone to her pocket. Then she retrieved the key, let herself into the small vestibule that provided access to the two apartments, and unlocked the door on the left.

37

There were no lights on in the apartment, but by the light from the vestibule, Louise could see a form in the center of the room. She groped along the wall until her hand found the light switch.

Andy McNally sat on a chair in the middle of the room, his ankles tied to the chair legs, his hands bound behind him. The unshaded light illuminated a face marked not only by the scrapes resulting from his abduction and a swollen nose and a pair of black eyes from the demonstration in the conservatory, but also by an unhealthy grayish cast. She suspected that his squinted eyes were as much a result of pain as from the unforgiving light.

"Doctor McNally."

"Doctor Mortensen, I presume." His voice was hoarse.

"I understand you've been injured."

"Yeah." He marshaled a ghastly smile. "Funny how those things happen."

Keeping her distance from him, she circled to the back of the chair. The middle and ring fingers of one of his hands canted back at a right angle. She tried to keep herself from wincing. "Dislocated."

"No kidding."

"We'll need to splint them."

After a pause, McNally said, "And who do you propose for that job? Emil?" His voice had lost its usual devil-may-care tone.

Louise stepped toward him carefully, although she couldn't imagine he could do much other than try to tip the chair back into her. If he did, he'd land on his injured hand, and she suspected that would be enough of a deterrent. She knelt behind him and probed his hand. His shirt was stuck to his back with sweat, and she could see his shoulder muscles tense when she touched him. She suspected it was not so much any pain she was inflicting with her touch, but his knowledge of what she could do if she wanted to add to the pain that had already been inflicted on him.

She stood. "If I untie you, can you do it yourself?"

He turned his head toward her, surprised. "Probably."

"I can bring you masking tape. Do you need anything else?"

"No, that should do it."

She stepped out of the apartment, locking the door behind her.

In the lab, she found a roll of masking tape in one of the desk drawers. Then she picked up a fire extinguisher about the size of a large Thermos and returned to the room.

She set the masking tape on the floor in front of McNally, then circled again to the back of the chair. Setting the extinguisher within easy reach of herself but not of him, she knelt and began working at the cords binding his wrists.

In a voice made hoarse by disuse—or, if Edmund were to be believed, by whatever noise McNally had made during Emil's visit to the apartment—he asked, "What makes you think I'm not going to overpower you and hold you hostage in exchange for your colleagues letting me and Lizzy and Philip go."

"You've been tied up for some time, and you'll be unsteady on your feet. One of your hands is useless. I feel confident I could knock you out with the fire extinguisher before you could get to me. Plus, we'd have two hostages to your one. I doubt my colleagues would consider saving me worth sacrificing the leverage having you and Ballard and Castillo gives them."

She had intended to say the last archly, but she was surprised by a pang of sorrow. Was there anyone at the compound who would care if she was killed? She didn't doubt Maja was grateful to Louise for releasing her from servitude to Theo Viklund, and for avenging, even if incidentally, Maja's brother's death. Lucas had decided to cooperate with her—so far, at least—even if it was mainly in order to attain his own ends. But she had no illusions that either of them would prioritize Louise's life over their own. Others at the compound, including Billy Chapel and Edmund Rinnert, would no doubt welcome news of her death.

There was a time not so long ago, sitting at the dinner table with Gerard in their comfortable Pocopson home or talking with him in her Vivantem research lab, that she would have found the situation in which she found herself completely unimaginable. Except for Gerard, Louise had never cared much whether or not other people liked her, as long as they respected her, but the idea that there were people who actively wanted her dead was sobering.

"Quite a company you've gotten yourself into," said McNally.

She raised an eyebrow. "Quite."

When she finally got the cord loosened, she stepped quickly back from the chair and hefted the fire extinguisher.

McNally pulled his arms forward slowly, his shoulders obviously stiff and painful from having been restrained, and gazed at his deformed hand. "Well, that sucks." He picked up the masking tape from the floor and fumbled at the end of the tape with his good hand. "I don't suppose you could help me with this."

"No. I'm sure you'll manage."

McNally got a couple of inches of tape pulled free of the roll, then set the roll in his lap and grasped one of his dislocated fingers. "Shot of whiskey?"

"Delay won't make it easier."

He drew a deep breath, then pulled, sucking in air in a hiss of agony. He bent forward, and she wondered if he was going to vomit. He held his breath for a long moment—she realized she was holding her breath as well—then let it out with a groan. "Goddamn."

Half a minute ticked by, then he pushed himself upright. His face was ashen, and his forehead was slicked with sweat. "Piece of cake," he rasped.

She was about to ask him if he wanted a drink of water when he grabbed the other finger and pulled it straight. "Fuck!"

She squinted in empathetic pain.

He fell back in the chair, his good hand gripping the wrist of the injured hand, as if he could form a tourniquet against the pain. "Okay," he said, his voice hoarse, "I have to admit I felt a little twinge with that one."

He sat breathing heavily for a few seconds, then set to work splinting the injured fingers to the uninjured ones on either side, encasing his injured hand in a mitten of masking tape. When he was done, his shirt was even more sweat-soaked than before.

"Do you need to use the bathroom?" Louise asked.

"The only thing that would make me happier than splinted fingers would be an empty bladder."

"Untie your feet."

He bent forward and fumbled one-handed at the ties at his ankles. It took him almost two minutes to get the ties undone.

When they were loose, she gestured with the fire extinguisher toward the door to the bathroom. "Leave the door open."

She sensed that he was trying to think of a snappy comeback, but instead he sighed, levered himself up from the chair, and walked unsteadily to the bathroom.

When he was seated in the chair again, he said, "I'd thank you ... but I'm still a little sore about you trying to kill my brother."

"Understandable. Retie your ankles—and tie them tight."

He bent and retied the bindings.

Then, still holding the extinguisher, she moved so she was once again standing behind him. She tossed a cord over his shoulder and into his lap. "Tie one of your wrists."

It took some time for him to get the cord tied around one wrist, then, at her instruction, he held his hands behind his back.

As she tightened those bindings and secured his other wrist, he asked, "Why did you do this?"

"You mean coming to the compound?"

"Well, sure, that, too."

"What did you actually mean?"

"Bringing me the tape for my fingers. Letting me use the bathroom."

"Because not doing so served no purpose."

"You tried to kill Owen," he said, and she knew by his tone that no matter what minor considerations she had shown Andrew McNally, he would always hate her for what she had done to his brother. When she was silent, he continued. "But I guess in your mind, that served a purpose."

She stepped back and examined the bindings. "Someone

from the security staff will come to make sure you're secure." After a moment, she added. "I regret that I wasn't here when that happened."

She had meant to convey that she might have put a stop to what Emil had done, but based on his even angrier tone, it was clear he had a different interpretation. "Too bad you missed the fun. At least you can watch it in replay."

"What do you mean?"

"They videotaped it."

Louise felt her stomach roil. "Videotaped it?"

"Sure. Easier than bringing Lizzy here to watch it happen—that wouldn't end well for anyone—and this way you can call it up and replay it whenever you need to make a point."

When she didn't respond, he turned his head, but she was too directly behind him for him to see her. He faced forward again. "You didn't know what they were going to do?"

"I knew Lucas had something in mind. I didn't know what. And I didn't know they would record it."

She picked up the extinguisher and circled to the door but turned back at his voice.

"I should give Owen a call," he said. "You can have one of your goons stand next to me with a gun to my head to make sure I behave. But he's going to start worrying if he doesn't hear from me." His clamped his lips shut for a moment, then continued. "And you of all people know why making Owen worry isn't a good idea."

She thought back to the drug George Millard had injected into the foil-topped fruit juice served to Owen McNally when he was trying to hide out as an inpatient at William Penn Hospital, and the fact that McNally was still alive only because she had underestimated his weight.

"I've done what I can for you," she said. "If you and Ballard and Castillo cooperate, perhaps you can make your call to your brother from outside the compound in the not-too-distant future."

She stepped into the vestibule and locked the door, then got out her phone and hit a number.

"Yes," Lucas answered.

"I let McNally splint his finger and let him use the bathroom."

"You ... what? What the hell were you thinking?"

"I was thinking," she said coldly, "that he needed to have his finger splinted and to use the bathroom. Please send one of your men to the lab to check that he's tied securely and to guard the room."

"Goddamned right," he snapped. "To keep McNally in ... and unauthorized visitors out."

Her voice rose. "Unauthorized visitors?"

"I thought we agreed—I let you take care of things you know about, you let me take care of things I know about."

She took a deep breath, preparing a retort, then let it out, slow and measured. "You're right, of course. I apologize for overstepping those boundaries. But there's a decision we need to make jointly. Meet me in the conservatory."

38

It had been hours since anyone had come to Lizzy's suite. Having no phone or watch, she periodically went to the kitchen to check the time on the microwave. She picked up one of the knives she had found on her first reconnaissance of the suite and tested its edge with her thumb, then slipped it back into its holder. As bad as she could imagine things getting, she couldn't imagine a scenario where her being armed with a kitchen knife wouldn't turn out even worse for her, Philip, and Andy than the alternatives.

And she hoped that there was an alternative—the squeeze— now that enough time had elapsed since her visit to Billy Chapel's suite for the juice to be out of her system.

She wandered listlessly into the bedroom. The bed was covered with a brilliantly white duvet and a mound of fluffy pillows, and the bone-deep ache of her fatigue made it almost irresistible. But she didn't want to be sequestered in the bedroom, even one as inviting as this one, if Philip returned to the suite—*when* he returned to the suite, she corrected herself.

She turned back to the living room. She could sleep in the

bed intended for Philip, but he would no doubt balk at taking the fancy bed while she slept in the makeshift one.

She pulled the duvet off the bed, grabbed one of the pillows, and returned to the living room. She arranged herself on the couch so that she could look out across the dark woods and also keep an eye on the door to the hall, through which she had been hoping for the last several hours that Philip would appear.

Her eyes drifted shut, but the absolute silence of the space was unnerving.

She shot upright at the sound of a knock at the door.

"Come in!" she called.

Elsa entered, looking almost as tired as Lizzy felt. Her normally rosy cheeks were pale. Her dress, which had been crisply ironed when she had picked Lizzy and Philip up in Pocopson a dozen hours earlier, was limp and wrinkled. "Doctor Mortensen has another assignment for you," she said.

Lizzy's gut tightened. "Billy Chapel?"

"No. Someone else." Elsa held up case containing the drug vial. "She asks if you need to take more of this?"

Her stomach clenching, Lizzy pushed the duvet aside and swung her legs off the couch. "I guess I better."

She injected herself with the last of the drug she had gotten from Owen, then followed Elsa out of the suite, down the window-lined corridor, and through the entrance hall to the house's main hallway. Elsa made a few turns, and finally stopped in front of door that wouldn't have looked out of place in a suburban tract home.

"The person in the room is asleep. Well, not asleep, but he won't know you're there. Once you're the room, Doctor Mortensen will give you instructions. When you're done, I'll take you back to your suite."

"Where is Philip?"

"I don't know."

"When will I get to see him?"

"I don't know."

"What's going on with Andy?"

"I don't know."

The drug had taken enough effect for Lizzy to be able to tell that Elsa did not, in fact, know. "Tell Louise that I'm more likely to be able to do my best on all these assignments she's giving me if I'm not worried about what's happening to Philip and Andy."

"I will."

Elsa opened the door and stepped back, and Lizzy entered the room.

Except for the fact that it was windowless, it looked like a normal bedroom, decorated pleasantly though modestly in Southwestern-themed decor. A man with untidy brown hair tinged with gray sat on the side of a bed. His eyes were open and turned in her direction, but her arrival caused no reaction.

She jumped at the sound of a voice, pitched low: "Hello, Lizzy." Louise.

She scanned the dimly lit room, but it was empty except for the man. In a moment, she saw a mobile phone propped on the bedside table.

"He's not aware of your presence," Louise continued. "I need some information from him. I'll ask questions, and you'll relay to me what you can gather about his answers. Don't say anything unless it's to convey what he's thinking. In the course of our conversation, I may mention the work we did at Vivantem, but he won't remember any of what we discuss. Your friend Philip could confirm that for you."

Back in Sedona, Louise's henchman, George Millard, had drugged Philip and then had Mitchell Pieda try to scan Philip's mind for information about Lizzy's location—apparently even Mitchell had needed help getting past Philip's defenses. She suspected that this man was under the influence of the same drug.

"I'm sure Philip could tell me all sorts of things," Lizzy whispered, her tone bitter, "if I could talk to him,"

Ignoring her comment, Louise said, "Pull a chair over and sit facing him."

Lizzy did as she was told. "Okay, I'm sitting in front of him."

"I know."

Lizzy glanced nervously around the room, although she felt sure she wouldn't be able to spot the camera.

"Edmund," said Louise, her voice pitched slightly higher. "Can you hear me?"

The man seated on the bed nodded.

"Edmund, I'm going to tell you about some work I did at the Vivantem clinic related to my area of specialty—fertility treatments—and then I'm going to have some questions for you related to your area of specialty—electrophysiology. My questions are going to be about how one might apply your area of specialty to my area of specialty. Do you understand?"

Edmund nodded once.

"Have you ever done any work related to mapping electrical signals generated by the brain to assess them for meaning?"

Edmund's expression morphed slightly, maybe to one of drugged enthusiasm.

Lizzy's ability to eavesdrop on his thoughts might be less than it would have been before Owen reduced the concentration of the juice, but whatever Louise had given him was helping make his thoughts more readable.

"He says yes," Lizzy said. "He participated in a study of ..." She tried to grasp the words Edmund was thinking. "... neural interface augmentation." There was a pause, then Lizzy said, "That's all I'm getting."

"Edmund, can you elaborate on neural interface augmentation?"

Edmund's hands rose—Lizzy noticed that he was missing a thumb on one hand—fluttered for a moment, then fell back to his lap.

"He's thinking something about electrochemical dynamics ..." said Lizzy. "And cognitive exchange. Diagnostic ... elucidation."

Louise sighed. "This might take some time."

IT TOOK a quarter of an hour for Louise to land on an approach for teasing the information out of Edmund. Lizzy realized that Louise was posing the questions in a way that ensured his answers would be as straightforward as possible, so that even a non-scientist like herself could relay the response. But regardless of how straightforward Louise tried to make the conversation, after half an hour, Lizzy's head was spinning.

But the general theme of the questions was clear: how electricity might be used to increase or even to create the squeeze or mind-reading abilities. Did this mean that there were more specially-skilled Vivantem babies out there—that she and Mitchell Pieda hadn't been the only ones? And was Louise searching for a way to tap these abilities even in people who were not the product of her Vivantem experiments?

Was Lizzy feeding Louise information that would enable her to create allies equipped with these skills—ones that might be more willing than Lizzy to help Louise pursue her agenda? If this was Louise's goal, Lizzy had no wish to help her achieve it.

In response to a question from Louise, Edmund had just thought a phrase that sounded like *nucleus tractus solitarius*.

Lizzy mentally scrambled for an alternate translation. "Solitary nuclear reaction."

"That makes no sense," snapped Louise. "Don't try to hide or distort what he's thinking. Andrew McNally's guard has already dislocated two of McNally's fingers—there are eight more we could use in response to any lack of cooperation on your part, and no reason we can't move on to other body parts as needed."

Lizzy's throat constricted with horror. "I can't believe you did that," she whispered.

"If you'd like," said Louise briskly, "I can show you video of the procedure when we're done here."

A wave of dizziness struck Lizzy, and she grasped the sides of the chair to stay upright.

"Are we done playing games?" asked Louise, her voice hard.

Lizzy nodded. Then, just in case whatever monitor was in the room hadn't picked up the motion, she said, her voice strangled, "Yes."

A quarter-hour became a half-hour, then three-quarters, and Lizzy felt her ability to read Edmund's thoughts slipping away. Her verbalization of Edmund's mental responses to Louise's questions became slower and slower, and Louise's tone more and more irritable. And over all this was the mental video playing through her head of one of Theo Viklund's henchmen breaking Andy's fingers.

Finally, voice trembling, Lizzy said, "I can't anymore. It's gone." Her voice pitched up. "It's gone and I can't do anything about it. Hurting Andy some more isn't going to help. I can't do it."

When Louise's voice came again from the phone, the irritation was gone, replaced by a tired sadness. "Very well. Elsa is waiting in the hallway. She'll take you back to your suite."

39

L ouise awoke to a buzzing and reached for her phone. She was momentarily startled when her hand encountered empty air, before she remembered that she was not in her suite, which was currently occupied by the odious Billy Chapel, but on the couch in Theo Viklund's quarters. She hadn't been able to stomach the idea of sleeping in Theo's former bed—it seemed both too intimate and too cold-blooded.

She located the phone on the arm of the couch and checked the caller.

"Good morning, Maja," she answered.

"Good morning, Doctor Mortensen. I'm calling to let you know that Doctor Rinnert is having breakfast in the conservatory."

Louise glanced at her watch: eight o'clock. "I'll join him shortly. How does he seem?"

"He complained that he didn't sleep well."

"That's all?"

"Yes, that's all."

"Good. Thank you." She ended the call and tapped a number.

"Yes?" Lucas answered.

"I'm just checking in to see how things are going. Maja told me Edmund's complaining of not having slept soundly."

"Does he have any suspicions about being drugged?"

"I don't think so, but I'll have breakfast with him and confirm that. Although I suppose it doesn't really matter whether he knows or not. As long as he cooperates."

"I suppose not." He paused. "You're sure you want to bring him along?"

"Yes. We discussed this. You agreed."

"Sure. But it's going to be a huge pain in the ass."

She sighed. "No argument there. How are our other guests doing?"

"Ballard's still in her suite. We gave McNally some breakfast. I'm expecting Chapel and Castillo to go to the front gate for their morning check-in pretty soon."

"Very good. I'll call you after I've spoken to Edmund."

"All right." Lucas ended the call.

Louise showered, put on her usual outfit of a tailored dress and low-heeled Christian Louboutin pumps, and hurried to the conservatory.

She found Edmund poking at a mound of scrambled eggs, and Maja topping up his coffee from a silver pot.

"Good morning," Louise said as she took a seat and unfolded the linen napkin in her lap. It was clean but not ironed, and Louise knew that the lack of staff to attend to such niceties was grating on Maja. At least she wouldn't need to worry about it much longer. "How did you sleep, Edmund?"

"Better than I would have out there ..." he said, waving in the general direction of the lab. His eyes were bloodshot.

"Yes, I can imagine," Louise said as Maja filled her cup.

"... but not great."

She suppressed a sigh. Same old Edmund.

"That'll be all," he said to Maja. "Louise and I need some privacy."

Louise raised her eyebrows at Edmund. "And I need some breakfast."

Maja set the coffee pot on the table. "I'll have something prepared for you while you and Doctor Rinnert talk."

After Maja left, Louise took a sip of coffee, then set the cup carefully back on the saucer. "Edmund, you'd do well to show Maja some consideration. I understand she went to some trouble to get you settled in the house last night."

"A little too 'settled,'" he said, eyes squinted but careful on her face. "You know what I mean?"

"No, Edmund, I don't."

"I often have trouble sleeping, and Maja provides me with NyQuil. She gave me some yesterday. The seal was broken. It knocked me out." He stared at her for a moment. "Know anything about that?"

"I didn't know she provides you with NyQuil, but I suspect that rather than going back to your apartment to get whatever supply you have there, she gave you a bottle she had at the house. I've used NyQuil myself from time to time. Perhaps she gave you the bottle I had in my quarters."

He smirked. "Wouldn't you have noticed if she had come in and started taking things out of your medicine cabinet?"

"I stayed at the lab for some time after you left. She might have gotten it then."

He stood. "Let's go check."

"No."

"No?"

"No."

"You're not curious?"

"Edmund why in the world would I be curious about

whether Maja borrowed my bottle of NyQuil in an attempt to provide you with a restful night?"

She could almost see him sorting through his options, then he dropped back in his chair. "What's going on at the lab? Who's the guy in the other apartment?"

"You don't have to worry about the man in the apartment, or about what's been going on. I believe our time here is nearing its end."

As she had hoped, this revelation took him by surprise. "Really?"

"Yes."

"Why?"

"I can't explain that right now, but I promise I will once we're away from here."

"When will that be?"

"Very soon. I can't be more specific."

"And then I can go home?"

His expression was so hopeful, so open, so unlike the sullen, surly Edmund Rinnert she had become accustomed to that she almost wished she could say yes. "I'm afraid not—at least not yet. I need your help with one more experiment."

His hopeful expression crashed like a brick building hit by a wrecking ball. "One more experiment? What the fuck do you think I've been doing ever since you got here other than helping you with 'one more experiment'?"

"Edmund—"

He jumped to his feet. "You don't think you owe me?"

She stood, gripping her napkin, trying to maintain her composure. "*I* owe *you*?" She glanced toward the door of the conservatory, through whose glass panes she could see down the deserted hallway, then returned her eyes to him. She lowered her voice. "Edmund, I killed Theo Viklund for your good as much as for mine, and I stood by my promise to protect you if the plan backfired."

"It didn't backfire."

"Exactly."

"In fact, it has all turned out pretty sweet for you."

"I would not characterize my time since Theo's death as 'pretty sweet.'"

"Better than mine."

She threw her napkin onto the table, where it knocked over her delicate china teacup, sending coffee spilling across the table. "Good lord, Edmund, what do you want? I removed you from a situation at the lab that you obviously felt was insupportable. I saved you from a lifetime as Theo's pet scientist."

Edmund's voice spiked. "*Pet scientist*?"

"A description that applies as much to me as to you."

He thrust his hand in her face, and she took a step back. "He cut off my thumb! He cut off my fucking thumb! I climbed over the fence, just like you—"

"I didn't climb over—"

"I got to the road, just like you—"

"Edmund—"

"Lucas and that gorilla, Anders, brought me back, just like you—"

She crossed her arms, glaring at him.

"—and he knocked me out, and when I woke up, my thumb was gone!"

She raised her hands in a conciliatory gesture, "Edmund, I know I was lucky—"

He stepped so close to her that she felt flecks of his spittle hitting her face as he screamed the next words. "Even a bastard like Viklund would treat his *pet* better than he did me. *You* were the pet. You were his lackey, you bitch."

He spun on his heel and strode across the conservatory. He

reached the door just as Maja stepped through it with a tray carrying Louise's breakfast. As he pushed past her, eggs, toast, and juice spilled across the brick floor. His footsteps thudded down the corridor toward the main hallway.

Maja surveyed the wreckage with some dismay, then composed herself with an effort. "Should I follow him, Doctor Mortensen?"

Louise sighed. "Please. Make sure he goes back to his room. I'll call Lucas and ask him to put someone at Edmund's door."

Maja nodded and hurried out of the conservatory.

Louise took a step toward the mess, having a momentary idea of picking up at least the larger pieces of china, then sighed and sank back onto her chair. She got her phone out and tapped a number.

"Yes," Lucas answered.

"I spoke with Edmund."

"And?"

"It didn't go well."

"Any change in plan?"

She sighed. "Much as I would like to say yes, I believe we still need to take him with us. He may be annoying, but he's valuable." She stood and smoothed her dress. "I'm going to the bunker to change."

"Okay. Chapel's getting ready to go up to the gate, and I have some work to do in his suite."

40

―――――

Lizzy woke on the couch to the sound of a knock at the door of the suite. Dawn light was just beginning to filter through the trees outside the suite's glass wall.

Before she could call *come in*, Elsa entered. She, like Lizzy, was still wearing the same clothes she had had on the previous day. She gripped an envelope in one hand and the case Lizzy had taken from Mitchell Pieda in the other.

"What's wrong?" asked Lizzy, as a seemingly endless list of possibilities unspooled in her head.

Elsa's laugh sounded a bit unhinged. "I don't know. I really don't know." She hurried across the room and handed Lizzy the case. "Doctor Mortensen has made more of the drug for you. She says she needs you to take one more dose, and then you and Doctor McNally can leave."

"And Philip."

Elsa flushed. "Yes, of course. Philip as well."

Lizzy stepped closer to Elsa. "What has happened to Philip?"

"Nothing has happened to him! At least not that I know of. They aren't telling me anything." She looked on the verge of tears.

"Last time I took the drug, I couldn't do what Louise wanted me to do."

"She says she understands."

Lizzy had hoped for more, but Elsa just stood staring at her, wringing her hands.

Lizzy lowered her voice. "Elsa, what's the matter?"

"Things are happening. That's all I know."

"What things?"

Elsa must have remembered that their conversation was no doubt being monitored and shot a panicked glance around the room. "Oh, nothing. Just things."

Lizzy looked down at the case. Why should she believe it contained more of the same drug she had stolen from Mitchell Pieda? Louise could have put anything in the vial. On the other hand, if Louise wanted her dead, she wouldn't need to resort to a doctored drug to do it. "One more dose, then we can leave?"

"Yes," Elsa said eagerly.

"Well," Lizzy said, dread balling in her stomach like a physical thing, "I don't have any reason to believe her, but I don't have many options, do I?"

Elsa dropped her voice to a whisper. "No. I don't think so."

Lizzy gave herself the injection, then gave the case with the vial and syringe back to Elsa. They stepped out of the suite and followed the corridor to the main entrance hall. Much to her chagrin, Elsa led her across the hall and down the corridor toward Billy Chapel's suite.

As they approached the door, bits of Elsa's thoughts began pinging into Lizzy's mind, confirming what Lizzy had sensed even before taking the drug: Elsa was afraid that her lack of understanding about the things that were happening at the compound didn't bode well for her own well-being. The drug was obviously enabling Lizzy to eavesdrop on Elsa's thoughts, but why would Louise think Lizzy would be any more successful reading Billy's mind now than she had been the first time?

But as they neared the end of the corridor, she realized that the effects of this injection were like those she had experienced when she had injected the drug she had taken from Mitchell. Her heart was beating even harder than could be explained by a return trip to Chapel's suite, like she had drunk too much coffee on an empty stomach. Sounds that otherwise would have been almost inaudible—the swish of Elsa's skirt, the pad of their feet on the carpeted floor—were like fingernails on a chalkboard. She closed her hands into fists and tried to concentrate on the pain of her nails digging into her palms. She couldn't afford to let these side effects undermine her ability to discharge Louise's assignment.

When they reached the door to Billy's suite, Elsa handed her an envelope. "Mr. Chapel isn't in the suite at the moment. Doctor Mortensen asks that you read what's in the envelope while you wait for him, and we will be monitoring the situation to make sure Mr. Chapel behaves himself."

Lizzy nodded, opened the door, and stepped into the suite.

At least she'd have a chance to collect her thoughts before Chapel arrived, and maybe she'd be better able to do that without the distraction of Elsa's panicked thoughts. But she couldn't possibly sit—she was too jittery. She crossed to the window wall and scanned the woods. Maybe she'd see Philip outside. If she did, could she bang on the window and get his attention? Could she call to him through the glass? But the woods seemed as deserted as the suite.

When she turned away from the window, her gaze fell on a smear of red on the couch. She stepped toward it to examine it more closely and realized that there were splashes of red on the cream-colored carpet as well.

If her heart had been hammering before, it was thundering now. What could it be except blood?

Then she remembered the envelope still clutched in her hands. She tore it open, and a piece of paper fluttered out. She snatched it up off the bloody carpet.

It was a crumpled receipt, and by the location and date printed on it, she knew it was from one of the gas stations she and Philip had stopped at on the drive from Arizona. Fingers trembling, she turned it over. On the other side, a note was written in a hasty scrawl.

Lizzy, you're on your own now. Try to get out with Andy. Louise isn't the enemy—Theo and Billy are. Philip

She stared at the message, mouth agape. Was this even Philip's handwriting? She couldn't remember ever seeing his handwriting. Their written communications had always been via email or text.

She looked back to the stains on the couch and carpet. What had happened here? Had Philip angered Billy Chapel one too many times? Had Chapel done something far worse than break Philip's finger?

She headed for the door, then stopped. Had Elsa said she had to stay here? Lizzy was supposed to wait for Chapel, but how long until he arrived? If she left the suite, would they punish Andy? Did Louise—and Theo Viklund, if he was still alive—know what had happened here? But Philip said Theo, not Louise, was the enemy.

She banged her fist into her forehead, as if she could settle her churning thoughts with a thump.

She'd at least see if the door was unlocked.

She was half-way across the room when the door opened, and Billy Chapel stepped in. When he saw Lizzy, his eyebrows rose. "What are *you* doing here?"

"What am *I* doing here?" she yelled—she hadn't meant to

yell—then pointed to the stained couch and carpet. "What is that?"

He crossed the room and looked down at the stains. "What the fuck ..."

"Exactly! What the fuck?"

His raised his eyes to hers. "What *are* you doing here?"

"I have no idea! Elsa brought me here," she waved the receipt, "and she gave me this note that's supposedly from Philip," she waved her hand toward the couch, "and there's blood everywhere! What did you do?"

She didn't know if she would have preferred to be able to squeeze Chapel, impossible as long as she was under the influence of the drug, or read his mind, just as impossible now as on her first visit to the suite. She stepped up to him. "What did you do to him??" She pushed him as hard as she could in the chest.

The push barely moved him, but his expression darkened from confusion to anger. He caught her wrists and jerked her toward him. "Keep your hands off me, little girl."

She tried to twist her arms away, but it was like trying to twist out of manacles. "Let me go!" She kicked out, and her foot connected with Billy's leg.

"Damnit!" For a moment, she thought he was going to take a swing at her, but instead he spun her around, shifted his grip from her wrists to her bicep, and propelled her across the room and into the kitchenette. He jerked open a few drawers, then gave a rough laugh. "I'll be damned—they took the knives."

He dragged her back to the couch, grabbed the neck of the champagne bottle chilling in the silver cooler, and swung it into the side of the coffee table. It shattered, sending a spray of champagne arcing across the room. It mixed with the blood on the carpet, sending runnels of red through its pile. The edges of the bottle were jagged claws of glass.

Lizzy screamed and tried to twist away.

His grip tightened further. He jerked her backwards, and she tripped over the leg he had positioned behind her. She would have hit the floor except for his iron grip.

He jerked her upright again and spun her toward him, his face inches from hers, the bottle held next to her ear. "You give me any more trouble," he snarled, "I'll cut you. You understand?"

She nodded, speechless with fear.

He started toward the door, dragging her beside him. "We're going to have a little chat with our host," he said, directing his raised voice into the room at large, "so we can find out what the fuck is going on." He stepped through the door and propelled Lizzy down the corridor. "Where the hell's the lab?"

"The lab?" she gasped. "The room that's like a doctor's office??"

"Maybe. Take me there."

When they got to the entrance hall, Lizzy turned down the hallway that led toward the back of the house, trying to remember the route Elsa had taken when she led Lizzy to the meeting with Andy. But none of the landmarks they passed now —a brightly colored painting, an open door revealing a formal dining room—looked familiar. When she recognized a marble bust in a niche, she wasn't sure if it was because she had passed it on her trip to the dispensary or because it looked like some piece of sculpture she had seen a picture of, maybe years ago.

She expected at any moment for Elsa, or maybe one of Theo Viklund's goons, to appear, and she wasn't sure whether to hope for or dread the encounter. But the hallway was empty, as were the rooms she glimpsed as Billy hurried her past them.

When she finally succeeded in finding the dispensary, Billy's face darkened with anger. "This isn't a lab. Plus, it's supposed to be in a separate building."

She said, her voice trembling, "This is the only place that's sort of like a lab that I know about."

He dragged her out of the room. "I thought Rey Viklund's baby sister would know her way around Uncle Theo's compound," he said, his voice taunting. He looked up and down the hallway. "How do we get outside?"

Lizzy pointed. "That way, I think."

Billy jerked her close. "You *think*?"

"I don't know. I've never been here before."

"Yeah, I figured." He started off in the direction she had indicated, his fingers digging into her arm, she struggling to keep up.

Lizzy was grateful—and almost surprised—that her route did take them to the back entrance.

In the upper canopy of the trees, a light spring breeze tossed the leaves, flickering in a dozen shades of green in the early morning sunshine. But the light stabbed Lizzy's eyes, and she winced at the call of a bird in the bushes topping the berm that protected the back entrance.

Billy stepped cautiously out onto the paved area, pulling Lizzy along with him, and scanned the surroundings. When he started off again, he caught her by surprise. She stumbled, and once again he jerked her to her feet. "Keep up, Liz," he growled. "You don't want me deciding you're more trouble than you're worth."

They hadn't gone far when they heard a man's shout. "Billy!"

Billy swung toward the sound, bringing the bottle up and using Lizzy as a shield between himself and whoever was approaching. She yelped in pain and fright as one of the jagged edges nicked her cheek. She was preparing to try again to twist away when Billy lowered the bottle.

"What the fuck is going on?" Billy called toward the approaching man.

It was Edmund, the man whose mind Lizzy had read for Louise.

"I don't know," he called back to Billy. "Mortensen just called me and told me to meet her in the lab." He reached them. "Where is everyone? There used to be a guard at my door in the house. They tried to pretend he was there in case I needed anything, like they had assigned me a valet, but he was definitely a guard. Now he's gone."

"Everyone's gone," said Billy.

"Who's that?" asked the man, gesturing toward Lizzy, his eyes drifting to the broken bottle.

Billy smirked. "Why, Edmund, you don't recognize Rey Viklund's little sister?"

Edmund rolled his eyes. "Theo wasn't going out of his way to introduce me to his relatives."

"Where's the lab?"

Edmund pointed. "Over there."

Billy turned to Lizzy. "Does Mortensen care what happens to you?"

"I don't know, but Uncle Theo—"

She cried out as he dug the tips of his fingers into the soft flesh of her upper arm. "Just stop with the *Uncle Theo* shit. And you'd better hope Mortensen doesn't want to see you cut up." He turned to Edmund. "Let's go."

Billy hustled Edmund in front of him and dragged Lizzy at his side. Lizzy could feel a trickle of blood running down her cheek and neck, but she didn't want to raise her hand to wipe it away for fear Billy would consider the move threatening and react violently.

A squat building came into view, its facade windowless, its mass as effectively camouflaged as the house in the rolling hills.

"That's the lab?" asked Billy.

"Yes," said Edmund. After a moment, he added, "We're going there?"

"Yes. I want to see him."

"Why? Don't you trust me?"

"Not as far as I can throw you, Rinnert."

"Who are we seeing?" ventured Lizzy, hoping that this might provide a useful piece of information as she struggled to formulate a plan while not angering Billy.

His smile was nasty. "Why, dear old Uncle Theo, of course."

41

———————

The three moved up the path toward the building. When they reached the front door, Chapel said to Edmund, his voice lowered, "You go in, and greet whoever's in there by name, so I know who's there. And if anyone has a weapon, say, 'Nice to see you.'"

Edmund paled. "What's going on?"

"I have no fucking idea, Ed—but we're about to find out."

"I don't know—"

In a sudden movement, Chapel thrust out the bottle and hooked the sleeve of Edmund's jacket on a jagged point of glass.

Edmund let out a yelp.

"If you piss me off," hissed Chapel, "I'm going to take your face off."

Edmund's fear-rounded eyes shot from Chapel's face to the still-bleeding cut on Lizzy's cheek and back. He raised his hands. "Okay, Billy, okay ..." He drew a deep, unsteady breath and turned toward the door. He pushed it open and stepped in, leaving the door ajar.

"Louise, Lucas, how are you doing?" he said in an unnaturally loud voice. After a pause, he added, "Lucas, nice to see you. And I'm afraid I don't know your name, sir."

Lizzy heard Louise's voice. "Never mind that, Edmund. Just come in and shut the door."

Lizzy guessed Chapel might have bided his time outside if Edmund hadn't turned a panicked look back at him, perhaps for guidance. She heard a Swedish-accented male voice from inside —"What's going on, Rinnert?"—and then Chapel, still gripping her arm, propelled her through the door, the jagged ends of the broken bottle next to her face.

She had a general sense of stainless-steel surfaces and tables crammed with complex machinery, but her attention was on the three people standing on the other side of the room.

Andy stood between a man and a woman. He looked even worse than he had in the photo Louise had shown her. The bloodstain on the gauze taped to his forehead had spread and darkened nearly to black, the skin around his eyes was a lurid purple, more blood flecked the skin under his grotesquely swollen nose. His hands, one of which was encased in a mitten of masking tape, were secured in front of him with a zip tie.

The man at his side must have been Lucas, the Swedish speaker whose voice she had heard from outside. His hand was on Andy's bicep, his gun trained on Andy's side.

Despite Edmund's roll call of the people in the lab, it took Lizzy a moment to recognize the third person, a woman whose raggedly cut brown hair, sweatshirt, jeans, and hiking boots were a far cry from Louise Mortensen's normal auburn bob, tailored dresses, and designer pumps. For the first time since Lizzy had escaped from the Pocopson mansion, she was in the same room as the woman responsible for her parents' deaths.

Louise's eyebrows shot up as her eyes ricocheted between Chapel and Lizzy. "What are you doing here?"

"Taking a little tour of the grounds with Rey Viklund's baby sister," said Chapel, "and wondering why I found blood on my couch when I got back from the front gate."

Edmund, who seemed as surprised by Louise's new look as Lizzy was, sidled toward neutral territory between the two groups.

Chapel shifted Lizzy so she was positioned more directly in front of him. "Drop the gun, Lucas."

"I don't see why I should," said Lucas, the gun steady on Andy.

"Because whether or not this girl is Theo's niece or not, I'm guessing you don't want me making a mess on your nice, clean floor with her."

Louise shifted her hand off the canvas messenger bag slung over her shoulder and raised it in a conciliatory gesture. "Billy, this is completely unnecessary—"

"Louise, I don't want to hear anything from you other than an explanation of how the blood got in my suite."

"I don't know. Perhaps Theo—"

Chapel lowered the bottle slightly and jabbed one of its points into Lizzy's shoulder, eliciting a shriek from Lizzy and a collective intake of breath from the other four people in the room. The fingers on Andy's unsplinted hand closed into a fist.

"Don't give me that bullshit about Theo," said Chapel. "I know exactly where he is. Edmund, let's take a look at old Theo."

"Now?" said Edmund. "I don't think—"

"Come on, I want to see my old buddy one last time."

Casting terrified glances back and forth between the two contingents, Edmund edged across the lab to a chest freezer. "He's in here."

"Edmund—!" exclaimed Louise.

"Shut up," commanded Chapel. "Open it, Edmund."

With an almost apologetic glance toward Louise, Edmund

spun the dial on a padlock securing the freezer's lid, removed the lock from the hasp, and lifted the lid.

"Step away," said Chapel.

When Edmund had returned to his position on the other side of the lab, Chapel worked his way toward the freezer, still using Lizzy as a shield.

When they reached it, Lizzy looked in, steeling herself for whatever was there.

A fog of super-cooled air swirled like a slow-motion pool of water, then began to dissipate. It took Lizzy a moment to orient herself to what she was seeing, but gradually she identified a shoulder, an elbow, a head, and hands drawn up under the chin. The skin was almost blue. From mid-torso down, the body was hidden under folds of purple and green fabric that looked like a piece of bedspread.

It was, of course, awful to see the body folded into the freezer, but Lizzy was reassuring herself that it wasn't as bad as it could have been when her stomach flipped at a detail the swirling air had at first hidden: one of the hands had been severed a few inches above the wrist.

"Took his hand to unlock his computer, eh?" Chapel asked conversationally.

Louise and Lucas exchanged looks.

"Am I right?" he asked his voice now harsh.

"What business is it of yours?" asked Lucas.

Chapel once again poked Lizzy's shoulder with the bottle, and she clamped her lips over a cry as she felt a second trickle of blood join the first.

Andy took a step forward, but stopped as Chapel raised the bottle toward Lizzy's head.

"Let's all just calm down," said Louise. "Billy, as you can tell, Theo has been dead for some time. He suffered an attack of some sort, and Lucas and I agreed to cover up his death because we were concerned what the other people at the compound would do if they knew. In fact, it probably won't surprise you that we were concerned about what people *outside* the compound would do. We removed his hand to access his computer so we could find out who he was in touch with. I apologize that we misled you, but—"

"Don't insult me," drawled Chapel. "If you could get to Viklund's email, you could get to his accounts. Are the three of you multi-millionaires now? And how are you splitting the money—one-third to each? I doubt it ... but I guess only the person doling out the proceeds knows for sure."

Edmund's eyes snapped to Louise.

"You have it all wrong—" began Louise.

Chapel jabbed Lizzy with the bottle again, and although she knew each jab was inflicting only a superficial wound, feeling the third trickle of blood join the first two—and imagining what other damage Chapel would wreak with his makeshift weapon —weakened her knees and she grabbed the edge of the open freezer to steady herself.

"Billy, stop it," said Louise. "Please."

"*I* could put a stop to this right now," growled Lucas.

"No," said Louise. "I think we can work this out. Billy, if I just knew what you were thinking ..." Her eyes drifted to Lizzy, and Lizzy realized that Louise expected her to be able to read Chapel's mind.

Was there benefit in letting Louise Mortensen think that she knew what Chapel was planning—assuming Chapel himself had a plan?

Then Lizzy realized that Louise was probably also wondering why Chapel was even still standing rather than lying screaming on the floor, clutching his temples, as had been the fate of so many others who had make the mistake of hurting Lizzy. Louise apparently didn't realize that even under the more benign drug that Owen formulated, Lizzy could only apply the squeeze when off the juice or read minds when on it, but never both.

Under the influence of whatever Louise had given her, she could do neither.

Lizzy tried to sort through whether trying to telegraph this fact to Louise was a good idea. Giving Louise more information seemed like a bad idea—but even if Lizzy didn't confirm her helplessness, Louise would surely have suspicions based on what was and wasn't happening to Chapel. In fact, Louise would have her suspicions based on what was and wasn't happening to herself. After all, Lizzy had just as much reason to want to squeeze Louise as to squeeze Chapel.

On the other hand, Louise seemed in the best position to resolve the current standoff without bloodshed.

"Who knows what Billy's thinking?" Lizzy said. Then she added, injecting a note of petulance into her voice, "I'm just trying to do what he tells me—I'm not about to give him any headaches." It was the best she could think of to convey to Louise that both her mind-reading and squeeze abilities were out of commission.

"Shut up," Chapel said, then asked Louise, "Why did you ask Edmund to come to the lab?"

Louise's expression darkened. "Because I believed Edmund was a colleague I could rely on. I suppose, since he evidently told you where you'd find Theo, I was wrong."

Edmund took a step toward where Chapel and Lizzy stood next to the freezer. "You know why?" he said to Louise. "Because I got tired of hearing your empty promises that things would work out for me."

"They *will* work out for you, Edmund," Louise replied. "They'll work out for you and me and Lucas—and Billy and Elisabet—if we can just keep our heads."

"I'm tired of waiting for things to work out. I ran into Billy on my way back to my room after I left the conservatory, and I decided that I'd rather throw my lot in with him than with you and Lucas."

"You forget, Doctor Rinnert," said Lucas, "that I'm the one with a gun, and I suspect you'll throw in your lot with the person who's holding an actual weapon, not a broken bottle."

"I think we can come to a mutually beneficial agreement without resorting to guns *or* broken bottles," said Louise.

Edmund took another step closer to Chapel and Lizzy. "You know what, Louise? I don't care if your lackey does have a gun— I'm sticking with the guy who hasn't double-crossed me."

"I did what I did for you as much as for me, Edmund," she said.

Edmund's laugh was harsh. "You say that, but as far as I can see, you care less about me than you do her—"

Edmund was now standing just a few feet from Chapel and Lizzy, and he reached for Lizzy's arm.

Lizzy flinched away from Edmund, and Chapel swung the bottle toward him. "Get your hands off—"

The moment the bottle was no longer pointed at Lizzy, Andy spun and, swinging his tied hands like a bat, smashed his forearm into Lucas's throat.

With a roar, Lucas swung the gun toward Andy, but Andy was on top of him, using his momentum to overbalance Lucas. As they fell, Lizzy heard a gunshot, then the two men hit the floor with a bone-jarring thump, and the gun flew out of Lucas's hand and went skittering across the floor.

Chapel dropped the bottle, which shattered. He pushed Lizzy away and dove for the gun just as Andy rolled off Lucas and slid across the concrete with the same goal. Andy's hand was on the gun, but Chapel kicked, connecting with his bandaged hand, and Andy roared with pain as the gun slid across the floor again. Lizzy was vaguely aware of Lucas struggling unsteadily to his feet, Edmund diving behind one of the lab tables, and Louise standing frozen, mouth agape.

The gun came to rest a yard from where Lizzy stood next to the freezer. She reached down and snatched it up.

She didn't know anything about guns—she didn't even know if pulling the trigger would fire a shot, or if she'd have to disengage a safety and, if yes, how she would do that. She doubted she could even get a shot off before Lucas or Chapel was on her, and if one of them got the gun it couldn't end well.

She spun, flung the gun into the swirling fog of the freezer, and slammed the lid down. Then she jumped up so she was sitting on top of the freezer, ready to fend Chapel and Lucas off with her legs as long as she could, hoping that Andy, and maybe even Louise and Edmund, would come to her aid.

"As long as she could" proved to be not very long, because Lucas grabbed one of her ankles and hauled her off the top of the freezer and onto the glass-covered floor. The impact rattled through every bone in her body, and she felt a dozen tiny stabs in her butt and back.

Lucas's action had momentarily cleared the way for Chapel. He reached the freezer and threw open the lid. He groped inside for the gun.

Lucas picked up a small fire extinguisher, swung, and caught Chapel in the side of the head.

Chapel dropped like a puppet whose strings had been cut.

There was a moment of silence that was broken only by Lizzy and Lucas's gasping breaths, a keening cry of panic from Edmund, and a snuffling snore from Chapel. Then Lizzy became aware of another sound—the thwack of helicopter rotors beating the air.

Lucas pulled a handkerchief out of his pocket, draped it over his hand, then cast about in the freezer. After a moment, he pulled out the gun. He stepped to Chapel's inert body and prodded it with his foot.

"What are you going to do with him?" asked Louise, taking in the scene with wide eyes.

"Leave him. If his men find him dead, it will be worse for us. I hear the chopper, and Chapel's men will have heard it, too. They'll know something's up. They'll be in the compound any minute. We need to get out of here."

Louise nodded and started for the door. "Come on, Edmund."

Edmund scrambled up from behind the lab table and started for the door.

"I don't think so," said Lucas, and he raised the gun and fired.

Louise and Lizzy both screamed.

Lizzy scrabbled across the floor, shards of glass cutting her hands, thinking she might be able to take cover behind the freezer, but there was less than a foot of space between the side of the freezer and the wall.

Louise had slapped her hands over her mouth. She dropped them and took a deep, gasping breath. "Lucas!"

"He betrayed us to Chapel. He'd betray us again."

After a moment, she nodded, wordless.

Lucas raised the gun again, and this time it was pointed toward where Lizzy cowered next to the freezer.

"No!" shouted Louise. "Not her!"

Lucas turned to her in surprise. "She can only cause us trouble."

"No. She's worth keeping alive."

Lucas glared at Lizzy, then shook his head. "Okay, fine. But this is on you if it doesn't work out." He crossed the lab and eased the door open, the throb of the helicopter's rotor even louder now. He poked his head out cautiously, scanned the area, then gestured for Louise to follow him. "Come on."

Louise hurried across the room to the door. Before she stepped outside, she turned back and met Lizzy's eyes. She opened her mouth, then clamped it shut, stepped outside, and pulled the door closed behind her.

Lizzy let out a gust of air. "Oh my God. They left. Andy, they're gone." She scanned the lab. "Andy?"

42

Rather than a response, Lizzy's call was greeted by a groan coming from behind one of the lab tables.

She rushed across the room and found Andy lying on the floor.

"Oh my God, you got shot?" she gasped as she knelt beside him.

A bloodstain was spreading slowly from where Andy's tied hands were pressed to his side, just above his hip.

"What can I do?"

"A towel ..." he croaked.

She looked frantically around the lab.

He gestured with his head toward a door at the back of the lab. "Back there."

Lizzy jumped up and ran to the door. Behind it, she found a small vestibule with two doors leading off it. She yanked open the left-hand door. It looked like an unoccupied dorm room, except for the chair standing in the middle of the room. There was a pile of folded bedding on the stripped bed, including a bedspread that looked like the material that had wrapped the corpse in the freezer. She was considering where she might find a pair of scissors to cut down the spread when she saw that the other door in the room led to a bathroom. A folded towel was draped over the edge of the bathtub. She snatched it up and ran back to the lab.

Andy was trying to pull himself into a sitting position, and Lizzy dropped the towel and helped him prop himself against a cabinet. There was no blood on the floor where he had been lying. Maybe he had just been grazed—maybe the wound wasn't serious. But when she knelt next to him, she could hear his breathing—shallow and rapid—and when she touched his hand, it was cold and clammy.

"I found a towel," she said.

"Fold it so it's thicker." His voice was raspy, barely more than a whisper.

She folded the towel a few times.

"Pull out my belt."

She unfastened his belt and pulled it out of the loops.

"Towel over my hands."

She placed the towel over where his hands were pressed to his body.

He quickly shifted his hands to the top of the towel. "Belt over the towel."

She worked the belt behind his body, then tried buckling it. "It's too short," she said, her voice spinning up.

"Pull it."

She shook her head. "It will be too tight."

"It has to be tight. Pull it."

She tried to pull the end of the belt, but the leather slipped through fingers slicked with blood from her crawl across the glass-covered floor. She wiped her hands on her pants and pulled again, trying to ignore Andy's shudder of pain. She managed to get the prong into the first hole. "I got it."

"It needs to be tighter."

She grabbed the strap and hauled, and this time Andy couldn't suppress a groan. Crying now, she released the pressure. "Andy—"

"Tighter. Lizzy. Please."

She pulled again and got the prong into the third hole. "I don't think I can get it any tighter than that," she sobbed.

He nodded. "It's good. Thank you." He raised his bound hands. "Can you cut this?"

Lizzy scrambled to her feet and yanked drawers open until she found a pair of scissors. As she maneuvered the blades around the tie, trying not to cut Andy's wrists, she asked, "What happened to you? You look awful."

"Just cosmetic. But you're bleeding."

She smiled through her tears. "Just cosmetic." The tie parted, and she tossed the scissors aside. "We need to get you to a hospital." She scanned the lab. "Do you know if there's a phone around here?"

"I doubt it."

She tried to marshal her swirling thoughts. "Hold on— maybe Billy has a phone."

Andy tried to sit up straighter, alarmed, then his face twisted with pain, and he fell back against the cabinet. "He's still here?"

"Lucas hit him with a fire extinguisher and knocked him out."

She scrambled up and went to where Billy lay, face down and now silent. Was he dead?

She bent over him and reached into the pocket of his jacket.

He twitched, and she jerked back. "He's waking up!"

She heard a movement from the other side of the lab table, then a thump. "Shit," hissed Andy.

"Andy, stay still!"

"The apartment," he gasped. "Lock him in there."

"I still need to get his phone."

"No—just lock him up."

She didn't need Andy to feel like he had to come to her rescue. "Okay, I'll lock him up." Gingerly, she reached down, fingers probing in Billy's jacket pocket.

He grunted and his arm moved.

She jumped back with a gasp.

"Lizzy—" Andy's tone was fearful.

"It's fine, it's fine—I can take care of it."

"Can you squeeze him?"

"No. Louise gave me some drug, and I can't squeeze anyone. I can't read minds. I can barely think."

"If he starts to come around, hit him with the fire extinguisher again."

Lizzy scanned the lab and located the extinguisher. She grabbed it and positioned it within arms' reach. "Okay, I've got it."

While Lizzy had retrieved the extinguisher, Billy had gotten one hand on the ground and was trying to push himself over.

Lizzy considered planting a foot on his back to keep him face down, then thought that Billy might be doing her a favor. Lizzy was fairly certain he didn't have a phone in his jacket pocket, and she could see it wasn't in a back pocket. If he pushed himself onto his back, she could check his front pockets.

It took Billy a few tries, but then with a grunt he managed to roll onto his back.

"Lizzy ..."

"Everything's under control," she called back, hoping she sounded more confident than she felt. She bent over Billy and reached into his front pocket, and just as her fingers touched what must be his phone, his eyelids fluttered.

She jerked at the phone.

His eyes opened, bleary and unfocused, then closed again.

She snatched the phone out of his pocket and slapped it onto the table next to the extinguisher.

"I got it! I got the phone!"

"Lock him up," pleaded Andy. "Now."

Lizzy grabbed Billy's ankles and tugged. It was like trying to move a man-sized sandbag—plus, her hands were still bleeding, and she couldn't get a firm grasp. She wrapped her fingers around the cuffs of his pants and leaned back. He slid across the floor a few inches.

His eyelids fluttered again. "What the fuck—" Billy groaned.

"Lizzy—what's going on?" asked Andy, his voice taut.

"Everything's under control!" she called, her voice tinged with a frantic gaiety.

She readjusted her grasp and leaned back again, and Billy slid another few inches across the floor.

His eyes opened, and she got the feeling that this time he was actually getting a sense, however hazy, of what was going on.

She looked wildly around the room. She should have tied him up while he was still unconscious, but she had thought he'd be out longer. She didn't see anything she could use to tie him, and she was afraid to waste the time searching in cabinets and drawers.

She ran to the apartment, grabbed the remnant of bedspread, then ran back to the lab and dropped it over his face. Maybe he wouldn't realize the darkness was because of a blindfold. Maybe any confusion she could cause would buy her a few seconds.

As she grabbed his pant cuffs and gave another heave, he reached a hand toward the cloth. She stopped long enough to kick the hand away.

"Goddamn," Billy rasped.

"Jesus—Lizzy," groaned Andy.

She heaved on Billy's legs again.

She had gotten him partway through the door to the apartment when his groping hand knocked the fabric aside. Her stomach flipped when his eyes met hers and the situation registered on his addled mind.

With a final heave, she pulled his head clear of the door and stumbled past him, out of the apartment. She slammed the door shut and fumbled at the knob, but there was no lock mechanism.

"How do I lock it?" she gasped.

"There's a padlock somewhere."

Lizzy saw that there was a hasp attached to the door, but no sign of the padlock, and no place for it to be hiding in the bare vestibule.

She heard a sound from the lab and turned to see Andy pulling himself to his knees.

"What are you doing?" she yelled.

"Looking for the padlock," he said through clenched teeth. He scanned the countertops, then pointed. "There." He let go of the cabinet and tumbled back to the floor.

Lizzy snatched up the padlock and turned back to the door just in time to see the knob turn and the door crack open. Billy Chapel, his face red with anger, his eyes squinted in pain, stared out.

Lizzy grabbed the fire extinguisher, ran to the vestibule, and kicked the door all the way open, catching Billy in the shoulder and sending him reeling back into the apartment.

He managed to recover his balance and took an unsteady step toward her.

She drew back the extinguisher and swung it, catching him in the bicep.

He roared and reached for her.

She swung the extinguisher the other way, and this time he grabbed it and yanked.

She lost her grip and her balance. She staggered but managed to remain standing.

Billy, no doubt still suffering the effects of the blow to the head, went sprawling to the floor.

Lizzy ran for the door, slammed it behind her, and slipped the padlock through the hasp just as the door shook with the impact of Billy Chapel's shoulder on the other side.

Lizzy waited through two more thumps, wincing each time the door shook under Chapel's attack. When it looked like the door would hold, she ran to the counter and snatched up the phone. She couldn't unlock the phone, but she knew there was a way to make an emergency call from a locked phone. She was racking her brain for how to do it when she saw the *No Service* message.

"Dammit!"

At the same time, she heard the pop of gunfire from somewhere outside—not right outside the lab, but not as far off as she would have liked.

She shoved the phone into her back pocket and rushed over to Andy. His face was now even more ashen.

"There's no service on Billy's phone. I could run to the road—try to flag down a car."

"Do you even know ... where the road is?" he wheezed.

She shrugged out of her bloodstained jacket and draped it over his chest. "There must be a driveway, right? I'll just go around the house until I get to the driveway, and then I'll follow it to the road."

"Liz, there's gunfire. Running down the driveway—probably not the best idea."

"Okay, then, I'll go to the house. They must have a landline somewhere."

"I don't think—"

"Andy!" she almost screamed. "I'm going to get you help!"

He moved one of his hands off the towel and reached for her. Lizzy saw that a spot of red had made its way through the layers of folded terrycloth. "Lizzy, if something happened to you—"

She took his hand, squeezed it, then placed it gently back on the towel. "Nothing's going to happen to me. I'll be back with help."

43

———————

When Lizzy peeked out of the lab door, she couldn't see anyone, but she could hear them: the sound of gunfire was joined by occasional shouted exclamations or commands from various directions, some relatively near, some more distant. What she didn't hear was the beating of the helicopter's rotor. Louise and Lucas must have made their escape.

She weighed her options. Sticking to the woods would provide cover, but the undergrowth would slow her down. She needed to get help for Andy as fast as she could. She'd try the path and jump off it if she heard someone coming.

Hoping that reception might be better if she moved away from the lab, she pulled Billy's phone from her pocket, then stepped outside and sprinted down the path toward the house. She slowed twice to checked for reception, but it remained stubbornly pegged at zero bars.

She had almost reached the back entrance, when she saw a dark-haired man, his back to her, peering around the corner of the building. She skittered off the path and knelt behind a bush, then cautiously raised her head.

The man held a gun extended in a shooting stance, and she saw that he was tracking a blond-haired man, also armed, who was making his way through the woods. The blond man's gait was a little uneven, and she realized with a jolt that he might be the person who had attacked her in Atlantic City. The dark-haired gunman's shot was currently blocked by a small copse of trees, but in a few more steps, the blond-haired man would clear the copse.

She clamped her hand over her mouth, with dread at what she knew she was about to witness and to keep herself from calling out a warning to the target.

As she had anticipated, as he cleared the copse, the shooter squeezed off a single shot.

The blond man dropped without a sound.

The dark-haired man ran to his victim and snatched up his gun. He fiddled with the gun for a moment, then tucked it into the waistband of his pants at the small of his back—Lizzy could see that he already had another gun stowed there. Then he bent and put his gun to the base of the blond man's neck.

Lizzy squeezed her eyes shut and clamped her hands over her ears, but she couldn't block out the sound of the execution shot.

When she looked up a moment later, bile bitter in her mouth, the dark-haired man was disappearing through the trees, no doubt looking for another target.

Lizzy scanned the area and could see no one else. She stood and ran for the house, stumbling once, her legs unsteady and her stomach roiling from the scene she had witnessed.

The back door was open, and she stood to one side for a moment, listening. All she could sense was the echoey silence of an empty building.

She slipped inside and tried to get her bearings. Where might she find a phone? Certainly not in her suite. Maybe the dispensary. But even after having led Billy there and back, she struggled to form a clear idea of how to get there. She started up the corridor toward the main hallway, hoping that her sense of direction had improved since she had passed through the house with Billy.

Suddenly, she heard rapid footsteps approaching—not the heavy footfalls she would have expected from the men shooting it out in the compound, but light steps. Before she could find a hiding place, the runner appeared from around a corner. It was Elsa, who shrieked and skidded to a stop. Her blond hair had escaped its usual ponytail and fanned around her face, her eyes were wide with fear.

Elsa was about to turn and run away when she recognized Lizzy. "What are you doing here?" Before Lizzy could answer, she threw a look behind her and stage-whispered, "You have to get out of here! We all have to get out of here!" Pushing past Lizzy, she ran down the hall toward the back door.

"A phone!" Lizzy called after her. "Where can I find a phone?"

But Elsa was gone.

Lizzy peered in the direction from which Elsa had come. Was someone chasing her? Should Lizzy be running, too? But she thought that the dispensary was in that direction, and she heard no more footsteps. She made her way cautiously forward.

After a dozen yards, she came to a familiar-looking corridor. She turned into it and, as she followed it, she became more confident that this was, in fact, the way to the dispensary. Just one more turn ...

She rounded the corner—and now it was her turn to shriek with surprise.

Standing in the corridor was a stout middle-aged woman in a loose-fitting cardigan.

Next to her stood Philip Castillo.

"Philip!" Lizzy ran to him and threw herself into his arms. "What happened? I thought you were dead!"

He gave her a gentle hug, then released her and stepped back. "What happened to your cheek?" He glanced down and saw the blood on her arm. His expression darkened. "Who did this to you?"

"Billy Chapel jabbed me with a broken bottle, but it's not serious."

He scowled. "Okay, I'm going to take your word for that." He gestured toward the woman. "Lizzy, this is Maja. I ran into her while I was looking for you, and she said she'd help. She also explained to me about the blood in the suite."

"That wasn't your blood?"

"No—in fact, it wasn't blood at all." He looked toward Maja.

"Cornstarch. Food coloring." Maja said. "Doctor Mortensen and Lucas had me stage it."

"But ... why?" asked Lizzy, her head spinning.

Philip answered. "I'm guessing that they hoped that when Billy showed up, you'd ..." His eyes drifted to Maja, then back to Lizzy. "... be mad at him."

Lizzy mentally completed Philip's message: ... *and squeeze him.*

"But how did you get away from Billy?" she asked Philip.

"I didn't. Billy's been taking me with him when he goes to the front gate to check in with his men. The last time we went, he left me with the guys at the gate. But when they heard the helicopter come in, they figured someone was making a break for it and crashed the gate. They're all over the compound now, shooting it out with Viklund's men."

She shuddered. "Yeah, I saw them."

"What are *you* doing here?" he asked her.

"Oh, jeez—I shouldn't be standing here talking. I'm looking for a phone. Andy's been shot. We need to call 911."

"You won't be able to reach anyone," said Maja. "There are no land lines, and except for Doctor Mortensen and Lucas, the mobile phones we have can only connect with the phones of other compound staff members."

"I have Billy's phone," said Lizzy, holding it up.

Maja snatched it out of her hand. "You can't keep that with you—he could use it to track you."

Lizzy flushed. "He's locked up in the lab."

"His men might be able to use it to find you, and you don't want that. Although as long as it's on the property, it won't matter in any case—the signals are blocked. You'd have to be well off the property to get a signal ... and the property is very large."

Lizzy ran her fingers through her hair and realized she must have left a streak of blood behind because Philip's expression darkened again. She wiped her hand on her pants. "What are we going to do?" she asked, her voice trembling. "Andy's in really bad shape."

"We can get supplies from the dispensary," said Maja.

"We put a towel on the wound, held in place with a belt. What else can we do?"

"There are sponges in the dispensary that help with clotting. And maybe other things that would be of use."

"Where *is* Andy?" asked Philip.

He's in the lab," said Lizzy.

"The lab?" asked Philip.

"A separate building," said Maja. "Where Doctor Mortensen and Doctor Rinnert worked."

"Where are they now?" asked Philip.

Lizzy answered. "Louise and another guy—I guess it was Lucas—left, in the helicopter, I think."

"How about Doctor Rinnert?" Maja asked Lizzy.

"Lucas shot him."

"It's just a matter of time before Chapel's men get to the lab," said Philip, "and we can't have Andy there when they do. I'll go to the lab and move him somewhere safer, and you guys get whatever supplies you can from the dispensary. I'll watch for you to come out of the house, and then I'll bring you to wherever I've stashed Andy. Plus, I can get rid of Chapel's phone."

Maja handed him the phone, and quickly described how to get to the lab.

Philip pulled Lizzy in for another quick hug. "Stick with Maja," he said. "I'll see both of you in a few minutes." He turned and jogged down the corridor.

"Come with me," Maja said briskly, before turning and walking quickly back down the corridor.

Lizzy hurried to keep up.

44

———————

When they reached the dispensary, Maja waved Lizzy to a sink in the corner. "You wash the blood off your hands while I see what there is here that we can use."

As Lizzy soaped her hands, Maja slipped off her cardigan and laid it out on the desk. She began opening drawers and cabinets, dropping items onto the sweater. By the time Lizzy was drying her hands, Maja was rolling the cardigan into a neat little carrier, using the arms as a handle. She picked it up and hurried out of the dispensary, Lizzy at her heels.

"Can Doctor McNally walk?" asked Maja, a bit breathless.

"Maybe a few steps, but not far."

"We need the golf cart."

"Sure ... but where would we take him?" After a pause, she added, "Can we take him wherever Elsa was going?"

Maja shot her a sharp look. "You saw Elsa?"

"She was running down the hallway. She looked scared."

Maja shook her head. "Silly girl. She could have been out of the compound if she had left when I told her to. I showed her a way to get to a break in the fence, but I don't know how I could describe it to you, and it wouldn't be possible to take the golf cart there." They reached the corridor that led to the back of the house. "The helicopter will be coming back for me. We might be able to convince them to take Doctor McNally, too, and to drop him somewhere he would be found and taken to the hospital. But there will only be one spare seat."

Lizzy felt a surge of hope—she had never imagined that medevacking Andy out of the compound would be an option. But she tried to temper her hope by reminding herself that, even if Philip seemed to have trusted Maja, Lizzy had known the woman for only a few minutes, and she must have been involved in whatever was going on at the compound.

"Who else will be on the helicopter?" she asked.

"Me. The pilot. One other person."

Lizzy wondered if the other person would be Louise, and if she should tell Maja that she didn't believe Louise would agree to allocating a seat on the helicopter to Andy.

Or maybe, she thought, the fourth person was Philip, since Maja and he seemed to have formed some sort of alliance. In any case, she didn't see that she had much choice.

"That sounds good—let's do that."

When they reached the back entrance, Maja peered carefully out of the door. Lizzy could hear the continued pops of gunfire, although it seemed to have tailed off since she entered the house. The golf cart was parked a few dozen feet away.

Maja moved cautiously out the door, Lizzy at her heels, but almost immediately Maja turned and hurried Lizzy back inside. "Herr Chapel is standing by the lab."

"His men must have found him and let him out of the apartment."

"Or Herr Castillo. He is by the lab as well."

"Philip? Is Billy holding him hostage?"

Maja eased back out the door, looked in the direction of the lab, then retreated back inside. "I don't think so."

Lizzy stepped cautiously outside. The paved area outside the door was flanked by raised berms topped with bushes, and she could observe the lab through their branches.

Billy Chapel stood next to the entrance. In one hand, he held a gun—Lizzy guessed he had gotten it from one of his men. In the other hand was a phone. Was it the phone Philip had said he would get rid of? Chapel wasn't talking on it, which suggested that at least what Maja had told them about the cell signals being jammed at the compound was true.

Philip stood beside Chapel, arms crossed, scanning the surroundings.

He didn't look like a hostage. He looked like an ally.

What was going on?

She realized that the effects of the drug must have worn off, because the sun didn't stab her eyes and the sounds of the surrounding woods didn't grate on her ears as they had when Billy had dragged her out of the house. That meant she wouldn't be able to eavesdrop on anyone's thoughts to figure out what was going on, and she wouldn't be able to use the squeeze unless she got a lot closer to a target than she intended to.

Lizzy stepped back inside. "I don't see Andy. Where could he be?"

"We weren't in the dispensary that long—Herr Castillo couldn't have taken him far." Maja thought for a moment. "I suppose Doctor McNally could be behind the lab building, but if he were anywhere else, I think Herr Chapel would have seen him. Perhaps Doctor McNally is still inside."

"Are there places where he could hide? Or where Philip could have hidden him?"

"Maybe in one of the apartments."

"I think we have to figure that's where he is."

"Maybe ... but I don't see how that helps us as long as Herr Chapel is standing by the door."

Lizzy shivered and crossed her arms. She winced as her hand came in contact with the cuts Billy had made in her arm with the broken bottle. "I'll—" Her voice caught, and she cleared her throat. "I'll get them away from the door if you look for Andy once they're gone and get him to the helipad if you can find him."

Maja gazed at Lizzy for a few moments, then said, "If you're willing, I'll try."

"Thank you." Lizzy started for the door, then turned back to Maja. "Can I ask you a question?"

"If you must."

"I know this is dangerous for you. Why are you helping us?"

Maja's expression hardened, and Lizzy was afraid she had offended the older woman with her question. Then Maja's eyes slid off Lizzy and toward the open back door. "Theo Viklund was responsible for the death of my brother, Nils. I should have avenged his death, but I was too afraid. I should have tried to leave the compound, but I was too afraid even to do that. Theo Viklund does not allow disloyalty to go unpunished. Billy Chapel is no better—he has killed no one close to me, but I'm sure he has killed many other women's brothers ... and husbands and fathers and sons. I don't want to see him kill anyone else." She scowled. "At least not anyone innocent." She turned back to Lizzy. "And you are doing the dangerous part. You are the brave one in this."

Lizzy's stomach flipped. "Where's the helipad?"

With the lab at twelve o'clock, Maja pointed to three o'clock. "That way. A few hundred yards."

Lizzy nodded. "I'll try to lead them away from it." She cleared her throat. "Once you get Andy away in the helicopter, do you have any advice on what I should do? Where I should go? Maybe to the break in the fence you showed Elsa?"

Maja pointed in the direction opposite the lab. "The place I sent Elsa to is that way, but, as I said, the way there is easier shown than explained. A fence surrounds the entire property, and even though the security staff maintains it, there might be other breaks in it. Look for a stream—you might be able to pass through there. But don't try to go through the front gate. I'm sure Herr Chapel's men are guarding it. "

Lizzy nodded. "Okay."

"If you find a way out, get as far as you can from the compound. Don't flag down a car until you are well away."

"All right." Lizzy paused. "What about Philip?"

"What about him?"

"Do you think ..." She swallowed, hating herself for even voicing her fear. "Do you think he's joined up with Billy?"

Maja narrowed her eyes at Lizzy. "You know him better than I do. Is he the kind of man who would do that?"

Lizzy felt a momentary shame at her doubt. "I *don't* believe he's the kind of man who would do that." She drew a deep breath. "Thank you again." Then she stepped outside.

Billy and Philip were still standing in front of the lab building. Billy was turned slightly away from where she stood, scanning the grounds. Philip was facing the house.

Lizzy stepped out from behind the bushes.

Even from this distance, she could see Philip's eyes widen. He glanced toward Billy, then turned back to Lizzy and shook his head.

She responded with an emphatic nod, then sprinted around the berm. She turned left, away from the helipad. She heard a shout she guessed was from Billy. She looked over her shoulder long enough to see that Philip and Billy were both following her, Philip sprinting, Billy only slightly slower. She turned and ran.

Lizzy was counting on the fact that Billy Chapel would be more interested in catching her than shooting her. Based on what had happened in the lab, he might think that Lizzy was cooperating with Louise, and he wouldn't be able to extract more information from a corpse. The thought of what Billy might be willing to do to get information from her if he caught her alive gave her an additional burst of speed.

Initially, she tried to run through the woods, looking for spaces that were relatively free of undergrowth. However, the turquoise loafers Elsa had given her didn't provide much traction, and she kept slipping on the leaf-strewn ground. She diverted to one of the paved paths. Its surer surface would be a greater benefit to her than to Billy, who must still be suffering the effects of the blow to his head.

It would also benefit Philip, and Lizzy had to admit that she wasn't entirely sure whether she should welcome or fear the possibility of him catching up to her. She hazarded a look back and saw that he was gaining on her. She heard Billy yell something but couldn't pick out the words.

With the time marked by the hammering of her heart, Lizzy sensed a minute ticking by, then another. Despite the coolness of the morning, sweat soaked her shirt. She scanned the trees, hoping to glimpse the fence that surrounded the property, but there was nothing but woods in all directions. Not only must the property be huge, but the path must be following a subtle curve to stay inside the perimeter.

More minutes passed, and her breath tore at her throat. She hunched over, bending into the pain of the stitch in her side. She had run so far on the curving path that she almost expected to find herself back where she had started.

She looked over her shoulder, dreading seeing the men right behind her.

The path, before it curved away out of sight, was empty. She veered off the path, pushing her way between branches that slapped painfully against the cuts on her arms. Then she fell to the ground, burrowed into the leaves, and lay as still as her heaving breaths and hammering heart would allow.

After a moment, she heard the rapid *pat pat pat* of feet—they must be Philip's—approaching and then passing her. Seconds ticked past, and then she heard the heavier and more uneven thud of Billy's footfalls, passing and then fading into the distance.

She took a deep, trembling breath, sucking in spores of mold from the bed of leaves and barely holding back a volley of coughs. How long could she lie here before they realized they must have passed her and come back to investigate?

Then she heard a noise that she at first took to be returning footsteps but quickly recognized as the thwack of helicopter rotors beating the air. The sound was coming from the direction she had just come—she must have run past the helipad.

She cautiously raised her head and looked down the path in the direction Philip and Billy had gone. There was no sign of them.

She had to know if Andy had made it to the helipad. She could watch from the woods, and if—she corrected herself—*when* he was safely out of the compound, she'd go looking for a break in the fence and make her own escape.

Jumping to her feet, she made her way back to the path and started a painful jog toward where she could hear—and now, through the tree branches, see—the helicopter descending.

45

———————

Lizzy reached the edge of the woods. The helicopter had landed, its blades still beating the air. The golf cart was next to it, Andy slumped in the passenger seat. Maja stood next to the cart, simultaneously trying to rouse Andy and arguing with Lucas, who stood next to her, hands on his hips. Their words were drowned in the roar of the rotors. The pilot at the controls—Lizzy thought it was the same man who had flown Philip and her to the compound from Pocopson—kept a nervous eye on the surrounding woods.

Lizzy also scanned the area. She could see no one else—not Philip, not Billy, not Billy's men.

She returned her attention to the drama playing out on the helipad. Lucas wasn't helping Maja with Andy, but he also wasn't taking any overt steps to keep Andy out of the helicopter. If Lizzy could help Maja get Andy into the aircraft, would Lucas give in?

But Lucas had seemed all too willing to shoot Lizzy in the lab. What would his reaction be if she started aiding Maja in an action that Lucas clearly disapproved of?

At the same time, the tone of the argument between Lucas

and Maja didn't carry the emotional weight of the events in the lab. It was more like a pair standing by a disabled vehicle, engaged in a low-level argument about whether to stay with the car or walk to the nearest service station. She imagined passing them on the highway and wondering about their relationship—the man looking a little too old to be the woman's son, a little too young to be her husband.

As Lizzy watched Maja tug at Andy's arm and Lucas throw up his hands in exasperation, she decided the vibe was more mother-and-son. If she was right about that, would Lucas really pose a danger to someone that Maja had put herself in some jeopardy to help?

And did it matter? Maja wasn't going to get Andy in the helicopter on her own.

Lizzy sprinted across the open space to the helipad.

When Lucas saw her, his hands balled into fists, but at least they didn't go to the gun she assumed was holstered under his jacket.

When she reached the cart, he said, "We're not taking McNally—and we sure as hell aren't taking you."

She pushed past him to Maja's side next to Andy. "You don't need to take me, but you *are* taking Andy."

At her voice, Andy's eyes opened. She hadn't thought he could look worse than he had back in the lab, but his skin was now almost white, highlighting in even more gruesome contrast the angry-looking scrapes from his kidnapping, the black rings around his eyes, and the flecks of blood under his nose.

"Andy, you have to help us," Lizzy said, her gaze darting around the field, on the lookout for Billy and his men. And Philip.

Andy tried to shift his legs, but his features bunched with pain.

"I'll lift," said Lizzy, wrapping her arms around his legs and lacing her fingers underneath his knees. "Try again, Andy."

"He's too badly injured," said Lucas, as much to Maja as to Lizzy. "He might as well die here as on the helicopter."

"We're taking him out of here," said Maja. She grasped Andy's shoulders and, as Lizzy lifted his legs out of the cart, rotated his body to follow them.

Lizzy could tell by the tremor that shook Andy's body that she was hurting him. "Just a couple of steps to the helicopter, Andy," she said, trying to voice a confidence she was far from feeling.

"*Vad fan*," Lucas spat.

Andy's feet were on the ground, and Lizzy draped one of his arms over her shoulder and hoisted him to his feet. He swayed, but Maja grabbed his other arm and, together, they managed to keep him upright.

"Lucas!" Maja called, her tone sharp.

Lucas groaned with frustration, but he stepped forward, took the arm Maja held, and looped it, none too gently, over his shoulder.

As Lizzy and Lucas dragged Andy forward, Maja opened the back door of the helicopter, then hurried around to the other side and climbed in. When Andy was propped up in the door, Maja hooked her arms under his. She pulled and Lucas and Lizzy lifted Andy's legs, while Andy did his best not to collapse onto the concrete of the helipad.

They had just gotten him into the seat, his legs still hanging out of the door, when a gunshot rang out.

"*Förbaske mig*," Lucas snarled, stepping back.

Andy began to slither off the seat.

Lizzy looked over her shoulder to see Billy lumbering out of the woods, a gun in his hand. Philip was right behind him, empty-handed. Billy raised his gun and fired, and Lizzy heard the *ping* as it ricocheted off the helicopter.

"*Kom in nu!*" the pilot yelled.

Lucas unholstered his gun.

"Don't shoot Philip!" Lizzy screamed as she tried to keep Andy from sliding out of the helicopter.

Lucas fired, and Billy's return bullet whined past her ear.

Lucas fired again, and Lizzy heard his triumphant exclamation: "*Fullträff!*"

As Lucas ran around the front of the helicopter and climbed into the front passenger seat, Lizzy grabbed Andy's legs, halting his slide, and looked over her shoulder again, afraid of what she would see. Had Lucas shot Philip?

Billy Chapel was hunched over, one arm hanging loose, the other hand grasping his bicep. In the woods behind them, Lizzy saw movement—men moving toward the helipad.

Billy lurched forward and bent, reaching for something on the ground, but Philip got to it first. When he straightened, he was holding a gun.

Lizzy felt a rush of hopefulness—Philip was armed!—then realized that it hardly mattered. There were too many men coming through the woods for one gunman to deal with—even for two gunmen to deal with, if she counted Lucas.

Then Philip raised the gun and fired—but not at Billy.

At the helicopter.

"Back off!" the pilot yelled back toward Lizzy.

"Andy's not inside yet!" Lizzy screamed back over the roar of the rotors.

She heard the engine spin up and felt the helicopter shift. Another gunshot cracked out. She wished she could summon the squeeze on command, but there were too many of them, and they were too far away.

"Lizzy!" Maja yelled, and Lizzy realized she was holding the strap of Andy's seatbelt out toward her.

Lizzy grabbed it. She pulled it across Andy's body and tried to fumble the belt's tongue into the buckle. His legs were still hanging out of the door, but if she could get the buckle fastened, she hoped it would be enough to keep him from falling.

There was another shot, and the pilot's-side window exploded.

The pilot threw his hands up over his head, but the shot must have missed him, because he grabbed the controls and a second later, the engine spun up again and the helicopter lifted a few inches off the ground.

"Get out!" Lucas bellowed at Lizzy.

Tears of terror and frustration blurring her vision, she fumbled with Andy's seatbelt and felt it click home.

"He's buckled in!" she screamed. "Go!"

She intended to step back, but at that moment, Andy opened his eyes, reached out, and clamped his hand onto her wrist.

"Let go!" Lucas yelled, squeezing off another shot toward Billy and Philip through the empty frame of the pilot-side window.

"No," rasped Andy, his voice barely audible.

"*Vi kan inte lämna med tjejen hängande på!*" the pilot yelled.

Maja reached over Andy, grabbed Lizzy's bicep, and hauled.

Lizzy yelled as Maja's fingers tightened on the cuts on her arm, but the sound was lost in the beat of the rotors. She tried to boost herself up, but the helicopter lifted, and her feet left the ground.

She kicked her legs and one of her feet found the skid for a moment, but the craft was rotating—maybe the pilot was trying to put the tail of the plane toward the shooters, and her foot slipped off.

"Let go of her," Lucas snarled at Maja.

Maja's mouth was a grim line. She grabbed Lizzy's shirt in her other hand, but the fabric tore, and Lizzy felt herself slipping again.

Andy's hand tightened on her wrist.

She was not going to have gotten Andy into the helicopter and then doom him by her presence.

"Let go of me, Andy!" she sobbed.

As best he could, Andy clamped his other, masking tape-encased hand onto her other wrist. "No, Lizzy," he whispered. "You're coming, too."

The helicopter rose a few more feet—it now must be two dozen feet off the ground.

"*Djävlar*," Lucas groaned. He reached back with his free hand and grabbed Lizzy's hair.

Lizzy shrieked. Was he going to push her out?

But Lucas pulled, and this time Lizzy's cry was a shout of pain as she felt the stitches in her scalp tear.

She was able to get a foot on the skid and boosted herself up.

Maja leaned over Andy and hooked her hands under Lizzy's arm and pulled.

Lizzy wrenched one of her wrists out of Andy's grasp and grabbed the headrest of the front passenger seat.

The helicopter turned again, and Lizzy felt herself slipping back, but Lucas grabbed the waistband of her pants, and hauled her into the helicopter.

Lizzy sprawled over Andy and Maja's laps, and she heard a groan of pain from Andy.

"*Åk!*" Lucas yelled.

The helicopter rose, more slowly than Lizzy remembered from the pickup in Pocopson—but then again, they hadn't had people shooting at them then.

She twisted to look out the still-open door, back toward the helipad, dreading the sight of Philip firing again at the helicopter. But he was bent over next to Billy. Her throat clamped shut. Had he been hit? But she realized he was talking to Billy, gesturing—but not shooting—with the gun, and Billy's confused gaze was shifting between Philip and the helicopter.

But now Billy's men were emerging from the woods, guns raised, firing toward the helicopter.

Philip made an even more emphatic gesture, and Billy turned and raised his good arm. He must have yelled something to the men, because some of them stopped firing and lowered their weapons, while others, too far from Billy to hear his shouted commands, continued to fire.

The helicopter was a hundred feet in the air and still rising, and as Lizzy watched, the rest of the men at the helipad must have either heard Billy's instructions or deemed the craft too high to hit. The firing slowed, then stopped.

A dozen men stood gazing up at the helicopter, some holstering their weapons, others jogging toward where Billy stood, supported by Philip.

The helicopter banked toward the tree line, and just before the clearing disappeared behind upper branches, Philip looked toward the helicopter and raised his hand in a fist.

To the other men on the ground, she hoped it looked like the gesture of a man who had been frustrated in his goal to bring down a helicopter.

She knew it was the closest Philip Castillo could get to a fist bump.

She raised her own fist ... then the clearing—and Philip—disappeared from view.

46

When the compound had disappeared behind them, Lizzy, with Maja's help, hauled Andy's legs into the helicopter and got the door closed. As carefully as she could, she shifted herself off Andy's lap and wedged herself into the narrow space between the two back seats. He made no sound, and, heart in her throat, Lizzy pressed her fingers to his wrist. She could just pick up the thready beat of his pulse. Not knowing what else she could do for him, she folded his cold, limp hand between hers.

With the broken window, the sound inside the helicopter was deafening. Lucas and the pilot were speaking to each other over their headsets—in Swedish, as far as Lizzy could tell—and she could only follow the intonation of the conversation. Lucas asked a question, the topic passed back and forth between the two, then the pilot made what sounded like a suggestion, and, after a moment, Lucas nodded.

Lizzy turned to Maja, who had also donned a headset. "Where are we going?" she yelled.

"Don't worry," Maja mouthed.

"We need to get Andy to a hospital!"

Maja nodded, then shifted her gaze out the window.

Unlike the helicopter trip to the compound, the pilot followed a straight route—to the east, as far as Lizzy could tell.

Eventually she became aware that the helicopter was descending, and when she looked out the window, she recognized their destination. The rolling hills dotted with woods and farmland, the specks of horses grazing in fields, the bucolic scene marred by the charred remains of a large structure, next to which she could see the white rectangle of a vehicle. The pilot was headed for Louise Mortensen's Pocopson property. She couldn't believe that she and Philip had been flown away from here just one day ago.

When they landed in the clearing next to the house, Lucas turned toward her and flipped the mic of the headset up, away from his mouth. "Bring the van up to the helicopter," he yelled to Lizzy. "You have two minutes, then I dump him out."

"I don't have the key—"

"It's in your duffel bag—remember? Go."

Lizzy eased herself over Andy, pushed the door open, tumbled out of the helicopter, and raced across the lawn. She wrenched the door of the Caravan open and emptied the contents of her duffel bag onto the floor of the cargo area. She swept her hands through the jumble of items and grabbed the keyring just as it started a slide toward the inaccessible space between the front seats.

She scrambled into the driver's seat. It took her three tries to get the key into the ignition, then the engine roared to life. She ground forward, panicking at the van's lack of acceleration until she realized she hadn't disengaged the parking brake.

She tried to calculate how much of her two minutes she had burned through. She wasn't as concerned about Lucas pushing Andy out of the helicopter—as long as it was still on the ground —as she was about her ability to get Andy into the van without help. Without a phone, her only recourse would be to drive off the property in search of help, then hope she could get back to the property, and to Andy, without a GPS.

Lucas and Maja were standing next to the open passenger door, and Lizzy realized when she saw Lucas's alarmed expression that she was driving too fast. She hit the brakes, and the van slid to a stop just short of the rotors.

She jumped out and opened the back door of the van as Lucas looped Andy's arm around his shoulders and hauled him out of the helicopter. Andy was conscious again, but just barely, and Lucas staggered as Andy swayed.

Lizzy rushed over, and she and Maja supported Andy from the other side.

When they reached the van, Lucas dropped Andy into the cargo area and swung Andy's legs in. Then he turned to Lizzy.

"I did this against my better judgment," he yelled, "because Maja insisted. If you make me regret it, I'll find you and McNally and I'll kill you both. And McNally's brother as well. Do you understand me?"

Lizzy nodded.

He turned and jogged back to the helicopter. "*Kom igen!*" he called over his shoulder.

Maja turned to follow him, but Lizzy grabbed her arm. "Wait," she yelled, "where's Louise?"

"Not far from the compound. She's alone now, but she won't always be alone. She'll get someone to help her, just like she got me to help her, but she'll turn on them, just like she turned on me. She left me behind to die in that compound. She's a cold-blooded bitch." Maja pulled her arm from Lizzy's grip and hurried after Lucas.

They climbed into the helicopter and were airborne seconds later.

Lizzy turned to where Andy lay in the back of the van. She bent over him and took his hand. "Andy?"

He groaned.

"Can you hear me? Can you tell me how to get to the hospital?"

She knew Mercy Hospital wasn't far, but she had no idea how to get there.

This time, she got not even a groan.

She had a horrible moment of thinking that he was gone, but then she felt a slight pressure on her hand.

She returned the squeeze, then extracted her hand, closed the back door, jumped in the driver's seat, and spun the wheel toward the driveway.

47

———

Louise sat in the lounge area of the airport's small terminal and assessed her options.

The helicopter had begun its descent only a few minutes after leaving the compound, and Louise could see it was headed for an airport.

"Why are we descending?" she asked Lucas.

"We're landing."

"Here? So close to the compound? Why?"

"To let you out."

"Me? What about you?"

"I'm going back."

"Why?"

"To get Maja."

"You can't go back there. They'll kill you."

"I'm willing to risk it."

She looked toward the pilot. "Why is *he* going back?"

"Because I'm paying him to."

Louise wasn't enthusiastic about the possibility that Lucas would fall into Billy Chapel's hands. She had done her best to keep the information she shared with Lucas on a need-to-know basis, but out of necessity had told him far more than she would have liked—not least, what Lizzy Ballard's special skills were.

Trying to imbue her tone with a sorrowful note, she said, "Lucas, with all of Billy's men overrunning the compound, do you really think Maja is still ..." She let the sentence drift into silence.

"Alive? Yes, I do. She would find a way." He turned in his seat, and she almost recoiled at the intensity of his expression. "You know what would have kept us from having to go back? If you had been willing to give her five minutes to get to the helipad when Rinnert's seat became available. Five minutes, that's all it would have taken. But you couldn't wait."

"I felt that ..." she began, then stopped herself. She couldn't imagine that any way she completed that sentence—*her usefulness was done, it wasn't important*, she *wasn't important*—would improve her standing with Lucas. "Very well. If you feel you must go back, then I won't stand in your way."

Lucas turned forward again. "You have no say in the matter," he said, his tone cold. He reached over his shoulder, hand extended. "Your phone."

With a sigh, she pulled her phone from her pocket and dropped it into his hand.

The skids settled, and Louise grasped the strap of the messenger bag on the seat beside her.

"Leave it," said Lucas, without turning around.

"What?"

"Leave it."

"It has the money I need to get to Philadelphia and pick up the documents."

"Leave it."

"But ... it has my research."

"Leave it."

"Why? What could you possibly do with it?"

"I don't know. Maybe nothing. But it couldn't hurt to have it."

Her hand tightened on the strap. She could do without the bit of money she had packed. After all, she had millions in an overseas account. In fact, she realized, she would end up with more than she had expected, since she could now move Edmund's share of Theo's money into her own account. She might even be able to do without the identity documents.

But he was keeping her research records—and just on the off-chance they would be useful to him?

"Lucas—"

He reached under his jacket, pulled out his gun, twisted in his seat, and pointed it at her head. "Get the hell out."

With her teeth clamped so tightly together she could hear her jaw pop, she released the strap of the bag, removed her headset, unbuckled her seatbelt, and climbed out.

She raised her hand to protect her face from the grit kicked up by the helicopter as it rose from the ground. She watched it until it disappeared over the tree line, then she turned and trudged toward the small terminal.

HER ANGER at Lucas had clouded her thoughts for a time, but finally she was marshaling her thoughts.

She regretted having turned the phone over without at least a bit of an argument—she realized it contained the audio recording of the information Ballard had been able to convey from Edmund about the use of electricity to create the type of extraordinary ability she sought in otherwise normal adults. But it hardly mattered—without Edmund's assistance, she didn't have the electrophysiological expertise needed to act on the information.

And she hadn't been completely surprised by Lucas's insistence that she leave the messenger bag behind. That was why she had a flash drive duct-taped to her ankle—a drive that contained Mitchell Pieda and Elizabeth Ballard's medical records.

Her false identity awaited her in Philadelphia, and those documents would enable her to access millions. But she had no money to pay for transportation to get there, or even to buy a meal.

And, for the first time in her life, she had no one to call on for help. No Lucas. No Maja. No George Millard. She twisted her wedding ring. No Gerard.

After a moment, her hands quieted. For several minutes, she sat stock still, staring straight ahead.

Then she stood and crossed to a reception desk, where a man about her age was tapping on a keyboard.

"Excuse me, can you tell me how far away the nearest pawn shop is?" she asked.

"Pawn shop? Not sure—hold on."

He turned back to the computer and typed. "About ten miles."

She sighed. "I realize I left my purse on the helicopter I came in on, and I need some money. I thought I could pawn my wedding ring, but I don't have a way of getting to the shop."

The man reached for a radio. "I can see if they're still within radio range—ask them to come back."

"No, please. I had a little falling out with one of the other passengers. I'd rather not see him again."

He raised an eyebrow. "You'd rather pawn your wedding ring than get your things back?"

"The passenger was my husband."

"Ah. Gotcha."

Louise reached up to tuck a strand of hair behind her ear, forgetting for a moment the haircut she had inflicted on herself back at the compound. She wished not only for longer hair, but also hair that hadn't been dyed a mousy brown. "Might you be willing to drive me there when your shift is over? I'd be happy to reimburse you for gas, and for your time."

He considered, then glanced at his watch. "It'll be a couple of hours, but if you're willing to wait around ..."

"Of course. Thank you so much."

She started to return to her seat but turned back when he said, "You hungry? My wife always packs two sandwiches—" he patted his ample stomach "—which is one more sandwich than I need. You're welcome to it."

A few minutes later, she was seated in the waiting area with a tuna sandwich and a soda that her new friend, Ron, had gotten for her from the vending machine.

"I'll just add it to your tab," he had laughed.

As she ate, suddenly realizing how hungry she was, she mapped out the next twenty-four hours. If she got a fair price for the ring, it should be enough for a train or bus ticket. Once she got to Philadelphia, retrieved the ID, and got some money, she could plan out a long-term strategy in comfort. There was a nice hotel near Rittenhouse Square where she and Gerard had stayed if they had a late dinner in the city. It has been long enough ago that she doubted anyone would remember her, but recent enough that she recalled their excellent afternoon tea.

She wondered if Lucas would have any reason to try to intercept her at the location where he had had the fake ID delivered, but she didn't think it was a serious risk. If Lucas wanted to harm her, he had had plenty of opportunities to do it before now.

And at least she didn't have to worry about Billy Chapel anymore—she couldn't imagine a way he could track her down.

She finished her sandwich and soda, then settled down to wait for the end of Ron's shift.

48

W hen Lizzy had reached the end of the drive leading from the Pocopson house to the road, she had picked a direction at random and driven until she spotted an oncoming vehicle, then pulled the van across both lanes, forcing the car to stop. She didn't know what she would have done if the barricaded car had taken evasive maneuvers and gotten away, but she was able to convince the vehicle's occupants, two elderly women on their way to a baby shower, that she had been in a car accident and needed to get a more badly injured victim to the hospital. The blood on her shirt, her arms, and her scalp—not to mention the long scrape down the side of the Caravan from Lizzy's first attempt to negotiate a highway on-ramp in what seemed like another life—supported her story.

The women gave her directions to Mercy Hospital.

When Lizzy pulled up to the entrance to the emergency room and scrambled out of the car, she found Andy completely unresponsive—only shallow, hitching breaths proved he was still alive. She stuffed the items she had strewn across the cargo space—at least the ones Andy wasn't lying on—back into her duffel bag, then leaned on the horn. When she saw an orderly approaching, she ran.

She couldn't hang around and risk having the police realize that she was the woman still wanted for questioning in connection with the Pocopson fire and George Millard's death. Avoiding the authorities altogether would also make it easier for her to comply with Lucas's parting command not to make him regret having helped her. She was sure the hospital security cameras would capture her face, but they'd have to find her to question her.

She ran until her pounding heart and gasping breaths forced her to stop, then hunkered down in a heavily wooded area and replaced her torn and bloodied T-shirt with a clean T-shirt and sweatshirt from the bag. She wrapped another T-shirt, turban-style, around her head to hide the blood from her re-opened scalp wound.

She was grateful that the weather was pleasant—the temperature warm, the sun shining in a sky dotted with puffy clouds. Under other circumstances, she might have enjoyed a stroll along the picturesque country roads. However, in Mercy's largely rural surroundings, it took her almost an hour to find someone she felt comfortable approaching to beg the use of a phone: a teenage boy skateboarding in the cracked parking lot of a closed farm supply store. She didn't know Ruby's number, so she called Owen.

He had arrived with Ruby, and after Lizzy had provided the sketchiest of descriptions of the events of the last two days, they had decided to make use of Andy's security guarded apartment rather than returning to Owen's Lansdowne house. Once there, Ruby helped Lizzy get cleaned up, and then Owen had restitched Lizzy's head wound—re-opened when Lucas had hauled her into the helicopter by her hair—with only the mildest signs of distress.

That had been three days ago, and Owen and Ruby had been dividing their time between the apartment and Andy's bedside. Lizzy stayed holed up at the apartment, away from the prying eyes and curious ears of the police who periodically stopped by to ask Andy about the circumstances that had landed him at Mercy.

She was working up a sweat on the fancy exercise bike in the master bedroom when she heard the beep of the front door opening, then another beep as the alarm was disengaged. She jumped off the bike, grabbed a towel off the bed, and went to the living room, where she found Owen shrugging out of his voluminous raincoat.

"How's Andy doing?" she asked.

"He's flirting with all the female staff, so I'd say he's on the road to recovery." He hung the coat on a rack by the door. "I'm going to make myself some tea. Want some?"

"Sure." Lizzy followed him to the kitchen and sat on one of the stools at the island. "I wish he didn't have to be flirting from a hospital bed."

"He's lucky he got to the hospital at all," Owen said, filling the kettle. He shook his head. "I still can't believe you got him into that helicopter."

She tried for a dismissive snort. "I can't believe I got him into a situation where he needed a helicopter."

Owen adopted his best approximation of a severe expression. "Lizzy ..."

She raised her hand, suppressing a wince at the still-sore cuts on her arm. "I know, I know. I have to stop beating myself up about it."

He put the kettle on the stove and began assembling teapot, tea leaves, cups and saucers, creamer and sugar bowl. "You realize you accomplished everything you did at the compound without ever relying on the squeeze or mind-reading."

"Not out of choice. I would have loved to have been able to tell what people were thinking ... and been happy to squeeze a few of them." *Especially if it had kept Philip out of Billy's hands*, she thought. She took a banana from a basket on the island. "What's going on with the police?"

Owen heaved a sigh. "As you can imagine, they're a bit skeptical of Andy's story, but he's sticking with it: he was kidnapped from the Mercy Hospital parking lot, he woke up in the ER with a gunshot wound and various other injuries, and he can't remember anything that happened in between." Owen shrugged. "His doctors have confirmed to the police that from a medical point of view, it's possible."

"Are these doctors buddies of Andy's?" Lizzy asked with a wan smile.

Owen returned the smile. "I suspect so."

"How about the Caravan?"

"Ruby's sticking with *her* story that she had driven the Caravan to Atlantic City, it was stolen, and she hadn't gotten around to reporting it missing."

"Did they question the fact that she's got two black eyes?"

"She told them she was helping me with physical therapy, and I fell and accidentally hit her in the nose as I went down."

"And they're buying that?"

"Ruby made it clear that she wasn't about to cover for someone who hit her on purpose."

"I wish you guys didn't have to keep covering for *me*—"

He raised a hand. "Lizzy, I won't hear it. We're the Four Musketeers, remember? You're Aramis—"

She smiled. "And Dad was Athos and you were Porthos." She cocked her head at him. "Although you aren't looking so portly these days. You're looking good. You had already lost a lot of weight with all the stress of everything I was getting you into—" Owen opened his mouth to raise an objection, and she hurried on. "—and then when you had the heart attack ... and then when you were stabbed. But you didn't look healthy. You're looking good now."

"Well, 'looking good' might be stretching it, but I feel good." The kettle boiled, and he poured water over the tea leaves in the pot. He sat down on one of the stools and laced his fingers over his still-substantial stomach. "You know, I think I was sick of being sick ... of being coddled and treated like an invalid. And when finally someone needed *me* to help *them*, instead of the other way around, I think it was what I needed."

Lizzy smiled. "Don't tell Ruby."

"I think Ruby already knows—she's letting me do more stuff for myself."

"Now she can be Sergeant DiMano to Andy."

Owen laughed. "Poor Andy."

Lizzy's expression sobered. "So, he's really going to be okay? He really got banged up at the compound."

Owen's smile faded as well. "I believe he'll recover fully from all his physical injuries. I think he's going to have a tougher time with the psychological recovery. The trauma of being held hostage, the stress of the escape, experiencing first-hand that there are people who are willing to cause pain for pain's sake ..." He shook his head. "It's a lot to deal with."

They sat in silence, each absorbed in their own thoughts, until Owen roused himself and poured out the tea.

"Still no word from Philip?" he asked.

She felt the thud in her stomach that came with any mention of Philip's situation. "No. Although he doesn't have my new number, so I don't know how he could get in touch, even if he wanted to."

"We owe him a lot for what he did," said Owen.

When Andy had regained consciousness after surgery, he

told Owen what had happened after Philip left Lizzy and Maja in the house at the compound.

Philip had arrived at the lab and, after a few unsuccessful attempts to get Andy on his feet, and with the sounds of the gun battle between Lucas's men and Billy's getting closer, Philip had dragged Andy into the apartment next to the one in which Chapel was locked, and stuffed him into the armoire, promising to get him out as soon as the coast cleared.

But as the gun battle neared the lab, Andy heard Philip begin calling to Chapel through the padlocked door of the adjoining apartment, acting as if had just arrived at the lab. Just before Chapel's men stormed the lab, Philip kicked in the door and freed their boss. From the little Andy heard before the men left the lab, Chapel assumed Andy had left with Louise and Lucas.

"Philip took quite a risk," said Owen. "Hiding Andy. Pretending to take sides with Chapel."

"Yeah." Lizzy's throat tightened. "Philip's a great guy." She forced a laugh. "And he and Andy don't even like each other that much."

"Why do you think that is?" Owen asked, his voice careful.

She shrugged. "Philip knows Andy didn't approve of me sharing a place with him in Arizona or driving back to Pennsylvania with him. After everything Philip had done for me, I think that lack of trust hurt him." Her laugh this time was less forced. "And then when I showed up in my casino outfit and Andy saw me—I think *Philip* didn't approve of *Andy's* reaction."

Owen blushed. "Andy feels awful about that—he knows it was completely inappropriate."

"I could tell he was embarrassed by it. I think it just took him by surprise, seeing me dressed up in a way that was intended to make me look older. I knew he'd do the right thing ... and not do the wrong thing."

"He thinks you don't know. He tried not to be around you when you were on the steroid drug."

She gave him a lopsided smile. "Uncle Owen, I didn't need to be a mind-reader to know how Andy felt."

Owen nodded and took a sip of tea. "And how about Philip? You've told me you can't read his thoughts. Are you sure you know how he feels? He has sacrificed a lot for you."

"I know Philip loves me, but not in a romantic way."

After a pause, he asked, "Do you wish he did?"

"Uncle Owen," she teased, "are you offering me advice about my love life?"

He blushed. "Not if you don't want it."

She was silent for a few moments, her smile gradually fading to an embarrassed thoughtfulness. "I guess I do wish he loved me that way—or would someday, when I was older. But he loves Olivia. I'm lucky to have him as a friend. I'm happy with that." She rolled her eyes. "Plus, I've never even been on a date with someone my own age."

They sipped in silence for a minute. Then Owen asked, "What do you want to do next?"

"You mean like dinner?"

"No, I mean like next steps."

She grimaced. "Once things settle down a bit, I need to go to Bethesda to see Olivia."

Lizzy thought back to the awful call she had had to make to Olivia, telling her Philip had been left behind at the compound with Billy Chapel. Olivia had been furious—more with Philip than with her, Lizzy thought—but eventually Lizzy had convinced her, at least temporarily, that calling in the authorities would probably prove more harmful than helpful to Philip.

"And what then?" Owen asked, his voice concerned.

Then she'd need to go to Baltimore and try to find Philip. But she knew that that wasn't what Owen wanted to hear.

"I want to find a place of my own," she said. "Andy's going to be home soon, and his apartment is too small for four people." She sipped her tea. "It's really too small for *three* people." At Lizzy and Ruby's insistence, Owen had been sleeping in Andy's bed. At Lizzy's insistence, Ruby was in the guest room and Lizzy was on the living room couch, which was hardly a hardship—it was as comfortable as it looked.

"I'm looking forward to being home myself," said Owen, "once we figure out how Ruby and I can do that safely—but I don't think it's the best place for you. Where do you want to live?"

"Not too far away. But before I get a place, I need to earn some more money. Maybe I'll try the Philly casinos, once the dust settles a bit."

"The 'dust' being all those people at Theo Viklund's compound?"

"Yeah. At least we know we don't have to worry about Theo himself anymore. And I'm not worried about Lucas or Maja— they could have killed me at the helipad if they wanted to."

"Louise Mortensen is still out there somewhere."

"Yes." She thought back to everything that had happened since she had seen Louise, awkwardly disguised, in the lab at the compound. It seemed as if Louise and Edmund had been allies at one time, but Edmund was dead. Louise had escaped with Lucas, but he had returned for Maja. And it was clear Maja would never forgive Louise for leaving her behind. Gerard Bonnay was dead. Louise's enforcer, George Millard, was dead. "But she's all alone now. That should count in our favor." She looked at Owen. "Right?"

"I hope so. That leaves Billy Chapel."

"True. But as far as he knows, I was just some teenager posing as Theo's niece. He probably thinks Louise hired me to make her claim that Theo was alive more believable. I can't imagine I have anything to worry about from him."

She wrapped her hands around the teacup, hoping its warmth would relieve the shiver that ran through her body. She might not have anything to worry about—but Philip was a different matter.

Theo Viklund had promised Chapel some service from Philip, and Lizzy was sure Chapel would make good on that promise.

It was dread over Philip's safety that kept her awake at night. He had come to her aid so many times.

How would she come to his aid now?

49

———

Billy Chapel turned the mobile phone contemplatively in his hand, then glanced up at its soon-to-be-late owner. Theo Viklund's bodyguard wasn't going to last much longer—Billy would have to get whatever he was going to get soon or not at all.

"The girl in the recording is the one you tried to pass off as Rey Viklund's sister," he said.

Lucas nodded.

"What's her name?"

"Elizabeth."

Billy nodded to Donny, who stood behind Lucas.

Donny drew back a blood-stained truncheon.

"It's true," said Lucas, sounding almost weary. "Elizabeth Ballard."

Billy flicked his hand, and Donny lowered the truncheon. "Who's Elizabeth Ballard?"

"Ballard's mother was a patient of Mortensen's fertility clinic. Mortensen experimented on her. Ballard was the result."

"What sort of experiments?"

Lucas cast bloodshot eyes back toward Donny. "You want me to tell you in front of him?"

Billy shrugged. "Donny's loyal ... and dumb as nails. He won't remember a thing you said by this time tomorrow."

Donny grinned.

Lucas's head lolled forward again. "To make someone who could read minds and kill a person with a stroke."

Billy laughed. "You know, an hour earlier, I would have given Donny the nod to give you a tap for feeding me that kind of bullshit. But that recording of Mortensen questioning Rinnert through Ballard? That's some crazy shit. What was Mortensen trying to get out of it?"

"She needed what Ballard could do, but she knew she'd never win the girl over as an ally, and she couldn't raise up a new batch of Vivantem babies. She was looking for other ways to get what she needed."

"What made her think of electricity?"

"Rinnert used electricity to get Viklund's hand to pass the biometric tests on the computer."

"And Mortensen has a fake ID—for Louise Gerard—waiting for her in Philly?"

"Yes."

"You think she's gotten it yet?"

"I don't know."

Donny raised his eyebrows questioningly at Billy.

Billy shook his head without taking his eyes off Lucas. "I appreciate you being so forthcoming about where your portion of Viklund's money is."

Lucas tried to shrug. "Won't do me any good now."

"And where's Maja?"

For the first time, Lucas was silent.

Billy nodded, and the truncheon swung.

Lucas let out a low groan. Then he said, his voice choked,

"She didn't do anything to you, and she doesn't know anything useful."

"I'll be the judge of that. Where is she?"

"I don't know where she is. I told her not to tell me. I knew this was a possibility."

The man drew back the truncheon, but Billy shook his head. "I'll bet you have a guess."

"No better guess than you."

Billy nodded, and the truncheon fell.

Lucas tried to speak, cleared his throat, and then said, "You and I both know she went back to Sweden. But that's all I know. And it's a big country."

"You weren't too shy about diming out Mortensen and Ballard."

"I don't owe them anything."

"What do you owe Maja?"

"The chance for a better life than the one I led her into."

"That's it?"

Lucas managed a single, tired nod. "That's it."

Half a minute ticked by, the only sound Lucas's labored breathing, then Billy sighed. "Okay, I believe you. We're done here—and Lucas, we'll make it fast for you."

Lucas's response was almost inaudible. "*Tack.*"

Donny set the truncheon on the concrete floor and drew a gun out of his shoulder holster.

Billy raised a hand. "Not you. You've had your fun."

Donny returned the gun to his holster, trying unsuccessfully to hide his disappointment.

Billy jerked his head toward the door, and Donny stepped out.

Billy raised a finger, and another man, who had stood leaning against the wall through the interrogation, stepped forward.

Billy pulled his own gun from his holster, handed it grip-first to the man, and jerked his head toward Lucas. "Take care of him. And make it quick."

The man nodded, took the gun, and flicked off the safety. He stepped behind Lucas, put the gun to the back of his head, and fired.

Billy grimaced. "Goddamn. I always forget how loud that is in here." He reached for the gun.

The man flicked the safety back on, then pulled a handkerchief from his pocket and wiped the barrel before handing it back to Billy.

Billy holstered the gun and extended his hand with a grin. "Welcome to the team, Castillo."

END OF BOOK 4

DID YOU ENJOY SCARE CARD? If you did, I would be so grateful if you would take a moment to leave a rating and review on your favorite online platform. For inspiration, check out what other satisfied readers have said!

Thank you!

Matty

NEXT IN THE LIZZY BALLARD
THRILLER SERIES …

Book 5: Drawing Dead

When Lizzy Ballard's enemies play their cruelest card, can she outsmart them before her life and the lives of those she loves are dealt a fatal blow?

For years, Lizzy Ballard has been running: from the fertility-clinic experiment that made her what she is, from the trail of bodies her power has left in its wake, and from Louise Mortensen, the brilliant, glacial scientist who engineered her. Now Lizzy is hiding out under a fake ID, bankrolling the handful of people she loves one rigged poker hand at a time, and letting herself believe she's learned to control the lethal gift she was born with.

Then Louise takes someone Lizzy can't afford to lose, and the terms are simple. Come to a fortress buried deep in the Maryland woods. Bring the one man who has kept her alive. But what waits behind those mirrored windows is even more dangerous than Louise: a thug who hides his violence behind easy charm, and a plan that means to turn Lizzy from hostage into weapon. The grounds are walled and guarded, the phones are silenced, and every person who loves her is now a chip someone else is holding.

SCARE CARD is a taut story of loyalty, complicity, and the brutal math of love that asks one unbearable question: how much of what Lizzy does is choice, and how much was decided for her before she could speak? For readers of Stephen King's *Firestarter* who like a cold, calculating villain at the center, Scare Card deals Lizzy into a game where the people she loves are the stakes—and she's about to learn what it costs to be holding the deadliest hand at the table.

Continue Lizzy's adventures in *Drawing Dead (Book 5)*!

Join Matty Dalrymple's occasional email newsletter at mattydalrymple.com and receive exclusive subscriber benefits.

ALSO BY MATTY DALRYMPLE

The Lizzy Ballard Thrillers

Rock Paper Scissors (Book 1)

Snakes and Ladders (Book 2)

The Iron Ring (Book 3)

Kill Box Checkmate (Book 3½)

Scare Card (Book 4)

Drawing Dead (Book 5)

The Lizzy Ballard Thrillers Ebook Box Set

The Ann Kinnear Suspense Novels

The Sense of Death (Book 1)

The Sense of Reckoning (Book 2)

The Falcon and the Owl (Book 3)

A Furnace for Your Foe (Book 4)

A Serpent's Tooth (Book 5)

Be with the Dead (Book 6)

The Ann Kinnear Suspense Novels Ebook Box Set - Books 1-3

The Ann Kinnear Suspense Shorts

A Year of Kinnear: 12 Suspense Shorts from the World of Ann Kinnear

All Deaths Endure

Close These Eyes

Ever Thanks

May Violets Spring

Ministers of Grace

More Than a Jest

Our Dancing Days

Sea of Troubles

Stage of Fools

These Hot Days

Wondering Eyes

Write in Water

Non-Fiction

Taking the Short Tack: Creating Income and Connecting with Readers Using Short Fiction with Mark Leslie Lefebvre

The Indy Author's Guide to Podcasting for Authors: Creating Connections, Community, and Income

From Page to Platform: How to Succeed as an Author Speaker with M.L. Ronn

Collaborate to Create: A Guide to Coauthoring Nonfiction with M.L. Ronn

The Podcast Guest Playbook: Turning Conversations into Connections and Community with Mark Leslie Lefebvre

ABOUT THE AUTHOR

Matty Dalrymple is the author of the Lizzy Ballard Thrillers, beginning with *Rock Paper Scissors*; the Ann Kinnear Suspense Novels, beginning with *The Sense of Death*; and the Ann Kinnear Suspense Shorts, including *Close These Eyes*. She is a member of International Thriller Writers and Sisters in Crime. Go to matty-dalrymple.com > About to learn more and to sign up for her occasional email newsletter.

Matty also educates and advocates for writers as The Indy Author. She is the host and producer of hundreds of episodes of *The Indy Author Podcast* and has spoken on topics related to writing and publishing at events such as the Writer's Digest annual conference, ALLi SelfPubCon, Author Nation, Authors Guild webinars, International Thriller Writers' CraftFest, and many more. She writes nonfiction books for writers, and her articles have appeared in *Writer's Digest* magazine. She is a Partner Member of the Alliance of Independent Authors. Go to theindyauthor.com > About & Contact for more information about Matty's non-fiction work and to sign up for her weekly email newsletter.

Matty lives with her husband, Wade Walton, and their dogs in Chester County, Pennsylvania, and enjoys vacationing on Mount Desert Island, Maine, and Sedona, Arizona, and these locations provide the settings for her novels.

facebook.com/matty.dalrymple

ACKNOWLEDGMENTS

My grateful thanks to all the people who lent their expertise to this story:

David Fried and Ken Fritz for advice on medical matters.

Jessica Feigley and Michael Strawbridge for advice on poker.

Wade Rogers for advice on Louise Mortensen's lab and experiments.

Chris Grall for advice on firearms.

Daavid Kahn for Swedish translations.

Jon McGoran for helping me tie it all together.

Any deviations from strict accuracy—intentional or unintentional—are solely the responsibility of the author.

ISBN-13: 978-1-959882-09-1 (Ebook edition)

ISBN-13: 978-1-959882-08-4 (Paperback edition)

ISBN-13: 978-1-959882-11-4 (Large print edition)

www.ingramcontent.com/pod-product-compliance
Lightning Source LLC
Chambersburg PA
CBHW070508310726
48976CB00002BA/383